A.J.COATES

The Askari System

BookTwo in the Extinct Company Series

First published by Turkana Press 2021

First edition

This book was professionally typeset on Reedsy. Find out more at reedsy.com

There are a million species at risk of extinction.
Hunting and illegal trafficking is considered one of the main threats.

This book is dedicated to those man and woman fighting poachers and the illegal wildlife trade.

Those on the front line—facing armed gangs
and those working quietly behind the scenes
gathering information, raising money
and raising awareness.

Contents

Acknowledgement

My greatest thanks to the person who has been my greatest supporter, my business partner and my wife for more than twenty years. Together we have lived and worked in a lifelong adventure, my writing is both part of the adventure and a reflection of it. I couldn't do it it without you. Thank you Beth.

Thank you to my children who are my first readers, listeners and provide me with large quantities of material for the relationship between siblings.

Thank you to my mother Hanneke Coates Hoorn for her ever lasting enthusiasm for my adventures.

Thank you to Johnny and Elaine Mizell, my parents in law, for all their encouragement and financial support in difficult times.

Thanks to my mate Alex (whose real name we can't mention because he works for Her Majesty's Government) for weapons and close combat advice plus turning out to be a whizz at spotting spelling mistakes.

Prologue

The underside of the acacia tree glowed fiery orange as the sun settled its way towards the distant hills on the dust laden horizon of the famous Maasai Mara.

Selina Styles meticulously rearranged her luxurious blonde hair so that it trapped the sun.

“Hurry Devon, it’s going down fast and I’m gasping for a drink.” Devon, her new and superbly proportioned husband, was fiddling with his iPhone, trying to get the tree, Selina, her hair, the distant sunlit hills, and a herd of elephants into the picture.

They married two months ago and had bought a new Mercedes 4x4 camper van to travel up the East Coast of Africa from Cape Town. Kenya was the fourth country they’d visited

, all funded by posting images under #Stylesvanlife on Instagram. They had amassed over a million followers already, and with each post they got more.

“OK, let’s do both of us.” They put their thumbs and forefingers together to make a heart around the setting sun, smiled, and let the phone shoot a burst of pictures.

“That’s enough, I’m tired of being out here, let’s go back to the lodge and get online. We haven’t had a signal for more than an hour.”

Although they were pretending to be living out of their van on a very frugal budget, they weren’t true Overlanders who survived using their vehicles. They actually spent virtually every night in an expensive hotel or lodge.

Tonight, they were staying at the Sand River Lodge. They would park their van by the staff quarters to keep it tucked away, and the staff would clean it and restock it for the next day.

As they buckled up and started their van, a family of elephants lumbered past, unnoticed by the couple.

"Hey, the sat nav says no data." Devon was tapping the big Garmin screen.

"Come on, let's just get going, it can't be too hard to find the lodge." The last slice of sun disappeared behind the hills. Devon flipped on the headlights, replacing the remaining warm glow of sun with harsh white light, and started driving in what he thought was the right direction. Selina took to tapping the sat nav. Almost instinctively, she opened the window and put her arm out to take a selfie. She managed a smile.

"Why didn't you bring a map?"

"Why didn't YOU bring a map?"

"Even if we had a map, you wouldn't know where we were. Devon, watch out!"

They crunched into a large rock. It made alarming screeching noises as it dragged under the van. Selina's cellphone dropped into the darkness.

"Bleedin 'ell." The Instagram star's tone clashed with her carefully manicured looks.

The sun had vanished, and they strained their eyes as they looked out of the windscreen. Devon was trying to see if there was any glow from distant buildings while Selina was trying to locate her cellphone on the ground, but she didn't want to leave the safety of the van.

Devon switched off the headlights so they might detect any distant lights more easily.

"Hey, that looks like someone's torchlight." A powerful beam moved erratically ahead of them.

Selina leaned out of her window to yell for help.

Without warning, the entire scene lit up with flashing orange balls of light and showering sparks erupted in the darkness. The shocking blast of multiple automatic weapons filled the air. It seemed to suck the night out of the sky. Huge dark shapes started running towards them, bellowing.

Selina screamed. Devon grasped for the lights and put his foot on the accelerator. Seconds before they barreled into the van, half a dozen bloody, massive elephants were lit up in a gruesome tableau of sheer terror in a desperate charge to escape the bullets. Some animals were already sinking to their knees. Others smashed straight into the sides of the van. It rolled over like a toy in a raging river.

The firing stopped. A ghost of cordite smoke drifted over the scene.

Devon and Selina, now lying on the upturned ceiling of the van, tried to crawl out of the smashed windscreen. There was a heavy smell of petrol.

The last thing they saw was a pair of black boots.

"Lala Salama," a voice said, and the van exploded in an orange ball which curled into the dark sky.

A chainsaw started.

1

The Askari System

Lt. General George Githere stepped up to the lectern and faced the ranks of cameras and reporters. In full uniform, the commander of the Kenya Wildlife Service silenced the room with his mere presence.

"Our Vision at KWS is to save the last great species and places on earth for humanity. Today we have taken a great step forward in realizing that vision. Allow me to introduce our Askari System. For those of you who don't speak Swahili, Askari is the word for watchman."

Lt. General George Githere flicked on the first slide of his presentation. It was a bloody picture of several elephants lying on their sides with their tusks hacked off.

"Poachers kill 100 elephants every day for their ivory. In the last ten years, the number of African elephants has dropped by 62%. At this rate, they will be extinct in the next ten years. Our Askari program will slow, then stop this slaughter. It will go into operation first here in Kenya and then across the great continent of Africa."

He flicked on another slide, which showed a video of an elephant lying on its side with a blanket over its eyes, surrounded by men and women in KWS uniforms and white coats. One man was using a drill on the tusk of the elephant. They were carefully collecting the ivory dust and one of the women inserted what looked like a small bean into the hole he had made. After mixing the ivory dust with a glue, another person sealed the hole with the mixture.

Finally, everybody stepped away, and the elephant rose shakily to his feet. He looked livid and stomped off into the bush, shaking his noble head.

The video ended.

"Ladies and Gentlemen, the Askari System relies on a GPS tracker inserted into each tusk of every elephant. The tracker has a life of 30 years. It not only gives us position but also heart rate. We monitor all of this at the KWS Askari Center. If the computer sees the heart rates rise amongst a group of elephants, signaling distress, we deploy the KWS Rapid Response Team. KWS-RRT."

To illustrate his point, sixteen heavily armed, and very fit men and women swept into the room. They wore full combat gear and face-masks.

"This is an elite force, trained by British Special Forces. There are several teams around the country on call 24-hours a day, ready to move in 10-minutes. They can deploy by helicopter or parachute to the location of the alarm. Under Kenyan law, they shoot to kill. Questions?"

There were several which the General answered clearly and precisely. A young, attractive blonde girl wearing combat trousers and desert boots stood up to ask a question when the general nodded at her raised hand. She spoke in Swahili.

"Lt. General Githere, what happens if poachers hack into the system? That would give them the location of every elephant in the country. Obviously, this would be a catastrophe."

He responded in English. "Thank you, Miss Stuart, this is a good question." He smiled at her. "Each elephant tracker has a unique signature which can only be accessed if you have a token_ it works like a bank account. If anyone else gets the token, apart from the one in the HQ, we will see it immediately."

2

Breakfast in Colon

Alistair Gordon Stuart walked through the streets of the Panamanian city of Colon with the confident air of a man who could handle himself. He also stood out with his messy blond hair, piercing blue eyes, and thick, dark eyelashes. Alistair understood Colon had a reputation for violent street crime, but he also understood that it was where he would find the best street breakfast on earth.

After a long morning of buying engine parts from a myriad of little shops, he was starving.

He turned down a narrow side street and the smell of coffee, pork and deep fried *hojaldres* filled the air and made his mouth water.

The buildings had a battered aura. Fallen chunks of plaster from the walls sat in trodden piles on the sidewalk, with scant evidence of varied and faded paint. Wooden doors showed where centuries of fingers had worn polished holes to simple latches.

The street was so narrow that the balconies above him almost touched. Loud music came from the open doors of the dilapidated houses. Each one blared a different tune, so as he walked, it was like scrolling through a car radio.

A woman on the balcony ahead of him was hanging out vast fuchsia bras on a line. She called down to him in Spanish, "Hey señor, want to see what I keep inside these?"

He politely declined and lowered his eyes, so he didn't look straight up her lurid green mini skirt as he walked under her balcony.

"Your loss." She laughed good-naturedly.

He rounded the corner, and a small, hooded man with a backpack launched himself from a doorway and stood in front of Alistair, blocking his path. Feet apart, a small stiletto knife flashed in his right hand.

"Give me your money, Gringo."

With the air of a tennis player moving to return a serve, Alistair didn't break stride and stepped straight into the man. Grabbing his knife hand, he landed double uppercuts to the thief's kidneys with his right fist while bending the other hand back until the man dropped the knife.

The would-be mugger fell to his knees, heaving for breath.

Alistair picked up the weapon, flipped it so he was holding the blade, and threw it spinning into the closed wooden door, where it stuck deeply, quivering with the force of the throw.

He looked down at the man, who was now also shaking.

"Actually, I am not a Gringo, I'm a Scotsman," he said in English, letting go of the man's wrist. He switched to Spanish. "Are you crazy? Why are you trying to rob someone twice the size of you with a pathetic little knife?" Alistair had learned Spanish from his nanny.

The man got up from his knees, looking like he was going to make a break for it.

"I am sorry. I thought you were a soft gringo. I am starving. I lost my job as a taxi driver," he said, backing away, looking for an exit.

"What is your name, ex taxi driver?"

"Miguel, Señor."

"My name is Alistair. Come on, I'll buy you breakfast, you look like you need it." Alistair could tell Miguel was torn between escaping and the promise of breakfast, the aromas of which were in the air.

Alistair smiled at Miguel, raised his eyebrows, and continued on his way, leaving the choice of whether to follow to the little desperado.

Miguel, who was very short, had to trot at high speed to catch up with Alistair's long strides. He looked nervous, eyes darting into every doorway.

The cafe was really just a counter top set in a hole in the wall, with four stools bolted to the pavement outside, but the smell drifting out was heaven.

Miguel was so small, only the top of his head appeared above the counter top.

"Hey, Señor Alistair, are you feeding strays too now?"

"Good morning, Juan, this is Miguel. He is hungry, please give him the works."

They chatted in the dialect of Colon, where all the words merged into one with all the words cut short at the beginning and end.

Juan piled their plates with food. Almost everything was fried and delicious. The coffee was thick, black, and sweet.

"So, Miguel, apart from trying to rob people, what else do you do?"

"I am famous for driving through traffic on my motorbike. I am fast, fearless and never late."

They talked about motorbikes. Miguel clearly had a passion and had Alistair transfixed as he described the tricks he pulled to get through a solid wall of traffic.

Alistair put his finger up and did a writing mime in the air. Juan held up a hand with an open palm. Five dollars.

"My wallet!" Alistair was patting all his pockets.

Miguel was holding Alistair's wallet in front of his face with a mischievous grin, and handed it back to him.

"My other skill is I can take anything from anybody. I knew you could take my knife from me—although I didn't expect you to hit so hard," he rubbed his kidneys, "but I also knew it was the only way I could get near enough to you to pick your pocket."

"Wow, maybe you and I can work together?"

"Sure Alistair, I don't have any pressing appointments."

Alistair roared with laughter and hailed a yellow taxi.

"Gatun?" He said to the driver.

"Excuse me, where are you going?" Miguel asked.

"I have a boat. I'm going to Gamboa, halfway up the Panama Canal, do you know it?"

"Sure, my dad was in the US military back in the Canal Zone days, my mother was Panamanian—I was 'unofficial'. Sometimes we would get permission to come in."

"Well, it belongs to the Panamanians now. If I give you the details, could you come to Gamboa with some supplies, tomorrow?"

"Sure, I am your man."

Alistair handed over pile of receipts for car parts that needed collecting the following day. Miguel put them carefully in his pocket.

They shook hands and Alistair got in the cab alone.

Ten minutes later, the taxi pulled up to a small dock on Gatun Lake at the northern end of the Panama Canal. Small, slightly abandoned looking yachts rocked in the water, cables slapping against masts with a pleasant tinkling sound.

Tied up at the end of the marina was a squat, matt green boat; it had the air of an old veteran about it. Written on the stern in neat military font was the word 'Marmalade'. Although unarmed right now, this was a floating weapons system, known as a PBR or Patrol Boat River, used extensively in the Vietnam war.

Weapons removed, and in the place where gunners normally stood, were piles of boxes.

Alistair fired up the twin jet engines and they purred and bubbled until he released the ropes and pushed the hammers forward until the motors roared and the boat shot forward.

He yelped with delight and sped along the side of the canal channel, jumping over the wake of ponderous tankers and container ships plying their way through the famous waterway.

3

The Magic Shop

Alistair left the main channel of the canal after ten minutes and entered a narrow waterway lined with thick jungle. Palms and vines dipped into the water, rolling up in his wake. Monkeys scuttled along the trees above the water's edge and dart-like toucans launched themselves from branches as he approached.

He eased off the throttles as the channel narrowed and fingers of soft leaves and branches swept the top of the cabin, emanating a gentle perfume.

Rounding the last corner, Alistair turned the PBR 180 degrees as a great metal door rolled open to reveal what appeared to be a large hole in the jungle.

He reversed the boat towards the opening. A woman in WW2 overalls and red lipstick was operating some levers which hooked the boat onto a winch. This was Charlie, the world's best mechanic.

"Welcome to Paddington Station. Did you get all my parts?"

"Yes, except the gaskets. They will be ready tomorrow and I found someone who can deliver them," Alistair shouted over the burbling engines. As the winch started to pull, he killed the engines, and silence filled the space.

The boat creaked up the ramp and the great door rolled shut and lights flickered on inside.

This was just one small section of the maze of underground bunkers known as The Magic Shop.

Alistair had found The Magic Shop one dark and stormy night when he got stopped by a fallen tree along the old 1930s track built by the American Army to provide an oil pipeline across the Isthmus of Panama.

The Magic Shop was a labyrinth of extraordinary discoveries and he and his associates were still finding gems. The PBR being one, along with a Huey gunship tucked into a secret hanger with an opening roof, an armory labeled The Dogs of War, a medical clinic lab and an enormous garage full of military vehicles.

The Magic Shop was the HQ of the Extinct Company Commando Unit.

The Extinct Company had been formed in Scotland, 1627, when the first known animal extinction was recorded. That was the Auroch, a great bovine creature that had once roamed the landscapes of Europe. The last one was shot for sport in 1627 and legend has it that the hunters were King Charles 1st of England and his friends.

Their symbol of The Extinct Company was an arrow pieced skull of an Auroch with its curved horns:

nine men and woman who signed a sacred book on the Isle of Mull in Scotland and founded the secret company. Now, this new team had inherited their book and inside the cover were written the following words:

'In the year of our Lord 1627, we men and women of sound mind and true do hereby declare the formation of the Honourable Extinct Company. We dutifully commit our souls, our swords, and our monies to the defense of those creatures of God who shall be struck down into extinction by the hand of man.

We commit ourselves to defend those creatures to the death and to destroy all of those who seek to take from this earth those creatures who hath been put here by God.

We shall not rest until our work is done.

We shall not be beholden to any other man, state, king or law whom shall bar our path.

6 day March 1627

Castle Moy, Lochbuie.

Their Motto was 'Nobis Non Est' We don't Exist

Since then, The Extinct Company had been dedicated to poaching the poachers of endangered wildlife. Fighting an unconventional war against those that sought to destroy wildlife threatened with extinction.

The Extinct Company fights the poachers at their own level, where governments, international agencies and charities couldn't, without rules.

The Extinct Company has two wings, 'Financial' and the 'Men at Arms'. Each wing operated independently of each other, in utter secrecy. The Men at Arms, or Commandos as they were now named, had been disbanded at the end of the Vietnam War because of a world wariness of fighting and treachery.

Alistair and his team of misfits had already been fighting this war and had found the Magic Shop when the 9th Earl of Godolphin, (code name Brandy), invited them to restart the Commando Wing of the Extinct Company and resurrect their operations.

Their Operations Center was the hub of everything, equipped with the latest technology that money couldn't buy and with a diverse team all dedicated to the same goal: to reverse the end of the natural world.

As Charlie and Alistair finished unloading the parts, Misha walked into the PBR dock. Misha was in her late sixties and wore elegant but practical clothes. As the former Director of Russian KGB cyber intelligence, she could hack into any computing system in the world and helped to fund their operation by "reassigning" funds from known wildlife traffickers.

Each commando had inherited a Sgian Dubh, a Scottish covert knife popular in the 1600s. It was a simple-looking knife, 10cm dagger blade, black, unadorned ebony handle except at the end was the Auroch symbol. One of Japan's most revered sword makers had made the knives, and they had marked the end of many a poacher over the last four centuries. There were just five of these exquisite weapons.

"Alistair, Paloma called from Nairobi. She wants to talk to the team at 10:00." Misha said in her strong Russian accent.

Paloma was Alistair's younger sister, ace pilot, and their ears on the ground in East Africa.

Alistair and Charlie lifted the last box and put it into a room with the words stenciled 'VEHICLE SPARES' on the metal door. Charlie punched the black numbered buttons set into a stainless-steel plate on the concrete frame and the door slid closed with a hiss of air.

They followed Misha down into a maze of corridors made of curved corrugated steel. They passed various doors on the way, all labeled with military looking letters, including one of Alistair's favorites, "UNIFORMS", which had a collection of uniforms and equipment dating all the way back to WW1.

They walked into the Ops Center, which looked something like a mix between the bridge on an aircraft carrier and MI5 headquarters.

On two walls there were screens, including one with a vast map which, for the moment, showed the world with a blinking red dot on Nairobi: Paloma.

Dr. Kitts-Vincent, or Dr. KV as he was known to everyone, was Alistair and Paloma's guardian. He had unexpectantly stepped into the role when their own father had been killed in operations. HDR. KV now also filled the role as leader of the Extinct Company's commando wing. He fit the part—a tall, ebony skinned, muscular man in his early 70s. He stood in front of the screen, feet apart, back ramrod straight and hands clasped firmly behind his back, reflecting his 30 years of military experience with British Special Forces.

"Right. Paloma has something she wants to talk to us about. She sent these."

His voice richly combined the education and breeding born of the British upper class, overlaid with the commanding presence of a senior army officer.

He flashed several images onto the screens, showing the bloody remains of six adult elephants and one calf. They all had their tusks hacked off. Another picture showed the burnt-out carcass of a Mercedes Camper van which was sitting on its roof.

There was a grim picture of two roasted human remains. In the screen's corner was the last image of Selina and Devon Styles alive, in the cab of their van, strained smiles on their faces. Part of Selina's arm was in the picture.

4

Moggy

Deep in the bowels of the Magic Shop, the team sat around the bank of screens until Paloma's face appeared on one. Paloma's high cheekbones and green eyes and normally framed a mischievous grin. But not today. The images of the blackened bodies of the Styles and their charred van remained open on the other screen.

Behind Paloma sat several aircraft while small vehicles with red and white checkered flags scurried from place to place.

"Hello, everyone, I'm at the Aero Club at Wilson airport in Nairobi. I am on standby." She lifted a cup of coffee and rolled her eyes. She was wearing a white shirt with black and gold shoulder tabs and a black tie.

"I've been flying police, CID, and British embassy staff to the Mara."

"Lt. General George Githere was there and he let me jump into a vehicle and see the scene. Poachers killed six adults and one calf elephant. They cut their tusks off. It looks like Devon and Selina Styles were nearby when the elephants were shot and the animals knocked over their van in the panic. It caught fire either by accident or by design.

"They were about 200m from the nearest track. Police found Selina's phone on the ground. That picture I forwarded was their last post, but there was no signal, so they never sent it.

"Sadly, we know that this sequence of events is not unusual, but what is unusual is that these animals had the new Askari System trackers in all of their tusks. The data recorded while they were killed shows them ten kilometers away. No heart rate rise. Around dawn, the signal from their trackers just disappears. Plus, Devon and Selina's photos have no GPS location for at least an hour."

"Somebody has blocked the signal from the satellites, messing up the GPS, then they drilled the trackers out once they had the tusks and smashed them." Misha concluded.

"I know you can buy GPS jammers, but they have limited range, max 20 meters. It is strange that both the elephants and the Styles were out of GPS signal for more than an hour. Unless the Styles were within 20 meters of the elephants and the jammer was in their vehicle, I can't see how this could work." Tatiana, Misha's granddaughter, was talking. Misha had been passing all her KGB training onto Tatiana since she had taken over her upbringing at aged six when Natasha, her mother, had been murdered by poachers. Although Tatiana was petite, she had the body of a gymnast and could reduce a grown man to a heap on the floor in seconds. Like her grandmother, she could hack into almost any computer in the world.

"Wow, so it looks like somebody has developed a GPS blocker that has a wide coverage area." Paloma was shaking her head. "Let me ask the safari guides around the region if they also lost their GPS signals. If that is the case, the whole Askari system would be completely useless."

"Wait, one of the KWS officers just ran into the club." They could hear Paloma speaking to him in an urgent voice in Swahili.

"That was Captain James Mwangi, Alistair. You remember he was in your service team during the Safari Rally you did with Leboo?"

As an 18-year-old, Alistair and his best friend from Prep school, Leboo, had entered one of the world's toughest off-road races. Although they didn't win, they didn't disgrace themselves either.

"Yeah, he is a brilliant engineer. What did he say?"

"Eight adults and two younger elephants just disappeared from the Askari System over in Tsavo—no sign of them where their GPS signal location indicates they are located."

"Tatiana and Alistair, I need you over here as soon as possible. This is already out of control and overwhelming the authorities."

"Roger that. We are moving. Charlie, we are going to need a vehicle that looks like we are just Overlanders cruising the continent."

"Paloma, can you see if you can meet with Leboo and get some local intelligence?" Leboo, who was Maasai, was now a chief and lived on the border of the Mara. He and Alistair still went on an annual expedition that always involved some remote place in the world.

Captain Mwangi appeared in the background and spoke to Paloma again.

"Got to go. They want me to fly a search grid and see if we can find the elephants."

"Be careful, it's a jungle out there Paloma." Alistair said. She rolled her eyes and signed off.

Charlie, Alistair and Tatiana were walking through the cavernous garage at the Magic Shop. This garage had been their first discovery beyond the hidden door in the old bunker. It was big enough to house twenty large vehicles and still have room for mechanics bays around the walls. Their collection of vehicles was enough to build a military vehicle museum.

"Let me take you to Moggy, your Overlander truck. Before Paloma left for Kenya, she and I had been working on the Unimog in the garage. We turned it into an electric vehicle and it has different modules that can be fitted onto the rear bed. Paloma has already named her Moggy," Charlie smiled.

Charlie was a huge fan of off-road electric race vehicles and had perfected the system for one Land Rover already.

The Mercedes Unimogs were medium-sized off-road trucks that had been improving since 1948. They could be found all over the world as military vehicles, fire engines, snow ploughs, expedition vehicles and even in the Paris Dakar race.

"The Unimog has fore-and-aft winches, self-inflating tires, it's bullet proof from small arms fire and there is a GAU-17/A mini-gun mounted in the cab hatch. It has four electric motors, one on each wheel, range in sunlight is infinite and at night it's around 750kms.

"As you can see, it has a twin cab. This means the rear cab can act as an extra sleeping area. I've made a roof top launch area for Biggles."

Biggles was their tethered drone, which could sit 200m above them for 24 hours, sort of like a sentry. It also gave them an amazing communications aerial.

"OK, let's look at the module that locks into the rear bed."

The module was still on the ground and

Charlie had connected it up to power and the internet.

As they stepped in, it reminded Alistair of the Millennium Falcon. There were three command chairs complete with harnesses for off-road use, banks of screens that locked onto the walls and every corner was padded. Keypads and buttons filled the sides. The compartment had its own mini air-conditioning unit.

There was a tiny sink, fridge, and cooker tucked into one corner.

"I love it Charlie, outstanding job." Tatiana sat down and fired up the computers.

"Charlie, not to be a softy or anything, but where do we sleep?" Alistair quizzed.

"Yes, good question. Well, the bench seat in the back should be OK for a small person." She opened the rear door and pulled out a canvas roll.

"And for the rest of you I found these excellent WW2 Australian army swag bags."

She undid the leather straps and rolled out a simple canvas bedding bag.

"They work on the ground."

"The scorpions will be thrilled," Alistair replied, shaking the bag out to check for local inhabitants.

5

Hong Kong

Poppy Cheng sipped her gin and tonic with relish. It had been a long but successful day. Standing up behind her desk, she looked out across the bay of Hong Kong at the pulsing, throbbing city. Small lights darted across the dark water as persistent little boats ferried passengers and goods to their destinations.

Slipping off her red and black silk dress, she dove naked into the subtly lit pool that ran the length of one entire side of her palatial penthouse. Her dive hardly made a ripple, and she reemerged at the other end of the pool. Her black hair shone like one of Poseidon's sirens.

Poppy's father, once one of Hong Kong's most desirable bachelors with global investments running into billions, had shocked everyone by marrying a poor student from the University of Edinburgh. Her mother, although almost penniless and working in the student bar, was not only devastatingly attractive but also at the very top of her class. Poppy had inherited her mother's blue eyes, her lithe figure, and the brain power of both her parents.

She swam ten lengths in a powerful, graceful crawl.

Getting out of the pool, she reached for a fresh towel and walked into her dressing room. The penthouse on the 68th floor of the exclusive tower known as The Cullinan, decorated in a subtle colonial tropical style with rattan chairs, lots of hardwood and long, drifting 'veils' that reached to the top of the 7m ceilings.

Putting on simple Chinese silk pajamas, she looked in her mirrors and smiled to herself then walked back to her desk and scanned the three, wafer thin, screens that glowed there. One showed CNN running a story about a double poaching in Kenya, pictures of a burnt-out van showed alongside portraits of Devon and Selina Styles. Picking up her phone, she punched the contact of a person simply labeled KP1.

"Why am I looking at the death of two Instagrammers next to the elephants? The whole point of this operation was that it was clean. The instructions were explicit, why didn't you wait for them to go past you? Now it's going to be a murder inquiry."

"I am sorry, they were lost because we jammed the signals for GPS for ten kms. We didn't realize where they were until we opened fire," KP1 lied. He knew that if he had waited for the Styles to keep driving, his team would have been spotted. Letting them be in the line of the fleeing elephants worked out perfectly.

"It looked like an accident?" He added hopefully,

"the operation in Tsavo went off perfectly. Our man in the KWS HQ told me it looked like the elephants were ten kilometers from their actual location on the Askari system."

Poppy closed the call in disgust. She knew KP1 was lying—she made another call to KP2.

"Have they found the elephants in Tsavo yet?"

"No boss, they were under a tree and KWS are searching from the air."

"Good, where are you?"

"Still in Voi, just 10km from the elephants. There are police roadblocks and sniffer dogs everywhere, and we can't move with our cargo." They had the bloody tusks of eight elephants tucked behind crates of bananas in a refrigerated 20ft shipping container which was sitting on the back of a battered truck, that was parked next to the bar where they were now drinking cold, Tusker beer. There had been several 'Tusker' toasts already.

"Listen carefully. I need you to do something. Where is KP1?"

"Uhmm he just went off with a, um, young lady." This road was the major artery between the coastal city of Mombasa and Nairobi. Dotted with truck stops that had bars and rooms serviced by 'available' girls.

"Good, here is what I need you to do." When Poppy had finished explaining to KP2 his eyes had narrowed and an evil grin crossed his face.

Pushing off the girl on his lap, he marched out of the low ceiling bar into the bright sunlight. He could hear grunting noises coming from one of the little zinc sided hovels behind the bar. Walking past a fly infested long drop toilet, he kicked open the door of the shack.

"The boss needs us to do a job, NOW."

KP1 swore and pushed the naked girl off him. She jumped up on the bed, sweat running down her back. She tried to slap him, but he caught her hand and bent it back until she was kneeling on the matted, pink sheets.

"You just lost your pocket money, little girl," she spat at him like an angry feline as he walked out the door, leaving it wide open.

"So, what's the job that's so important?"

"We need a safari bus; I'll explain as we drive." KP2 was walking towards a minivan with a roof hatch that opened, 'Jambo Safaris, The Best in Kenya' in colorful letters on the side. They had seen the driver with his 'Jambo Safaris' hat, sinking lower and lower into the bar stool as the day progressed. KP1 followed, doing up his trousers as he walked.

KP2 stepped back into the bar. Putting his hand in the drunken man's pockets, he pulled out a set of keys. The driver didn't move.

"Lala Salama." said KP2. Walking back into the sun, they crossed to the safari van, used the keys they had just stolen, and drove off.

They left the third member of their team to guard their truck.

They drove through Voi gate into the low Leleshwa scrub of Tsavo East National Park. They had found safari jackets with the logo embroidered on the chest pockets and put them on. Several police and KWS Land Rovers raced past them in both directions.

"The boss says one tracker must have fallen out and she can't turn off the jammer until we destroy it." KP2 explained.

"That makes little sense. As long as it's not in the tusk, it doesn't matter where the trackers are, they'll find the bodies pretty soon anyhow. I don't trust her, let's go back. "

KP2 ignored him and kept driving.

"Do as I say. That's an order," KP1 said, as he reached for his pistol. It was gone.

"Looking for this? I do what the boss says not what you say. Move and I'll blow your nuts off." The missing weapon was in KP2's hand and resting on his leg, he pointed the barrel at the other man's hips.

He scanned the track and then drove off into the scrubby bushes. Tsavo was a landscape of low thickets that reached just above the top of their vehicles. Once off the road, you could disappear for days with nobody seeing you.

Within minutes they came to the great hulks of elephant bodies. Their blood had turned thick and black and was swarming with flies.

"Get out and find the tracker." KP2 waved the gun in a 'move' motion.

Stepping out, KP1 looked around for a place he could run to. As he did so, KP2 stepped behind him, put the pistol up to the back of his skull and squeezed the trigger. He slumped to the ground, blood pooled out from the exit wound and mixed with the dust on the ground. The assassin stripped his quarry of all his clothes, including his boots, threw everything in the van and drove off.

Twenty minutes later, he was back on the road.

"Mission Completed."

"Excellent. You are now in charge. Drive to Mombasa, find an empty space and burn the van, throw the pistol into the sea, get another vehicle, and drive back to the truck. Await future orders."

The line went dead.

Poppy's eyes went to CNN on the screen. Footage of the press conference about the Askari System was playing, General Githere was speaking, then Paloma asked a question.

Poppy jolted upright.

"Paloma-bloody-Stuart, I thought I'd seen the last of you.... you meddling, little bitch," Poppy said to the screen, her lips curled back. Holding up her right hand, she looked at it, glaring at the end of her middle finger where the tip was missing.

6

Into the Bush

From Paloma's plane, Captain Mwangi had spotted the vultures homing in on the now putrid flesh of the elephants. There were so many that she'd needed to make some evasive maneuvers while circling the site so Mwangi could send the coordinates back to KWS HQ.

They landed close by and caught a lift in a KWS Land rover to the gruesome pile of bodies.

The rangers were visibly shaken, several were from the Tsavo Park, and they knew this family of elephants well. They gave no sympathy to the naked and now bloated body of KP1. He was a known poacher and petty criminal.

Someone reluctantly put a tarp over his body to stop the vultures from pulling him to pieces before CID got there.

Paloma took several paces back to avoid the swarm of flies now engulfing the entire scene. White maggots could already be seen writhing in the bloated carcasses. If there was one thing Paloma hated, it was maggots. The very sight of them made her retch. As she walked hurriedly away, hand over mouth, her foot knocked on something that was not gravel. She knelt to 'tie her boot laces', picking up a dented cellphone with a smashed screen and slightly guiltily put it in a Ziplock bag inside her pocket. Although she had great respect for Kenyan CID, she knew their resources were limited and processes slow. She would give it to them later with the data that she hoped Misha would harvest.

A safari guide with an empty van stopped close to where she was standing. She walked over to him.

"Hey, terrible, isn't it?" She was wearing her pilot's uniform and speaking in Swahili, giving her instant credibility.

"Horrible, it will be all over the news again, very bad for Kenya, very bad for tourism. What's under the tarp?"

Paloma shrugged her shoulders, not wanting to give away too much information. She asked her own question instead, "Hey, were you out with clients last night?"

"Sure. French family, we saw a leopard about five kilometers from here."

Paloma knew safari guides sometimes WhatsApped their location to other guides when they found something interesting, usually with a picture.

"Did you happen to send your location by WhatsApp to other guides?"

"Young lady, I have been guiding here for twenty years. I don't need WhatsApp to tell me where I am."

She tried another tack.

"Did you take any pictures of the leopard?"

"Sure, I got a great one," he held up his phone showing the excited French family with the leopard walking close to the window of the safari van.

"Would you mind sending it to me? We need all the pictures we can get near the incident. I'll pass it on to Captain Mwangi."

"Certainly, give me your contact." She handed him a card.

The captain was walking towards them. "Right Miss Stuart, let's get back to Wilson, I have a lot to do."

That evening under instructions from Misha she connected the phone she had found and let Misha 'do a little ice fishing.' She also sent the picture from the guide which, as suspected, had no GPS data, just cell triangulation for its location. She sent it to Captain Mwangi, showing the metadata.

Next morning, she hitched a lift with a British Army major in one of their Puma helicopters who was flying up to their training base near Nanyuki in Northern Kenya.

Major Taylor was a rather nervous, ruddy faced man and clearly rather taken with Paloma. She was taller than the Major's five feet, six inches and as fit as a professional boxer. Wearing desert-colored tactical trousers and boots, a green tank top with the words 'Step Aside and Nobody Will Get Hurt' stenciled on it, she had a Glock sidearm and was carrying an MP5. On her left side, like a shadow, was Jeeves, her German Shepherd who was wearing a matching tactical harness. Together they made quite a sight.

She put hearing protectors over Jeeves ears and gave the major a cheeky thumbs up, her green eyes sparkling. She could see the crew in the front of the aircraft chuckling as the major's face went even redder.

An hour later, landing at the shared British/Kenyan airbase brought them into a world of extremes—ordered ranks of parked military equipment contrasted sharply with the untamed red savannah beyond the fence.

As the broad rotors wound down to a stop, Paloma jumped out of the helicopter and pulled her grey rucksack onto her back from the open door. Jeeves sat patiently inside with the major, who also appeared to be waiting for instructions from her.

"Come Jeeves." He bounded out, tail sweeping.

"Thank you, Major Taylor, I owe you one," she said with a warm smile and started walking towards the control tower.

He rather awkwardly stepped out of the helicopter and trotted after her.

"Uh hm, Miss Stuart, I was, err, wondering, if you would like to join me in the mess later, I have got a rather good...."

An incredible roar drowned his voice out. A huge, plump shape swept over their heads, shaking the very ground as it passed.

The rest of the team had arrived. In the distance, the flat gray Atlas military Airbus performed a neat aerial turn, lined up with the runway, and lowered itself until its eight chunky wheels touched the tarmac. The plane came to a halt in what seemed like an impossibly short distance, all four massive propellers screaming.

The Atlas headed towards them, did a 180 turn, and stopped, rear loading ramp descending before the aircraft had finished moving.

As soon as the ramp touched the ground, four black uniformed women wearing hearing protectors ran out in a perfect drill.

The major's mouth was slightly ajar. He looked at Paloma and then back at the plane.

"Thanks Major, I am afraid I already have an appointment. Maybe next time?" She shouted over the noise of the plane.

As she and Jeeves doubled over to the massive machine, a green twin cab Mercedes Unimog inched down the ramp and onto the tarmac. A door opened and the two of them clambered in.

Driving past the major, who was glued to the tarmac, Paloma waved, smiling out of the back window. They headed for the gate of the base, hardly hesitating as the guard hurriedly opened the barrier. The name MOGGY was stenciled on the rear of the truck.

The Atlas was already moving as the rear ramp shut. It blasted down the runway and popped into the sky, wagging its wings like a gigantic dragon as it passed over the Unimog, which was already creating a contrail of red dust.

In the sudden silence, the major stood alone, shaking his head, and staring at the rapidly disappearing red cloud on the road beyond the camp.

The team had concluded that the only way to stop a GPS signal over an area as big as ten square kilometers would be from the sky. They had tested out several theories by trying to calculate how they would do this. It had taken the considerable brainpower of the entire company to narrow it down to three methods: tethered drone like their own Biggles, fixed-wing aircraft flying in a pattern above the site, or fixed wing drone.

They had dismissed the tethered drone because they believe the ground unit would have been spotted. Likewise, the fixed-wing aircraft would need to register a flight plan and it could be tracked to an airfield when it landed. That left the fixed wing drone taking off at a remote airfield and flying at high altitude. But even with the price of Ivory at $100 a kilogram, it would take more than all the world's elephant tusks to buy and operate a drone with those capabilities.

The only lead they had was from the data on KP1's phone that Paloma had picked up. It had several calls from an area close to Lake Turkana, also known as the Jade Sea because of its remarkable color.

That was more than 300 kilometers north of their present position, close to the border of Ethiopia and Southern Sudan.

They couldn't have landed any closer. The Atlas was a large, military looking plane, its arrival at the British Base in Nanyuki was unremarkable. The RAF had several but landing further north would have got the bush telegraph lit up. Plus, the team were pretending to be Overlanders, so they needed to leave a fairly obvious trail. The further north they traveled, the less dense the population, making them more and more conspicuous.

The heat here was like an anvil. Nothing moved except the odd gray dove. Even the camels knelt, sagging in the sparse shade of thorn trees that were shrouded in wind-borne plastic bags. The ragged bunting fluttered slightly as Moggy went silently past. Charlie had considered adding a little speaker that mimicked the sound of an exhaust because the silence of such a big vehicle was a shock. Alistair had voted no, but he knew that Charlie actually had a collection of engine sounds on her iPhone.

This part of the country was on the limit of human existence. Tatiana had an old colonial map open on her lap. The title of the map was East Africa Kenya or EAK, the part that they were in was marked in large letters, 'Not Fit For Human Habitation.' Presumably this was for colonial settlers, not the native Samburu and Turkana people who had existed here for hundreds of years. She was looking for old airstrips, big enough for a large drone.

"Let's overnight at Johansson's ranch, it's just beyond Rumuruti. Johansson always has his ear to the ground." Alistair and Paloma had gone to prep school with the Johansson children, but the family had gone back to live in their native Norway, leaving the grandfather Len Johansson to run the vast 100,000-acre ranch. Len was a tough old hunter and he knew Northern Kenya better than almost everyone.

An hour later they stopped in the shade of a pepper tree on the dusty street of Rumuruti. Emaciated stray dogs scattered as Jeeves was allowed to jump out of the cab before accompanying Paloma into a *duka*, one of many shops that lined the road. There were rows of big plastic buckets, wheelbarrows, and neat rolls of barbed wire hanging from string in a cheerful display around the front door of each shop.

Speaking Swahili, she asked for five bottles of Navy Rum that were securely displayed behind the unsmiling face of the Lebanese shopkeeper. They had fond memories of old Mr. Johansson regaling them with hunting stories—the stories were always punctuated with pauses while the old man took healthy draughts of Navy Rum from an enamel tin mug.

7

Len Johansson

They turned off the main 'road' into a rough drive marked with two acacia tree trunks painted dusty white. There was a faded sign which read 'Rumuruti Ranch' neatly written on a slab of wood.

A dozen assorted dogs came wheeling down the drive, barking and trying to attack the chunky wheels of the Unimog. Jeeves lifted his elegant nose a little higher and ignored them.

"Good boy Jeeves, they're just a bunch of ruffians," Paloma said, rubbing his ears.

As they rounded boulder that marked the entry to the farmhouse, they were shocked at the state of the place. A wide, shallow crater lay before them. Jagged rocks peppered the entire scene, including the house where several had lodged themselves in the doors and wooden siding. Every single window was blown out, and shards of glass were sticking out at odd angles.

Standing in front of the rock-decorated door was a tall, boney man in baggy shorts and an almost colorless shirt. He wore suede safari boots and had a large, drooping, gray mustache. His eyes were such a light blue color that they competed with the clear sky. In his hand was a navy and white tin mug of tea. He was heaving with laughter at their faces.

"Len, what the hell happened here? Were you bombed?" Alistair asked.

Len laughed some more and told his dogs to go into the house. They obeyed instantly.

"You two wild hooligans. Welcome back, I see you brought an extra one in case one of you gets injured. Nice hound." Jeeves was standing to attention on Paloma's left. Len spoke in the clipped tones of a white man whose has spent his life in Africa, but his voice also still held traces of Norwegian Fjords.

"Len, this is Tatiana, our good friend, and Jeeves."

"Also a good friend," Paloma added.

"Tatiana, my kids all left for their Scandinavian sofas. They were too soft, not like these two. These blighters would have camel races that lasted for three days... or until one of them broke something. How's your arm, Paloma? Did I do a good job setting it?"

Paloma laughed and held up her arm, "perfect, thanks Len. I think the rum helped a lot."

"Come in, come in, I'll tell you about my landscaping efforts."

He handed them each a cold White Cap beer from a fridge and threw Jeeves a hunk of meat from a pile under a fly screen on the big table in the middle of the room. The other dogs growled but didn't move.

The ramshackle room was cool, dark and held the rich smells of tobacco, coffee and stew that was bubbling away in a Poiki three-legged pot on the hot embers in the fireplace.

Paloma ran back outside and grabbed the bottles of rum and placed them on the table. Len smiled and nodded thanks.

He said something in Norwegian to the dogs and they jumped off the sofas and chairs that were scattered around the fire. Sweeping his hand across the air in front of the furniture, he sat down on the biggest armchair. The lumpy sofas were covered in threadbare sacking cloth and white dog hair. Paloma caught the look on Tatiana's face and grinned, bouncing down on the nearest one.

The beer tasted good after their long, dusty drive.

"You remember the British Special Forces do their training up here? Well, three of them rocked up in a Landy one afternoon and I gave them a few beers and we put some zebra meat on the *braai*. Yeah, well, it was getting dark, and the beers were going down nicely, and we were talking about how relaxing it would be to be sitting in a pool and drinking those beers. Then one of those buggers, Captain Danning was his name, says he's got two kilograms of plastic explosive in the Landy, and we could make a nice pool with it. He claimed to be the best plastic explosive bloke in the whole British army, and he could make a pool with jacuzzi and an infinity edge if I wanted to. I said I just wanted a big hole. Thing about plastic is you must drill a hole, a deep one, but I only had an eight-inch drill bit... cut a long story short, several beers later, we buried the plastic in an eight-inch hole and fired it off. Turns out that the explosive just blows to the bottom of the hole that you make... and everything above it becomes a million pieces of rock shrapnel."

He drank deeply from his mug. Paloma topped it up.

"So, now I have an eight-inch deep swimming pool and a windowless house!"

He roared with laughter.

"Captain Danning said it was the worst hangover he'd ever had. His head was ringing for days afterwards."

They were all laughing.

"So, you didn't come here to get my landscaping expertise, I assume?" His blue eyes drilled into them.

They explained what had happened to the elephants, the blocked GPS signal and their theories. Len had a sharp mind and was a brilliant inventor. Alistair and Paloma had spent many happy hours working with him in his fully equipped machine shop at the back of the house. He was very up to date on drones and had been using one to create GIS maps of his property.

"Do you remember the Norwegian government NORAD decided to 'save' the Turkana people from famine by teaching them how to fish and building a fish tinning factory on the side of lake Turkana?"

"Yeah, it was a complete failure because Turkana culture revolves around cattle and wants nothing to do with fishing," Alistair answered.

"Exactly. The factory closed down before it even started. I was up there just under a year ago. I was leading a camel safari and as we got close to the old factory, these guys came over in a pickup with AKs and told us to sod off. Well, you know me, so I crept back at night to have a better look and they had added big wide doors to the principal building and that crappy airstrip that was there was now very nice concrete. Paloma, would you mind handing out more beers, I'm too old be popping up and down every time your beers evaporate."

"Wow, that sounds exactly what we are looking for. You have good internet here, don't you?" Paloma said as she collected more beers from the fridge and popped their lids off.

"Yup, built the system myself."

"Let me grab our computers." Tatiana hurried out to Moggy. The sun was losing some of its heat.

Len had built the house around a 20ft shipping container. Invisible from outside and clad in 'normal' walls. He led them through a wood covered steel door. The interior walls of the container were covered in unpainted plywood and a long desk ran all the way along one side. It was loaded with computer gear and screens almost filled one wall. It felt like the inside of a mini sub.

"Wow," Tatiana was looking at the scruffy old man with fresh eyes.

She hooked up their computers and connected to Misha in Gamboa. They introduced her to Len, whose eyes lit up when he saw her and heard her Russian accent.

"So, Misha, what are you doing this evening? Fancy a little chess?"

"I don't think I want to embarrass you by thrashing you when we have only just met."

Tatiana cleared her throat. "Grandmother Misha, we need to explain something to you."

Clearly, she considered her grandmother far too ancient for this kind of flirting, but Len went right on. "Grandmother hey? Looks like your granddaughter is a darn sight tougher than my Gameboy-playing, soft handed grandsons."

They explained the ex-fish factory in Lake Turkana and Misha immediately started sharing information. She pulled up a very recent sat image, which revealed several smart looking 4x4s, new buildings and a perimeter fence.

"One minute, I am finding the owner." She was scrolling through shell companies in Panama and then cross-referencing them.

"The—Bingo—owner is Poppy Cheng, Hong Kong, Billionairess."

"You are kidding me? That evil nasty, vile... bitch."

"Paloma are you knowing this woman?" Misha said in surprise.

Alistair left the room.

8

Old Scores

They were sitting round the table the following morning. Toast, butter, coffee, and marmalade was laid out in front of them. Over Len's excellent stew the night before, they had made their Plan of Action, or P of A, as Alistair called it.

Outside, the turtle doves were just starting their soft, early morning coos and they could hear the zebra making their high-pitched barking in the distance.

"Paloma, can you pass the butter, please?" The moment Alistair spoke, a cheetah came flying through the open door and leapt onto the table, sending everything flying. Her paws flew in four different directions as she skidded off the table, the butter dish clamped in her mouth.

The three visitors jumped up from their seats, mouths open as she disappeared out the door.

"Oh, sorry, I should have warned you about that. Gussy has a thing about butter. She's the laziest cat in the world unless it comes to butter. They killed her mother when she was a cub and I couldn't bear to put her down. One dachshund had just had puppies, so I put her in with them. I tried to teach her to hunt, but she's too smart to do that when

I am walking around with a rifle."

Gussy walked back in. Beautiful orange and coal eyes, underscored by distinctive black teardrops, scanned the table for more butter. Paloma knelt down and stroked her behind the ears. Her pur was like ten domestic cats all added together.

Half an hour later they were back on the dusty road with a promise to return to spend more time with Len.

Traveling north, the track got rougher and the population thinner. The Samburu people here stood on the landscape tending their goats in their red *shukas*, holding long thin spears. Children chased the truck with their palms outstretched.

The odd bush taxi rattled past them in the opposite direction, often piled high with what sometimes looked like the entire contents of someone's house, including goats.

"I think you should tell me about Poppy Cheng. You both obviously have a history?" Tatiana, who was sitting in the front, turned and looked from Paloma to Alistair.

Paloma turned away resolutely.

"OK, I'll tell you."

"Yeah, from your perspective Alistair, perhaps we should start with the facts."

"The facts: Paloma and I were at boarding school in Scotland, Gordonstoun. I was 17, Paloma was 15. She was starting her GCSEs—I was starting my A levels. It was not long after our father had been killed. He was an officer in the SBS and he was killed on an operation. Our mother died giving birth to Paloma. Admittedly, we were both a little wild during that time, don't you agree, Paloma?"

"I guess so."

"Gordonstoun is a terrific school that encourages outdoor adventure and individual characters. It's one of those places where you have some very wealthy and well-connected people but loads of decent down-to-earth kids too. Our father had been a student there. Our grandparents lived in Scotland then, on the West Coast. We still own a lovely house there. Wynards Estate. Anyhow, we were boarders. Gordonstoun is on the East Coast, a long way from our grandparents' home.

Poppy Cheng joined the school in my year to do A levels. She was a boarder too. Everyone knew she was the daughter of a billionaire."

"Yeah, she would arrive in a helicopter with bodyguards. How tacky is that?"

"Facts, Paloma." Alistair interjected.

"But this is where it gets fuzzy, right?" Paloma continued. "So, Alistair falls for Poppy BIG time. Poppy was his first REAL girlfriend, his first love and you know what they say about your first love. You never get over it. Ever since then, he's gone for smart, gorgeous, and exotic girls. Before that the locals were fine."

To his credit, Alistair laughed.

"And Poppy 'falls' for Alistair. It's all snogging behind the bike sheds and heated notes."

Tatiana looked confused

"Kissing, writing love letters, stuff like that."

"But what he didn't know is that when he wasn't around, she was this huge flirt around all the boys. She didn't notice me because I was just a skinny kid with ripped jeans. So, I decided to catch her at it and show Alistair what she was doing. I had tried to tell him, I wanted to look after him, she was going to break his heart."

"I could look after myself and you were spying on her."

"Why was she toying with you? Anyhow, I discovered she was breaking into the gym with other boys, so I set up an OP."

"OP?" Asked Tatiana.

"Observation Post. Yeah, Paloma went into full military combat mode to protect her poor helpless... OLDER brother."

"You didn't realize, blinded by love. Anyhow, I filmed her bonking this Russian boy in the gym."

"And what did you do, Paloma, instead of just showing it to me?"

"OK, so it was movie night at the school and I slipped the footage into the machine."

"So, the entire school saw Poppy and the Russian. How do you say... 'bonking'?"

"Yes."

"Including Alistair? You were watching?"

"Yes, can you imagine what that felt like, the entire school watching my girlfriend humping some Russian kid?"

"Oh, that is bad."

"OK, so maybe I shouldn't have shown the entire school. Maybe I should have just sent it to the headmistress."

"They expelled her and the Russian boy. After three days, her father came and took her away in a helicopter. I have never seen anyone so angry,"

"Did she know it was you who made the film?"

"She couldn't prove it but before she left, she attacked me in the girls' loo with a knife. But Dad had taught us to defend ourselves since we could stand, and she ended up losing the top of her finger. I had just come from gardening club and I had an excellent, and very sharp pair of secateurs in my pocket. She wouldn't let go of the knife that was at my throat, so I cut off the top section of her middle finger. She dropped the knife and legged it and so I flushed her digit down the bog, like a little, bloody, poo. I pruned the Poppy!!" Paloma held up her hand and bent her middle finger down. She had a triumphant look on her face.

"Wow, now I understand. If that had been me, I would have slit her throat." Tatiana drew two fingers across her throat and made a gurgling sound.

"She really was a nasty creature. She was such a bully to the juniors, even to the teachers."

"But Paloma, you went too far with the movie... but at least it wasn't a Ukrainian," Tatiana said optimistically.

There was silence in the truck for the next hour.

They drove through one last town before reaching Lake Turkana. 'Town' was perhaps an over generous description, it was more a line of battered-looking shops or *dukas* all selling slight variations of the same stuff—sardines, rice, soap, '007 whisky' in small plastic sachets, tea and variations of lurid colored nylon blankets and bowls. Shacks where people lived clustered around the shops and two ramshackle bars. There was a butcher selling fly-covered carcasses of goat and bits of camel. A small hill of rubbish was piled up at one end of the town and wretched goats were attempting to chew on the fetid heaps.

They were glad they didn't need to stop at the petrol station, which was three faded pumps standing in the sun: petrol, diesel, and kerosene.

But there was a cell tower here, which meant they could easily connect to the Ops center back in Panama.

Connecting to the humid, rich, green world of Panama made them all feel rather homesick.

They gave Misha a quick situation report or SITREP on their position and progress.

"Any updated intel since last night? Should we proceed to the site?"

"Yes, proceed, as planned. First, there is a police roadblock 20 kilometers ahead. From the radio traffic we have intercepted, they basically give out details of every vehicle that goes through, IDs of passengers, car, destination, etc. This is easy to intercept and we expect whoever is at the fish factory will listen, so you need to make a detour and go around. This is the position of the roadblock." Misha gave them GPS coordinates.

"Second, our friend, Brandy," (this was the Earl's code name) "has been monitoring flights in the area and it looks like a small, slow-moving aircraft took off from the fish factory at around 10pm last night. There was no flight log registered. The plane disappeared over Lake Victoria this morning."

"Third, at 10am Kenya time, rangers found five more recently shot elephants in Marsabit National Park; that's only 100 kilometers from you now. The Askari system showed them 10 kilometers from where the bodies were found. So, they blocked the GPS. We are pretty sure it was that plane that took off from the fish factory. It looks like they cut the tusks off with chainsaws."

"That leaves us with two questions, how are they blocking the GPS signals and what are they doing with the tusks? As you know, as soon as there is a hit on elephants, the police and KWS shut down every access to the area and inspect every vehicle with ivory sniffer dogs."

"Questions?"

"Yeah, what the hell has that bitch Poppy Cheng got to do with this?"

"I'm working on it, and I know what happened between you three. Dr KV said I needed to know, and he was right. Don't let it get personal, Paloma. If she is guilty, we'll get her."

Tatiana drew her fingers across her throat again, making exaggerated, throttled, gurgling noises, which made Paloma feel better. Alistair shook his head.

Abruptly pulling off the track and heading off at a 45-degree angle, Alistair announced, "and now, for something completely different." He was making a wide detour around the roadblock.

They pushed forward through the scrubby bush, branches dragging lines along the paintwork of Moggy. The electric motors gave them much more torque and control than a traditional engine. All the power was going directly to the wheels rather than through a driveshaft and unstoppable as the Unimog was before, it now felt like they could handle anything.

From now on, they would avoid existing roads all together.

9

The Jade Sea

Alistair, Paloma, Tatiana, and a rather hot Jeeves fought their way through the scrubby, rock-scattered landscape. Lonely trees struggled out their meager existence. Heat came in waves, blurring the distant hills. Moggy was not equipped with air-conditioning in the cab, just the rear module.

Planning their route, they realized they had two choices: one was to pretend they were Overlanders doing a little site seeing, the other was to sneak in at night and set up an OP. They decided on the latter. If they behaved like real Overlanders, they would drive across the open scrub during the day, but then they would be easily spotted and probably followed.

Based on this information they had to pick a route in, a place to hide up and, most importantly, an escape route if things got hot. The airstrip was a little way from the factory, and that's what they needed to watch. Settling on an escarpment just off a dry riverbed, Tatiana plotted a route. It was severe and would test their vehicle to the limit, plus they would go under cover of darkness.

Estimating an hour of light left, they pulled under the meagre shade of the biggest tree they could find.

Alistair made Lapsang Souchong tea in the little kitchen that was part of their command module.

Tatiana was teasing him about his British habit of making hot tea in the desert, but when she drank a cup of the sweet, smokey liquid, she asked for more. He told her it was also Winston Churchill's favorite tea.

As darkness fell, the wind picked up, blowing from the east. It would help to mask their sounds, even though there was no engine—the truck was big, old and made plenty of noise as it crawled over rocks. The satellite images revealed no habitation on their route or near their OP.

The rising excitement of going into action made them all jumpy. Paloma took Jeeves for a short walk. They were heading out in an hour. As she walked, she could feel the heat emanating from the ochre rocks beneath her feet, but at least the wind was cool. Before sundown, it had been like standing in front of a hairdryer.

Strapping on their Kevlar vests and Jeeves' harness, they joked about adding layers for the cold weather. Paloma picked up her 1915 Webley Mk. VI pistol, strapping it on with an old Sam Brown belt. The weapon had a short range, but a huge.455 round that could stop a charging man in his tracks.

Climbing aboard, they strapped themselves in. Paloma sat in the hatch so she could look ahead and Alistair was driving; they both wore SPi x28 full color night vision goggles. Tatiana was navigator.

After an hour of traveling, they came to the back of the rocky escarpment they needed to climb to reach their OP. Treacherously, it combined loose rocks and small ledges. There was a danger that if they slipped sideways, the vehicle would roll.

"Let me run up ahead with a strap and winch cable." Almost the only thing that Paloma was truly afraid of was a rolling vehicle.

"There's nothing to tie onto by the look of it." Alistair was scanning the top of the escarpment.

"Let me see, we can't afford to roll down here." Even with Moggy stopped on the start of the slope, there were ominous scraping gravel sounds as the vehicle slipped backwards an inch.

"Come Jeeves. Radio check?" she turned on her set and headed up the rocks with Jeeves at her side.

About halfway up, Jeeves froze, ears forward, looking into a crevice to their left.

Paloma whispered into her mike, "Alert. Jeeves has found something." Tatiana put on her goggles and popped out the hatch. Her silenced Russian machine gun at the ready. Alistair put a round into the breach of his MP5.

Paloma and Jeeves crawled forward and looked over the edge of the crevasse. Bundled in the bottom was a harness and what looked like a parachute. It had smears of blood all over it. They waited to see if there was anything moving. Bloody drips made a trail over the other side of the rock valley.

Together they carefully searched the area, finally collecting the parachute and taking it back to the others.

"What the heck is a parachute doing here? The blood looks pretty fresh."

Nobody had any answers. "I found a dirty great boulder to attach the winch to." Paloma started pulling the rope cable back up the hill, Jeeves on full alert, checking ahead.

After reaching the top with the winch, they could see the place they had selected as their OP: it was perfect. Two hundred meters down a steep but not undrivable slope was a wadi, or dry riverbed, that disappeared in both directions and was wide enough to get the truck down. This connected to a much bigger dry riverbed further on. It was like a system of motorways.

Alistair picked his way down to the site, using the controls of each individual wheel with precision, so the vehicle never slipped.

The OP had large boulders and overhanging rocks which would keep them in shadow during the day. They spread the camo over the vehicle and sent Biggles, their tethered drone, up.

The rear module of Moggy was a fully functioning remote Ops center. Tatiana fired up the computers and communications systems. Once Biggles had reached 200 meters, they could see the airport four kilometers away on their screens. As she zoomed the 50x lens in, they counted ten single engine light planes with registration numbers from across the world. They all looked battered.

On one screen, they were monitoring the GPS signals from the satellites. Right now, it was reading a normal 80 percent. She had set an alarm if it dropped below 65 percent.

Misha's face appeared on one screen. They gave her a SITREP, including the discovery of the bloody parachute and the old single-engine planes.

Together they scanned the live feed from the drone.

Over by the old fish canning factory, there was a fence and, as Len had described, a pickup was patrolling the perimeter.

Parked on the side of the old building were six Toyota Urvans with pop-up roofs, the ubiquitous safari vehicle for the less expensive lodges.

There was writing on the sides, but they couldn't make it out. Beyond the vans were six battered-looking lorries with nondescript 20 ft. containers on the rear bed of each one. These trucks were so common in this part of the world that nobody noticed them until they had an accident. Each container had a faded jade and yellow paint job.

"Why would they put those vehicles there with armed guards and a fence? Nobody goes on safari this far north." Paloma asked.

Equally perplexed, Misha suggested they have a closer look.

10

Recon

Tatiana and Alistair put on their dark combat equipment and rubbed camo cream into their faces. There was no moon yet, and the wind was blowing hard—perfect conditions for a nighttime reconnaissance.

Misha had loaded the Unimog with an array of useful equipment, including several high-performance tracking devices, which would work as long as there was a GPS system. They could attach these to vehicles with powerful magnets. They loaded everything into their packs. Tatiana carried a Vintorez silenced assault rifle, which was used by Russian special forces and a silenced pistol. Alistair carried a Magpul 870 combat shotgun and Glock sidearm.

Paloma handed them some snacks. "I am going to make steak and kidney pie for supper when you get back." They had a good supply of British Army rations, known as Rat-Packs, which included several classics; Alistair and Paloma had grown up using them on every expedition with their father, and Tatiana had surprised them by becoming a fan.

"Can we finish with treacle pudding?" Her favorite.

It was good to have something to look forward to after returning from a dangerous mission.

Strapping on their backpacks and flipping down their night sights, they headed down the escarpment to follow the dry riverbed which came out right next to the old fish factory and airstrip. Paloma would monitor their progress. They both wore cameras which would send live video.

The air had cooled and they hastened down the dark tunnel of trees arching over the riverbed. A few dik-diks trotted out of their way but apart from that they were on their own.

Nearing the factory, they saw crude fences made of thorn bushes pulled in a circle around flimsy looking huts where the indigenous Turkana people lived. The remains of houses built by the well-meaning Norwegians lay unused.

They needed to get into the compound so they could attach their trackers to the vehicles and planes. Lake Turkana is so far North of any large population and the operations in the fish factory so well disguised that the guards took a relaxed attitude to their patrol, that when the pickup patrol drove around the fence close to them, they could see both occupants in an animated conversation with each other with hardly a glance outside. The cab was fogged with air-conditioning and cigarette smoke.

After the vehicle passed, Alistair and Tatiana clipped a small slit in the chain linked fence that surrounded the airfield then crouch-ran towards the parked vehicles. Rolling under each one, they attached the trackers, which locked on with a metallic thud. Activating the devices once they were in place, Paloma back in the Moggy confirmed the location lock when it went live over their radio. She labelled each one with the number plate and type of vehicle—"KDK667G URVAN is live."

'Safari Nzuri' was written on the sides of each van with a cartoon of a smiling elephant.

Completing all twelve vehicles, they were heading back to the fence to wait when a door in the factory's side opened, spilling light across the vehicles and out towards their position. Dropping and facing the door, weapons pointed, they froze. Six men carrying AK47s, a chainsaw, and wearing backpacks walked out. Four of them got into the first Urvan. They were all dressed in Safari Nzuri khaki uniforms. The other two, scruffily dressed, got into a blue and battered Isuzu truck with a 20ft jade and yellow shipping container on the back. It started up with a cloud of black smoke. Alistair and Tatiana tried to make themselves invisible by flattening closer to the earth.

The headlights of the truck came on, but they were so cracked and filthy they only illuminated a shallow pool in front of the vehicle. Pulling out, it blocked the lights of the Urvan which had also started, and Alistair and Tatiana found themselves in the deep shadow of a 20ft container. The Urvan whipped past the truck and headed for the gate, which was being opened by a guard. The lorry lumbered on behind.

Alistair and Tatiana quickly retreated under the fence and set themselves up in a spot 100m beyond under a scraggly thorn bush. Nothing, apart from the pickup patrol, moved. After an hour, they went back in to add trackers to the four planes parked on the taxiway.

"I want to just blow the bloody things to bits." Alistair still had the images of dead elephants in his mind.

"Me too, but old planes are easy to replace. We need to find out what they are using them for."

Hiding a tracker on a small plane proved more difficult than expected, apart from the fact that most of the aircraft was aluminum so their magnets wouldn't work, and all the surfaces were so smooth that foreign objects would be easy to spot. Tatiana solved it by picking the locks on the doors so they could stuff them into the fabric of the seats from below.

They relocked the doors and crept back under the fence to their hiding place, beyond the wire.

"Bloody Mary, do you read me?" This was Paloma's call sign.

"Loud and clear Whisky, go ahead." Alistair's was more obvious.

"Any sign of loss of GPS signal? Are those two vehicles giving clear positions?"

"Affirmative, all systems are working perfectly."

"Vodka and I will stay here for one more hour and see what else happens."

"Roger that, standing by."

Sixty minutes later, apart from the patrol going by twice, nothing else had stirred.

Alistair turned to Tatiana. "Ready for steak and kidney pie?"

"And treacle pudding?"

"Absolutely."

"Bloody Mary, do you read me?"

"Loud and Clear Whisky."

"Put the steak and kidney on please, we are heading back."

"Roger, that."

Fifty minutes later, they were enjoying a hot supper under the camo net that made a tent and covered the Unimog.

Paloma had an iPad set up in front of them showing slow moving red dots. The truck was well behind the Urvan. They were both heading south on the main road.

"You guys go to sleep—Jeeves and I will take first watch." Jeeves lifted his head from the sandy ground when he heard his name.

Alistair and Tatiana rolled out their swag bags onto the sandy ground. Jeeves lay his noble head on Alistair's lap and he tucked into his bag.

"Hey, aren't you on first watch?" Jeeves opened his eyes, then shut them again with an added sigh.

Just as they were settling down, they heard a plane starting up over at the airfield. It spluttered, coughed, and finally fired.

Tatiana and Alistair leapt up and climbed into the Ops center on the back of Moggy. Paloma had already zoomed in on the plane, which wasn't yet moving.

"Hey, they have removed all the registration numbers from the fuselage."

"That plane must have been inside the factory because it wasn't parked outside when we were there. Damn. That means it has no tracker."

"Paloma, did you get footage of the pilot getting in?" She opened a video on the other screen and scrolled backwards until they saw someone walk towards a plane being pushed out of the factory by four men.

"Yeah, and he doesn't look like the type of chap that registers a flight plan."

"What's he wearing on his back?" Tatiana was pointing at the screen.

"Mark four parachute!! just like the one we found." Paloma grabbed it. "Look, here's the harness." She was right, it was the same.

"Maybe the planes are so old the pilot needed to bail out?"

"Yeah, but this guy is taking off in the dark in a plane that is not rated for night flying. I saw the cockpits of those planes from your video feed—something strange is happening."

The plane taxied to the head of the runway, and the pitch of the engine increased.

11

The 'Drone'

The little plane bolted down the runway, cracking the silence of the night as it rose up. There were no lights on the plane or ground. Biggles, however, was equipped with night vision, and the team could watch as it lifted off the concrete and peeled left in an arc.

The plane, a Cessna 182, continued upwards in its slow circles around the airfield. Eventually it disappeared out of the top of the screen in Biggles' cameras.

They ran outside but even their night goggles showed nothing. The plane had reached such an altitude that it was beyond their vision.

"That little thing has a ceiling of around 18,000 ft, looks like he's heading up there?" Paloma, the pilot, was giving commentary.

The wind had dropped and they could hear the aircraft climbing, then it changed pitch.

"Oh, hang on, he's leveling out, can anybody see him?" There was no sign.

Tatiana went back in to check the feed from Biggles.

"Quick, look at this," they ran back inside to join her.

On the screen, a white parachute was drifting slowly downwards towards the airfield.

"Mark 4 parachute. The bugger jumped out but the plane is still going, can you hear it?"

They could. The parachutist landed on the tarmac—he pulled in his chute and started walking—he was limping as one of the Urvans peeled out from the side of the factory and picked him up.

"Wow, so that plane has no pilot, right?"

The other two nodded.

"Would you agree he sounded like he was heading Southwest? Where are the vehicles, Tatiana?"

She clicked on the red dots, "heading Southwest, toward Mt. Elgon National Park."

Paloma was dialing a number on her phone. She waited a long time before someone answered—it was nearly midnight.

"General Githere, I am sorry to bother you so late. This is Paloma Stuart. We have intel that you have a group of poachers going to hit elephants in Mt. Elgon Park. They are in an Urvan, registration number. KDK667G, and an Isuzu lorry with a 20ft container on the back. Their position is..." she related the coordinates and spoke for a few more seconds, nodding her head.

"They are sending a KWS Rapid Response Team out now, they will intercept them on the road."

"What has the plane got to do with it? Let's see if my grandmother has any ideas."

Tatiana connected to the Ops center in Gamboa and they updated her, although she had been watching their video feeds.

"You know we were looking for a drone—but maybe the plane is the drone? The pilot performs the take off and then jumps out. Unmanned, it somehow flies over the site and blocks the GPS. The complicated part of any air mission is takeoff and landing. A pilot does the takeoff and then when the plane completes its mission, they just let it crash. By the look of them, those planes are worth less than a compact car. If they have worked out how to pre-program their flight so that at a certain point is just flies in big circles, that could be when the GPS signal is blocked. It is actually brilliant. Can you imagine if they flew over a city, the damage that would be caused? Deliveries would stop, people would get lost, trains would crash into each other, it would ground planes, ambulances wouldn't know where to go. Did you know in the first Gulf war when GPS was still in its early days and there wasn't always a signal, tanks would simply stop and wait until the signal came back?" They could see the implications shocked Misha.

"This could have a profound affect, not just on elephant poaching but the entire world of conservation. I think there is a bigger picture that we are missing."

"But right now, I am watching an armed gang heading straight towards a group of elephants that live in Elgon and we need to do something." Alistair had his eyes on the flashing dots on the screen representing the two vehicles they had tagged earlier.

As they watched, both dots disappeared.

"That's it, the plane must be overhead, blocking the GPS signal."

Paloma called the General again, giving him the last known position of the trucks. She dropped her head as she listened to his response.

"The Rapid Response unit hasn't left the ground yet; they had a problem with their heli."

They all looked at each other, knowing what was about to happen and feeling like they had failed the elephants.

They knew they had no way to reach the elephants before the poachers, and even if they could, they were unlikely to find them without a GPS.

They had the image of the last lot of elephants killed, seared into their minds. The thought of the wisdom and gentility of the elephants made the possibility of their violent death all the more heart wrenching.

There was a long silence, as if they were almost waiting to hear the shots.

"We have to nail those bastards. We will poach the poachers, gun them down in the same way." Alistair's voice was hard and cold.

12

Ambush

Alistair, Paloma, and Tatiana quickly packed up their camp and drove forward down the dry riverbed. Tatiana was in contact with Misha in Gamboa to work out a good ambush point. They knew that there was only one road out of Mt. Elgon based on the entry route of the vehicles.

They expected the tracking devices to come back online as soon as the plane disappeared. It would not make sense for the Urvan and truck to drive together, the truck being much slower.

Tatiana held up her iPad to show Paloma. Alistair was driving with night goggles on, so he couldn't look.

"Here?" She pointed to her screen. There was a high-resolution map with contours.

"If we stop here, we can hit them with the mini-gun and one of us can be on the other side behind this boulder to create crossfire." The area she was showing was a road cut into a hillside. There was a flat space with trees where they could turn, but the Urvan would be stuck on a single-track road.

"After we hit them, we could push them off the cliff here." She pointed to a wooded bank that ended in a deep gulley.

"And then wait for the Isuzu. Ideally, we capture them with the ivory and hand them over... but we can't let them see us or the truck,"

"Let me ask you something. What is the purpose of killing the poachers, is it revenge or to stop them doing it again?" Alistair spoke up. Despite driving at high speed, in night goggles, over extreme terrain he had been listening carefully.

"Revenge and to send a message. We want them to suffer." Paloma was unequivocal.

"We want to stop them doing it again and, if possible, find out some information from them. I am worried that if we blast them to hell with a mini-gun and push them over a cliff, we will simply alert the rest as soon as they find out." Tatiana was more measured.

"So could we make it look like an accident, or even create an accident?" Alistair offered.

"Sorry Alistair, I still want to blow them into little chunks with the mini-gun."

"Would a slow death in a burning vehicle satisfy you? That would also be a way to get the truck to stop and maybe even a way to get the guys out so we can question them."

"Bastards, they are probably cutting the tusks off the elephants as we speak."

"Look Paloma, there is an entire crew that we have to take out and don't forget about Poppy. We have to link it all back to her," Alistair was pleading.

"You don't think you might go all gooey when you see her and her lovely dark hair being dragged away by INTERPOL and want to save her?"

"I'm over her." His voiced told her the subject was closed.

"OK, so have you got a plan to make a van have an accident and burn all the occupants to death?"

"Nope, Tatiana?"

"No."

"Hey, the red dots just came back. That means the GPS is on again." The dots were as they expected, heading along the single road out of Elgon. The Urvan was pulling away from the truck.

"Tatiana, what is our ETA at the ambush site and theirs?"

She was estimating time, speed, and distance.

"We will be there in about 30 minutes if we keep up this speed, the Urvan will be there in, hang on," she was scribbling, "fifty minutes and the truck, maybe one and a half hours, although there are some steep hills which may slow him down."

"So, let's make a P of A: we have 30 minutes. Paloma, is there any tea left in the thermos?"

"Yup," pouring some for each of them she asked, "So how do we create a crash, make sure they don't get out of the vehicle, set fire to it and make it all look like an accident then capture the guys in the truck behind?"

"Bond, James Bond," Tatiana said it with her Russian accent and a sideways grin on her face, that made her quite adorable, Paloma and Alistair grinned expectantly. "Aston Martin DB5, remember how he squirted oil out the back and the car chasing him spun off the road?"

"We have a whole twenty liters of spare oil—we could spread it on the road. If we could get them to brake just before they hit it, maybe a fallen tree?"

"We could pull one over with the winch, so it looks like it fell?"

"They would slide into the tree at high speed... nasty."

"Perhaps if we spread a little napalm across the tree and light it when they hit, it would finish the job?"

"Where do we get napalm at this time of night?!"

"You can make it, just add bleach and polystyrene together then diesel, we have all three, then... puff the magic dragon."

"Are you guys serious?"

"Yes," Paloma and Tatiana said together.

Arriving at the spot, they realized they had chosen well—a gnarled cedar tree hung over the road just beyond the bend. Paloma scuttled up its branches trailing black para-cord.

"That should do it," Alistair spooled out the winch rope attached to the cord wrapped around the tree as Tatiana pulled it down. When the hook reached the tree, Paloma clipped it over the rope and scrambled down. Alistair put his boot on the brakes and pressed the switch to wind in the 20,000lb winch, the tree's roots in the soft sandy bank were no match for the machine and soon the earth around the base was ripping out of the ground, the tree reached its tipping point and smashed to the road.

They spread the oil starting 20 meters from the tree—they estimated the van would brake as soon as they rounded the bend and saw the tree.

"Incoming ten minutes." Tatiana was watching the dot get closer.

"Blimey, I hope some old bugger on a motorbike doesn't show up first...."

Paloma was mixing the napalm. When it was ready, they spread it on the tree, leaving a line to the other side for Alistair to light.

Tatiana moved up the bank with her silenced assault rifle. They tucked the Unimog out of direct sight, but with a line of fire from the hatch with the mini gun.

The van was coming along at high speed. Rounding the bend, the driver panicked the instant he saw the tree across the road, slamming on the brakes as he wrenched the steering wheel over. The boxy vehicle went into an instant full 360 spin before gravity took over and it flipped onto its side. There was a screeching, smashing noise as it slid, almost without slowing, into the tree. Sparks flew as metal met tarmac. The ancient tree shuddered as the van crunched into it, the upper part and windows instantly squashed as they impacted the solid timber.

There was a fraction of a second of utter silence and then a whoosh as everything turned into an inferno. Ammunition from the poachers' weapons started going off in uneven pops from inside the van. The team took cover as random explosions scattered bits of hot metal into the air.

"Looks like they went straight to hell, the bastards," Paloma told the others from her radio.

"How long have we got until the truck with the ivory gets here?"

"We can't be sure it has ivory, but it looks like it will be here in 20 minutes, no chance of getting cell phones from that mess." Tatiana was moving down the hill to inspect the Urvan which had settled into a gentler fire, belching black smoke.

After seeing there was nothing to salvage, they returned to Moggy and sent a message to Misha back at the Ops center in Panama.

Just as they got in, a massive explosion lifted the van off the ground, ripping it apart and blasting most of the tree out of the way. Paloma dropped instantly into the cab as shrapnel peppered the front of the Unimog, which had jumped backwards with the force of the blast. Without her ear protectors, it would have deafened her.

"Shit, they must have been carrying explosives. There goes our roadblock." Alistair looked at the small crater where only parts of the van were remaining. It pockmarked the armored windscreen of Moggy where shrapnel has struck it.

"If the truck was carrying ivory, you would have thought the Urvan would stay with it, to guard it, as least fairly close to it. Yet those guys seemed to race away from it." He added.

"Unless they have another escort? A Safari vehicle escorting an old truck would look strange and they may want to separate the poachers from their loot? Five minutes. We need to get into position." Tatiana was looking at the red dot getting closer.

"I'm going back up the hill. We want them to get out and inspect the van so we can capture them, but this no longer looks like an accident and they may get spooked and run for it. With the tree gone, there's nothing to stop them."

"If they don't stop, we open fire. Tatiana, take some frag grenades with you. Paloma, if you drive, I'll man the mini-gun. Agreed?" Alistair was climbing up into the hatch. Paloma put an MP5 in her lap and started the engine. Tatiana disappeared past the flickering glow that once was a minivan and started climbing back up the hill. The blinking red dot was almost upon them.

13

Ivory Battle

The first thing that came around the corner was not an Isuzu lorry with a 20ft container unit on its back. It was a Toyota Land Cruiser which skidded to a stop just before it hit the remains of the Urvan and four armed men jumped out almost before the car stopped moving. They fanned out in a professional choreograph and tucked in behind the cover of the remaining tree trunk.

Tatiana, now on the other side of the hill and never one to hesitate, opened fire with her silenced weapon, neatly slotting two of the men in the head before the others even registered what was going on. The remaining two poured automatic fire into the woods, far beyond where Tatiana was concealed. The Isuzu lorry came around the corner, full brakes already on. It slid unceremoniously into the Land Cruiser, which lurched forward under the impact. The lorry stalled and there was silence. The smell of burnt rubber from the truck tires hung in the air. Then Tatiana took out the other two men. Alistair and Paloma heard the twin thwacks of the heavy rounds hitting flesh as they crumpled to the ground. The driver of the Land Cruiser floored it, driving over one of the prone bodies with a sickening bump.

Alistair lit up the mini-gun, and the windscreen of the car simply vanished, revealing the dancing corpse of the driver as the rounds poured through him, through his seat and into the radiator of the Isuzu behind.

The crew of the lorry were desperately trying to restart it. Black clouds of smoke coughed out of the exhaust until Alistair adjusted his aim and they, too, were plastered against the back of their cab at 3000 rounds a minute. They had no chance.

Running down under the watchful eyes inside the Unimog, Tatiana checked each of the bodies carefully. As she looked for signs of life, she also removed all personal items she could find which they would use later.

"Clear. They are all dead. I found a laptop in the Land Cruiser that survived Alistair's lead storm!"

"Great, come Jeeves, let's find some ivory." Paloma, bolt cutter in one hand and powerful torch in the other, jumped down and headed towards the container on the back of the Isuzu with Jeeves at heel. Misha had been training Jeeves to sniff out ivory and rhino horn, a game he loved. Alistair kept watch using his night goggles behind the mini-gun.

Paloma's German bolt cutters went through the two padlocks like cheese and she and Jeeves scrambled in. The container was half full of sacks of rice covered in blue and red stamps that read, "A Gift from the United States of America." Many had leaked their contents. Neat lines of holes from the mini-gun studded sides of the metal box and Alistair and Tatiana could see shafts of light appearing and disappearing in a mini laser show as Paloma swept her torch around inside.

Jeeves immediately sat down with his eyes glued to one spot that told her he had already found something. They trained him not to bark and bring possible unwanted attention.

"Good job, Jeeves." Pulling a few sacks aside, she soon revealed several still bloody tusks. Any doubts about killing the men outside evaporated instantly.

"Yes, it is full of tusks, and I am looking at holes where they drilled out the GPS trackers." Paloma was speaking on her headset.

"Come back to Moggy, we will ask Misha to make an anonymous call to report the ivory so that the KWS can find it." Alistair said, "Tatiana will start running tests on the laptop and phones. Quick, I can hear more vehicles coming." They were wearing headsets that increased small noises but suppressed loud noises like gunfire.

Alistair pulled Moggy into the road as Paloma and Jeeves jumped in. Just as they started down the road, a ten-tonne Kenya Army truck appeared around the corner, the driver braked and skidded but most of the oil had burnt off, so he controlled it, before bumping into the Isuzu with its container which was still blocking the road. A figure pushed open the roof hatch, cocked the GPMG on a swivel mount, and opened fire at the stern of the disappearing Unimog. Several camouflaged men disgorged from the rear, dropping to their knees as they also opened fire.

Inside the Unimog, they could hear the heavy rounds clattering against the armor plating at the rear. Once again, they said a silent thank you to Charlie's planning. Alistair saw another truck appear in his mirror before they rounded a bend, and the firing stopped.

"What the hell is the Kenya Army doing opening fire on us without warning? There was no hesitation!" Paloma was indignant. She had several good friends in the army and frequently worked with them flying supplies to remote communities during times of drought.

"If you needed to move large groups of heavily armed men around the country the best way to do it would be to disguise them as the Kenyan Army, just like they did with the poachers as safari guides." Tatiana was simultaneously cracking into the laptop she had found, keeping up with the conversation and hanging on as Alistair belted around corners.

"I think Tatiana's right. They arrived before we even sent our message and they weren't there to ask questions. In that case, they will unload the ivory before they push the Isuzu off the road so they can chase us. Let's update Misha." Alistair was using all his rally skills to keep the 12-tonne truck on the road. With its electric motors the Unimog was much faster than the army ten-tonners, but they weren't sure what else they might encounter.

After giving Misha a SITREP using a satellite phone, she asked for thirty minutes to do some enquiries and talk to The Earl.

Feeling safer, they drove more slowly through increasingly densely populated areas and eventually Alistair took off his goggles and turned on his headlights. There was still an hour before dawn. Paloma dismounted the mini-gun and closed the roof hatch, then passed out mugs of tea and gingersnaps.

They called Misha and put her on loudspeaker.

"According to my sources, there are no active Kenya Army units operating in and around Mt. Elgon. There was no order given to open fire on anyone, there are strict protocols regarding live firing and even stricter ones inside national parks. In fact the army can only operate in a national park with permission of Lt. Gen. Githere, he did not give that permission."

"We can therefore assume it is a rogue unit or not an army unit at all and it was just a disguise."

"We don't think they will attack you in a populated area in daylight. Nowadays everyone has cell phones and it would trigger a nationwide hunt." They agreed.

"The Earl has invited you to join him for supper at the Muthaiga Country Club tonight. He has set up one of the family cottages for you. You can park Moggy around the back behind the cottage. Meet him at the Pinks bar at 5.30pm for sundowners."

They passed through Eldoret, once a sleepy agricultural town but now a busy hub. Alistair pulled over by a road vendor and they bought Farmer's Choice sausages in hot bread rolls slathered in spicy Kenyan ketchup and ate them for breakfast on the move. Jeeves got one too.

Now they were driving at a more sedate speed along a less potholed route, Tatiana climbed into the Ops module mounted on the rear and fired up all her computers. An hour later, she climbed back into the cab through the connecting hatch and opened her laptop between them.

"I think I have worked out what they are doing, and it's much more serious than we thought."

14

MCC

They pulled into the calm garden car park of the Muthaiga Country Club in the early afternoon. Alistair jumped out and registered them, getting the keys to their cottage. He and Paloma had been there frequently when they were students at the upcountry prep school. Many parents of their friends were members and they allowed children free range within the gardens.

MCC was once a bastion of white colonial maleness, a drinking hole for politicians, hunters and government officials. Nowadays, there was a healthy mixture of society, at least a healthy mixture of the upper echelons. Getting membership was notoriously difficult.

The rules were limited and allowed for the slightly rebellious nature of the members. You could party as hard as you liked but any damage was billed at three times the cost of repairs. Briefcases, firearms and cellphones were forbidden in the main dining room and bar, where gentlemen also had to wear a jacket and tie.

They received some sideways glances as Paloma drove their bullet scarred and muddy lorry down the neat gravel driveway to the cottage behind the tennis courts. Paloma spotted one of her old mates from school sitting having Pimm's on the lawn and called to her out the window as they passed. Jeeves stuck his head out at the same time.

"Grace, Grace Kenedje, who's that good-looking chap you're with?"

Paloma was still in full combat gear minus her helmet, and Grace's expression reduced her to squeals of laughter.

"Paloma Stuart! You get out here and have some Pimm's. What on earth are wearing and what's that thing you are driving?"

"Don't go anywhere, I just need to have a bath and put on some fresh clothes."

At school she and Grace had been on the winning Hog Charge team, an extreme national mountain bike event for kids. They had won three years in a row, an unbeaten record.

The cottage had once been a colonial farmhouse with deep verandas, cool slate floors and high ceilings. They each had their own rooms with lovely, enormous bathrooms. The contrast with their last few days made them feel like they had just gone to heaven.

After a quick bath, Paloma put on a fresh summer dress and went out to see Grace. Shouting behind her as she shut the door,

"Alistair, don't forget you have to wear a jacket and tie... or they make you borrow one of their nasty ones..."

"Thank you, I know the drill... I'm just thinking about what's on the Trolley tonight," he shouted back from his steam filled room.

Somehow the Earl had convinced MCC committee that Jeeves was a working dog and therefore should be permitted to join them inside the club, so Paloma took him along, shocking some guests until they saw how beautifully he behaved.

Grace had already ordered her a Pimm's, which came in a pint beer mug.

Alistair had a long bath, then fell into a deep sleep in the crisp, sun-dried sheets.

Tatiana quickly washed and changed and was back in the Ops module within half an hour.

The Earl arrived early and settled himself into his favorite corner at Pink, the outside bar at the MCC. The Earl was in fact the ninth Earl of Godolphin, a retired British army general. His position as head of the anti-poaching unit at INTERPOL was a well-guarded secret. As an Earl, he was a member of the House of Lords, and he played the role of a rather boring and slightly right-wing politician. The Earl was their commanding officer in the Extinct Company. He used information and resources from INTERPOL so that The Extinct Company could do what INTERPOL could not—poach the poachers.

He was wearing an immaculate three-piece linen suit that made him look vaguely like Winston Churchill.

Calling the red-uniformed waiter over, he ordered a pink gin and tonic. No money was exchanged at the club, you simply signed a chit and received your bill at the end of the month.

A copy of *The Nation* newspaper lay on the table with the headline. "Third Group of Elephants Killed in Mt. Elgon National Park" It explained how the bodies of eight elephants had been found with their tusks cut off. Authorities had caught no poachers yet, but they were actively pursuing several leads.

The four of them walked in, Jeeves trotting neatly beside Paloma. Alistair looked slightly uncomfortable in his tie and tweed jacket. Tatiana looked great in a long safari dress, silk scarf and knee-high suede boots that laced all the way up.

They ordered pink gin and tonics, although Tatiana had hers with vodka.

The Earl had organized little white triangles of bread with Marmite and butter.

"Sort of tradition," he said by explanation. "So run through everything that has happened. I assume you saw the headlines?" Nodding towards the paper.

They told their war stories.

"Tatiana hacked into the laptop we found in the Land Cruiser, she and Misha have been working on it nonstop since we got it, Paloma and I had a little R&R while she was working, Tatiana do you want to explain what you have found?"

"So, there are many pieces of the puzzle and this is how we think they fit together."

"Number One. Funding and organization seem to come from Hong Kong, specifically Poppy Cheng. It is well hidden, but we have traced it for certain."

"That Dragon bitch,"

"Thank you, Paloma. "

"Number Two. Their main operational base is in the old fish factory in Turkana.

"Three. They are using unmanned planes as drones to mess with the GPS trackers implanted in the elephants' tusks: the Askari System. A human pilot takes off—presumably because this is the most complex part of the flight—and then bails out as soon as the plane hits the right altitude.

"Four. And this is the smart bit. They then command the plane from the ground using simple servos which handle the controls. It has a powerful GPS blocking device which points downwards so the plane can still receive the GPS it captures and basically hijack the data from every device below it and then block it. It is a bit like hacking into thousands of bank accounts and then blocking the users.

"Five. We think this is the actual goal. They have basically stolen not only the live position of every elephant but of every device within the radius of the flight."

Tatiana took a sip of her drink and looked at the Earl.

"This means they can choose when and where to hit the elephants. They will know the location of every ranger, every vehicle, every cell phone?" he asked.

"Exactly. We think hitting the elephants is just a diversion that came with a bonus of ivory. You can expect the same thing to happen in each park and then they will start taking out individual animals. Our guess is that they will roll this across Africa just as the Askari System is being completed."

"Wait, let me get this straight. Once they fly around an area for an hour, they can basically 'own' the location of every device forever?" Paloma was looking at Tatiana.

"Yes, Misha and I believe that's how it works. You know when you want to log into your bank account online and you have to use a unique token either from a device or an app on your phone?" Everyone nodded.

"Those are almost impossible to hack because they are dynamic, they change and the number on the token only lasts seconds."

"Yeah, bloody things, I'm always too slow and have to do it multiple times." The Earl was shaking his head.

"Well, unlike the token, the GPS requires a constant signal to update the position. But each device has a unique signature, so if you get that signature it is like getting the token from a bank account, except it's not dynamic, so once you get it you can see where that device is whenever you want. Does that make sense? It is how we know where our trackers are. We already have the 'token'."

"Thanks, Tatiana, that makes sense, but why hasn't someone done this before?"

"Well, the Askari system has a military grade encryption, and it's really hard to hack into and you have to be within 10 meters, by which time you might as well just see the elephant. What these people have done is intercept the communication between the satellite and the device from 3kms in the sky. Nobody thought that possible." Tatiana looked at everyone's faces to see if they understood. The Earl's held a dark expression.

"You said the Askari System had a military grade encryption?"

“Exactly, the same as you would... find... in... a... tank or military vehicle... oh my god, that means they could use this for....”

“A military application.” The Earl Finished. “Or a terrorist organization. Imagine the damage that could be done if the wrong people got hold of this in somewhere like Afghanistan.”

“I don’t think Poppy is after the ivory at all. I think she’s running a live demonstration of her system with ivory as the sweetener.”

“She’s using a budget version of the system, flying it in old planes, but imagine if it was attached to a high-level drone above a battlefield, it would be chaos. You could stop missiles, tanks, antiaircraft fire, everyone would get lost.”

“Tatiana, you and Misha need to find out if Poppy Cheng has any connection or is in contact with a high-level official that would A: be shopping for such a system and B: has a taste for large amounts of ivory. I will give you everything we can find at INTERPOL.”

“Finally, and this will be our job to investigate. They can move the ivory because they are using what looks like Kenya Army escorts, although they may not be real. Let’s move to the dining room and make a P of A.”

The sun was setting.

“Good, I’m starving. It has been a long day. What’s on the trolley this evening?” Alistair was asking a waiter.

“Roast Beef, roast potatoes, Yorkshire pudding, Brussel sprouts, parsnip and gravy.”

“Thank you ‘I’ll have that. The advantage of the trolley is you can go back for seconds.” Alistair explained the obvious.

The Muthaiga Country Club was an island of constant calm in a sea of chaos and the food was excellent, as always. They sat at a quiet table on the veranda.

The team was in a state of shock at what they thought they had discovered. Having the Earl’s commanding presence gave them confidence, and the planning went well.

At the end of the meal, the night air had become chilled. They moved inside and sat around a crackling fire in deep and well-worn leather armchairs. A waiter appeared, pushing a highly polished silver trolley loaded with colorful ranks of after-dinner drinks.

"Ahh, the sticky trolley. What will you have?" The Earl raised his palm to the girls.

When they had all been served and the waiter glided away, Alistair said, "excellent, so tomorrow night, we HAHO into a spot five clicks from the fish factory, plant limpet mines on all the planes and anything else interesting, get into the factory, see what we can find, blow it up, and shoot anyone who asks questions. But how do we get out of there when we are finished?"

15

The Raid

After a day of preparing equipment and making plans, they had a short sleep. Getting back into Moggy at 1am, they headed out to Thika, 30 kilometers away, where a friend of The Earl's had a coffee plantation and a dirt airstrip.

The air was crisp, the moon a mere whisper of a white smile when they parked next to the hanger surrounded by earthy smelling coffee plants. Nobody from the farm came to meet them, Alistair assumed this was deliberate.

Somewhere out in the dark night came the roar of powerful engines and the noise grew as if some vast beast were coming inexorably towards them. Suddenly, a massive black shape swept over them, shaking their bones. It peeled away and then reappeared, stubby nose bearing down on the dirt strip.

Taboga and her team had arrived in the Atlas. Taboga was the brilliant pilot of this almost magical plane; her all woman team came from Central and South America. Taboga was a stunning woman and had Alistair tongue tied every time they saw each other. The plane seemed to stop moving forward almost as soon as the wheels touched the ground. Clouds of dust filled the air as the plane taxied towards them and turned on the spot, presenting a slowly descending ramp to the Unimog.

Alistair reversed Moggy into the red lit cargo bay, guided by black-clad figures wearing helmets and headsets. They strapped her in and the vast aircraft bumped its way back to the head of the airstrip. Everyone found a seat and the plane seemed to perform a vertical takeoff, leaving their stomachs on the ground.

As soon as the plane was making a steady climb, the team started preparing for their High-Altitude High Opening, or HAHO, jump. This would allow them to leave the aircraft (and noise) a good forty kilometers from the target and basically fly in close using their parachutes. This was the fastest way to get back to the fish factory without being spotted. They would jump out at around 10,000m. At this height they would need oxygen. Jeeves had a special dog's mask to do the job.

After an hour's flight, the rear ramp lowered and wind filled the cargo bay. Beyond the glow of the red lights of the plane, there was just blackness.

"Two minutes to jump site."

They waddled awkwardly to the ramp. Paloma had Jeeves strapped to her chest and Tatiana and Alistair had kit bags strapped between their legs. This was going to be tough—they would drop off the back of the aircraft and their parachutes would deploy immediately, but they couldn't jump together because in case they got tangled in each other's chutes, so they would have to 'find' each other in the dark sky before navigating their way, in the air, towards their target.

"Bloody hell, it's freezing up here." Alistair shouted at the others.

Paloma looked at the bag between her brother's legs. "Hey Alistair, I think you need to change your nappy there."

"Five, four, three, two, one goooo." The light above them turned from red to green.

Paloma stepped off the ramp at the back of the plane and rolled into the black night, closely followed by the others. Their chutes popped open automatically on exit.

She spun around, looking for the other two. A dark shape passed over her like a bat in the night. It wheeled around and came back towards her, Alistair—she stacked above him so they could fly together, making a bigger shape for Tatiana to spot. They couldn't use their communications systems with oxygen masks on.

Jumping from that altitude meant they could fly for nearly twenty minutes. They navigated using their eyes, following the land.

Alistair, Paloma, and Jeeves landed quietly in the dry riverbed just below where they had set up their OP in Moggy when they were last there. That would be their RV and they hiked the short distance, hoping to find Tatiana already there. She wasn't.

Carefully stashing their parachutes and harnesses behind a rock, they put on their night sights and checked their weapons. After ten minutes, as agreed, they set off to the fish factory, trying to reach Tatiana by radio.

"Do you agree we must keep going, even without Tatiana? I hope she is OK but we have to stop these bastards and there is nothing we can do to help her." They were halfway there and Alistair wanted reassurance.

"Yeah, we are ready" she patted her HK MP5 SD and then Jeeves.

"OK. Let's go."

Keeping to the darkest shadows, they passed through the 'village' and onto the perimeter of the airfield.

Pushing through the cut in the fence they made last time, they headed towards the planes.

Alistair jumped up on the first one and found it unlocked. Searching inside the cockpit he found no unusual equipment. They had expected this—it seemed they prepared the planes just before each flight in the fish factory. Clamping a mine under the seat, he jumped down and they moved to the next one, Paloma scanning for unwanted visitors with Jeeves.

As they finished rigging the last plane, they saw the pickup patrol car heading up the runway. This time there was a man in the back with a huge spotlight. He was sweeping it back and forwards as it approached. Lying flat under the plane, they tried to make themselves as hidden as possible, their silenced weapons tracking the pickup.

Alistair whispered, "If they spot us, you take the guy with the searchlight, I'll take the driver."

As the vehicle got closer, they could hear muffled West African music coming from the closed cab. Alistair and Paloma held their breath as it reached a point on the runway parallel to them. The spotlight swept over their plane, stopped, and then came back and stopped again. The man banged franticly on the cab roof and fumbled for his weapon.

"Take them out."

Twin double shots thunked from their suppressed MP5s. The man in the back crumpled to the bed of the pickup but the driver convulsed violently as Alistair's rounds hit his chest, his foot pressed hard on the accelerator. Falling forwards on the steering wheel, it spun under his sagging arms. The car careened straight at the plane they were under. Springing up, they ran as hard as they could, jumping into a drainage ditch on the other side of the runway.

There was a screeching, crunching sound as the pickup barreled into the plane, the dead man's foot wedged on the accelerator, the unwieldy mess of metal began sliding across the taxiway, sparks flying out of the tail as the pickup lodged itself under the wing. Then the fuel tank ruptured. A yellow ball of flame rolled up into the night sky as the lot exploded with a massive bang.

Flood lights all around the airfield popped on and armed men spilled out of the fish factory. Alistair and Paloma picked their targets carefully, squeezing their triggers in neat, silent double taps. The figures crumpled to the ground.

Several ran back inside—the others quickly dived for cover and began wildly firing at random shadows on fully automatic.

"That mine we set in the burning aircraft will explode from the heat any second now. When it does, let's make a run for it." Alistair was pointing to the place in the fence where they had come in.

"They are still not sure where we are but it won't take long to find us."

"Roger that." Paloma put a fresh magazine in her weapon.

Just as she spoke, a Kenyan Army truck burst through the gate. A camouflaged soldier was manning the GPMG, mounted in a hatch on the cab with a powerful searchlight attached to the weapon. One man taking cover jumped up on the running board and pointed in their direction. The gun and searchlight swung and the soldier opened fire with the machine gun as the driver started towards them.

"Down, down!" Bullets zinged over their heads, sending up showers of rocks and stones as the lead hit the surrounding ground.

As they buried their heads in the sand, they heard a jet taxi and takeoff. They looked up and saw a white Citation jet pass over them. They couldn't see the registration numbers.

"Oh Shit." Paloma said quietly over her radio.

The truck had stopped and a dozen soldiers poured out, fanning each side.

"Bugger... do you think you can reach the truck with a frag grenade, Alistair?"

"Too bloody far and they will see my arm."

The machine gun stopped abruptly and the truck seem to lurch sideways of its own accord, then the cab exploded.

"You guys are having the party without me?" Tatiana was on the radio.

"Tatiana, thank god you're OK."

Paloma and Alistair both started firing at the advancing figures, knowing Tatiana would have worked out where they were and stayed out of their line of fire.

The mine they had planted on the plane exploded, sending shards of metal zinging across the scene, taking out two of the soldiers standing nearby.

In the chaos, two more had almost reached them by crawling forward. One jumped up and ran towards them, pistol in hand. Jeeves launched forward from the ditch, clamping his jaws around the man's gun hand and bringing him down with the force of his jump. A bullet from Paloma's Webley cut the man's scream of surprise short. The second man stood up and was bringing up his weapon as she fired a second shot at his chest. His feet seemed to lift off the ground with the power of the shot and he crashed backwards. Her brother had said WW1 officers called the weapon a man stopper and now she understood why.

There was no more movement from the soldiers.

"Looks like we got them all," Alistair said advancing forward in tactical steps. They met Tatiana on the other side of the burning truck.

"Thanks. You saved our butts. What happened to you? We lost you as soon as you jumped."

"I jumped maybe one second late but when my chute opened an enormous bird went up into it, very bad, I was falling with the bird inside my chute."

"Really? That's crazy, most birds don't fly at night, at least not high."

"Yes, but there was this hot air coming up and then this ugly bird with no feathers on his head appeared."

"Gosh, that was a vulture having a late-night thermal ride."

"Very ugly. I tried to shoot him but this is a mistake in a parachute, so I released and use my reserve. I am lucky, I am tiny, no damage done, but I had to run a long way because I was late for your party!"

They laughed.

Figures from the factory began running out of the gate. Some had got into vehicles and were already disappearing down the road.

"Let's check the fish factory. Our remaining mines should go off in six minutes."

Running inside the lit building, they found a mess of upturned desks, workbenches, and filing cabinets. They quickly searched for anything useful. Alistair noticed a stainless-steel cabinet that looked like someone had pulled it across the concrete floor. Putting his shoulder to it, he pushed it aside, revealing a door. They had locked it.

"Thank you, I will open this for you, Sir." Tatiana was smiling. She loved breaking into things. Pulling out a suede leather roll, she selected a small metal tool and had the door open in seconds.

Concrete stairs went down to a basement.

Paloma and Jeeves tucked in behind the steel cabinet, on sentry duty, as the other two worked their way down the stairs, weapons ready and torches burning bright tunnels into the dark space.

"All clear." They found the light switch. Sitting in the center of the floor was a demolition explosive attached to a timer. It was counting down—9.55 minutes remaining.

The owners obviously hadn't expected anyone else to make it inside.

Above them, a neat roll of explosions lit up the night sky as the mines hidden in the planes went off. Paloma could see the devastation through the giant open doors of the factory.

"And that, ladies and gentlemen, is the end of the flying circus. Please take all of your belongings as you exit," she announced over the radio.

"Paloma, find us a trolley."

"Alistair, trolley finishes at ten pm, even you know that."

"Paloma, stop pissing about. We have a mountain of computers we need to move and there is a bomb with a timer down here."

Alistair appeared at the top of the stairs, his arms full of computer hardware. Paloma was already waiting with a luggage trolley. Jeeves swept his tail from side to side when he saw Alistair.

"May I help you with your baggage, Sir?"

He laughed as he piled the computers onto the trolley, patting Jeeves on the head once he'd emptied his arms.

"Don't expect a tip," he said over his shoulder as he went back down for another load.

"Atlas incoming in five," Tatiana alerted them—Taboga was coming into land. She had told the crew that the LZ was clear and it was safe to come in.

Appearing at the top of the stairs with one more armful of computers, she said, "OK, that's all the good stuff. We need to move."

Pushing the trolley as fast as they dared, they got outside just in time to see the Atlas blast down the runway at 30 meters' height to check it was clear. Taboga banked the plane into a turn and started its final approach. As she did so, a Scout armored car raced through the gates driving almost parallel to the plane along the taxiway, its stubby little turret with an M60 machine swiveled up to aim at the descending aircraft. The occupants of the vehicle never had time to realize their mistake: the side mounted 6,000 round per minute M61 Vulcan machine gun locked and fired like a chainsaw, ripping men, machine and road into a thousand pieces. The armored car simply disintegrated as the Atlas continued its descent, as if it had needed to swot a fly out of its way.

The plane landed and taxied over to where they were standing, its ramp descending as it moved, pushing their trolley up and inside. The moment it stopped, they climbed aboard.

On takeoff, they looked out of the windows as the demolition bomb went off inside the fish factory. Flames were shooting out the doors, burning planes, bodies and vehicles were scattered about and they remembered their pledge to destroy the poachers, make them extinct.

16

Back at the Magic Shop

Three days later they were back in the Ops center of the Magic Shop, hidden deep in the Panamanian jungle. The well-equipped series of bunkers were the perfect safe location for their headquarters.

The Earl had sent a team of INTERPOL investigators to what remained of the fish factory to work with the Kenyan CID and see what further information they could find. They were especially interested in the Kenya Army truck and armored car that had appeared.

The carcasses of disemboweled computers spread out across a series of stainless-steel tables along one wall of the Ops center. Colored wires and cables connected them to a large computer. Misha and Tatiana were operating on them.

"Looks like all the hard drives were wiped just before we got in the building, but crudely done because they were in a hurry and because they assumed the drives were going to be blown to pieces. It'll take us a couple of days, but I think we can recover everything. We already have the basics. "

"Brilliant, Misha, and the good news is they won't have any idea that we have hacked into them." Alistair turned and an enormous spread across his face. McDonnell their Glaswegian chef had just appeared, his great bulk filling the doorway. Pushing what looked like a gurney, he whipped off a white cloth to reveal dozens of perfect little sandwiches.

"I thought you might like a wee snack while yer work. "

Dr. KV looked up from his computer with a smile. "Thank you McDonnell, you heard my stomach from inside the kitchen."

The sandwiches—smoked Scottish Salmon, Gentleman's relish, Marmite and cucumber, tasted wonderful washed down with large mugs of tea.

Misha finished her sandwich and walked over to the big digital map. "You made correct assumptions. They designed this system to 'capture' the GPS signature of everything in its range. It can also shut down the locating systems of the same devices. They named it 'Mengbi Weapon' which is Chinese for blinded. It looks like they have been testing for over a year. Knocking out the Askari System was the last test. We think they had intended to close the fish factory once they were sure it would all work. You are also right that they could scale this up using military drones or even bigger civilian aircraft. Finally, it connects back, at least financially now, to Hong Kong and Poppy Cheng. She financed the development of the system and ran the demonstration."

"So, if Mengbi Weapon is now for sale, how do we find out who is buying it?" Alistair asked.

"They may not be connected, but it's all we have to go on. If we can find out where those elephant tusks are going, we may find the buyer. Clearly, the buyer of Mengbi Weapon is also very involved in the illegal ivory market. We are working on the assumption that the ivory goes by shipping container to the buyer, just because of the container trucks that seem to be involved in every poaching incident. We looked at the bill of loading for all the ships leaving Mombasa in the next few days and tried to match it with the invoices we found on the computers in the fish factory and found this little beauty."

Misha clicked her mouse and the labelled picture of a large container ship came up. "Morning Glory, built in 1992. At 32.3 meters wide, she just fits through the old Panama locks, hence the Panamax label. Her capacity is 5,000 containers. It looks like 'Turkana Fish Company' loaded three 20ft refrigerated containers on her last week in Mombasa. Once we have finished with this lot," Misha swept her hand over the bodies of computers on the table, "we hope to confirm the connection."

"Her first destination is Genoa, Italy, through the straits of Gibraltar, then she'll cross the Atlantic and then on to Colon, Panama. Now it looks like all the containers are to be offloaded in Colon, which is the last destination of the Morning Glory voyage. But as we know, it is unlikely that is her final destination. 99% of the containers will either be taken by train across the isthmus and loaded on another ship in Balboa Port, Panama or a new one in Colon, which will either go through the canal or back into the Atlantic."

"I know where you are going with this. We need to get on that ship, find the three containers among the 5,000 and then put a tracker on them and then maybe stick with them." Alistair was looking at the map.

"Hopefully, you don't have to get on the ship, if we can get more information we will see if they come off the *Morning Glory* in Colon, then we either tag them in Colon or we get them on the way across the isthmus on the train."

"Good, I have had enough jumping onto moving ships for a while, and Paloma and I have already perfected the art of jumping on a train. We used to ride it illegally to get back to Gamboa at night. How many days do we have before she reaches Colon?"

"She's due to dock in ten days."

"Great, I think I need to talk to my man Miguel in Colon. I am sure he can get us into the port."

17

Chasing Containers

Dr. KV, Alistair, Paloma and Tatiana sat at their favorite table under a Myrtle tree at the GAS57 pub, watching the tugs power their way through the brown water of the Panama Canal.

GAS57 was the halfway point along the famous canal in the village of Gamboa, an unchanged tropical paradise built by the Americans in the 1930s during the heyday of the old Canal Zone. From here on it was jungle and twenty minutes in the jungle lay their hidden bunkers, The Magic Shop.

The pub sat on the site of the town's original gas station, building number 57, hence the name. The ground floor accommodated the pub. Its interior featured high ceilings, mismatched chairs, tables, and comfortable sofas. The pub was owned and run by Dr. KV. The floors above held apartments with deep overhanging roofs and wide, cool verandas. Alistair and Paloma had their own places on the top floors.

They were waiting for Miguel, who was proving to be a very handy asset. He showed up on a motorbike with a box tied to the back. Looking furtively around, he handed Alistair, Tatiana, and Paloma three very official-looking ID cards on lanyards. On the front were the letters CCT,

Colon Container Terminal, above a head and shoulder photograph, in which they were each wearing the distinctive blue overalls with reflective shoulder patches of CCT. He had given them alternative names.

He pulled a uniform, boots, and helmet out of the box for each of them and said in Spanish,

"They will fit you perfectly." Each uniform already had a name badge on them.

He sat back, looking very pleased with himself.

They congratulated him and Dr. KV handed him a coffee.

"I can get you the gear and the IDs but you still have to make sure they are in the CCT computer so that when you turn up at the gate, they can verify you. I can't do that part, I am sorry... but if you do it, you will get paid from the time you enter until you leave.

And you girls must be careful, few women work there, and the men are very rough."

"Thanks Miguel, we are really ninjas in disguise so we can look after ourselves, right Tatiana?"

"It is true. Miguel, do they have metal detectors when we enter?"

"No, but you can only carry your lunch."

Miguel was well paid for his services. They expected to need him again. Driving off on his bike, he left with a big smile.

The next day, they borrowed a white, twin-cab Toyota Hilux—a vehicle more in line with their assumed identities than Alistair's Land Rover.

Tatiana was laughing at Paloma who was doing a 'man's walk' in her heavy boots, overalls with reflective tape and helmet. She stopped and did an exaggerated scratch of her crotch while saying with deep toned Spanish, "Give me beer, woman."

Alistair shook his head, walked over, and picked up her ID badge. "Paloma, you are 'Ana De Lucia'? The name female, no?"

They got in the car and headed over to Colon. Reaching the massive fences and gates of Colon Container Port, they drove to Gate 15 as instructed by Misha, who had hacked into the port's human resources database and added them.

Gate 15 was the section where the three containers they needed had been unloaded during the early hours. *Morning Glory* was having the last of her cargo removed.

They got through the gate with no problems and the three of them switched to speaking Spanish while they parked the pickup in one space marked 'Empleados'.

"How much do we earn an hour?" Paloma asked.

"Ask Misha, I think it pays well. I wonder what McDonnell packed for our lunch."

Tatiana brought them back to reality. "I just hope that the containers we need are not on the top."

Looking in the direction Tatiana was pointing, they realized their problem. The containers were stacked five high, while climbing them would not be physically impossible, it would be both dangerous and, importantly, getting caught would get them arrested.

"Watch out, this is a very hazardous environment." As if to prove his point, an enormous forklift truck carrying a 40 ft container swept past them in efficient haste.

They made their way over to section 15-22, the area where the containers were stacked.

"I don't understand how we know where the containers have been parked, but we don't even know what the destination or name of the ship they are going on." Paloma asked as they walked.

"We discovered it is fairly common for a container to become 'lost' during the transshipping process. This allows the owners to send the container on without it being in the official, tracked database. Sometimes this is a genuine mistake, sometimes it is deliberate."

Misha saw that as soon as the containers touched the ground in Panama, they 'disappeared.'

"In fact, if we hadn't been watching—grandmother set an alarm that notified us the moment they were being unloaded—we wouldn't know where they are now." Tatiana continued.

"Obviously, this is highly illegal. But it means that with a valuable cargo, whoever is responsible may be watching, or even guarding them, so we have to be really careful. Don't forget there are CCTV cameras all over the place."

Alistair pulled out a clipboard, which had an official CCP logo marked on a sheet covered in numbers. He started inspecting random containers and making Xs on the sheet. White numbers written in large font were emblazoned on the ground in front of each stack of containers, dividing them into the different types. 15-22 were all 20-footers. The team tried to look like they were busy and knew what they were doing but as they hesitated to read the ID numbers of the container in the stack, a burly man carrying what looked like a pickaxe handle immediately appeared around the side of the stack and walked towards them. With studied nonchalance, they kept moving.

He looked at them menacingly as Paloma did her best to make up what she considered 'being a Colon Container Port employee' chat in Spanish. "So, Fabiola, in accounting, said that Miguel had been caught in the backseat of his pickup with Jose from HR and that was the last straw. Last night she threw all his belongings out the window of their apartment...but you know they are on the 5th floor and one of his cactuses hit an old lady on the cheek...there was blood everywhere and the lady called the police, then Jose turned up and...... what? Why are you looking at me like that?"

"Thank you, Paloma, he can't hear us anymore."

"But I was just starting to enjoy myself and I'm not Paloma. I'm actually Ana De Lucia," she said, holding her ID card to his face. "Don't you want to know what happened to Fabiola?"

"No, thank you Ana De Lucia. I think we need to talk to Misha urgently."

Alistair activated the radio in his ear. "Misha, have you got into the CCTV system for the ports by any chance?"

"Almost. Give me 30 more minutes and just one thing: the ID number of any one of the containers in that stack. The containers are stacked according to their next movement. It will be train, or Colon. And if we assume that the Turkana ones are there, all we need to do is find one in the same stack and then we will know what the next step is."

"Roger that, we'll go back and get one. Based on the containers on the trucks in Turkana, do you think we could guess the color at least?"

"I'll check the body cam footage for the colors," Misha answered.

"OK Ana De Lucia, you can continue telling us about Fabiola." He explained they had to walk back to the stack and get the number from any container.

"I am going to distract the nasty man," Tatiana smiled. "KGB style!"

Undoing her bootlace, she cat-walked off in the stack's direction ahead of them, giving a remarkably good impression that she was modeling an Yves St Laurent silk dress, not overalls and boots.

The 'nasty man', hooked by the bait, followed her.

"Let's go."

"So, then Miguel came downstairs in his dressing gown to see what had happened to all his belongings but when he saw Jose, he started running towards him. But he forgot he wasn't wearing anything underneath and people were filming with their phones." Paloma continued her tall tale.

Misha came on the radio. "The containers in Kenya were all jade color with a with a yellow stripe around them. They look pretty battered and old."

"Makes sense. We know Lake Turkana as the Jade Sea. Thanks, we'll look now." Alistair took a quick photo of the ID number on the first container as they walked past it.

Paloma kept telling her story while watching Tatiana, who had bent over to tie her bootlace, presenting her very athletic bottom to the 'nasty man' who was close behind her. He did what they knew he would and put both hands on her and squeezed hard. In a single fluid movement, she whipped around, put a hand on each of his shoulders and brought a knee up between his legs. Dropping to his knees with his hands between his legs and mouth agape, Tatiana put her palm on his forehead, pushed him backwards onto the concrete, and marched away.

Taking the opportunity, Paloma ran around the side of the stack and searched for jade containers with a stripe. She found them all on the top of the stack. Taking a photo with a location, she sent it to Misha.

"Got them, let's move." She and Alistair hurried past the groaning man on the ground and caught up with Tatiana.

"Time to leave. We got everything we can—let's get back to the car." Paloma took the lead.

Alistair looked at his watch. "Hey, what about our lunch break?"

Paloma and Tatiana shook their heads and continued to the pickup. When they got there, Paloma got in the driver's seat and handed Alistair his lunchbox.

"Happy now?"

"Aye, McDonnell made us Scotch eggs!"

They got out through security without a hitch and headed back to the Magic Shop on Pipeline Road.

18

Panama Canal Railway Company

Entering the cool interior of the Ops Center, they saw Dr. KV and Misha watching the CCTV screens so intently that it looked like they were playing a video game.

Putting their helmets down on the table, they joined them at the screens.

Misha spoke without taking her eyes off the images. "So, if we are correct, the containers you got the ID from should all be moved to the yard in a few minutes and loaded onto a Panama Canal Railway carriage to cross the isthmus at 7pm. We just want to watch and make sure our three jade ones go with them. Sometimes this is the point where they 'disappear' out the back door."

The screens showed the topmost jade container about to be picked up by the massive forklift, as the vehicle extended its arms and plucked it off the pile. Leaving the stack, it seemed to defy gravity.

Swaying slightly, container and forklift trundled over to the railway yard, disappearing, and then reappearing on different screens as it moved across the yards to the trains.

The team cheered in relief. It would be fairly simple for them to attach the trackers as the train passed through Gamboa in the darkness of night.

"…. twenty-seven, twenty-eight, twenty-nine, thirty." Paloma was counting railway carriages back from what they assumed was where the engines would connect when loading was complete.

"OK, so the first one is on the 30th carriage back from the engine, that's perfect. If we stop it at the STRI dock railway crossing, the 30th carriage will still be on the line in the jungle." STRI was the Smithsonian Tropical Research Institute.

Alistair and Paloma used to get the train to stop here so they could board carriages by getting a friend to stage car trouble on the railway crossing that led to the STRI dock. The train always slowed down to a crawl at this point, so the 'breakdown' was in no danger. They would jump off just before it entered the container yard in Balboa.

"Dr. KV, would you mind playing the doddery scientist and break down on the crossing for us?"

"My pleasure, I will borrow a STRI truck for the job."

Misha would stay in the Ops Center and monitor the progress of the train.

Night falls fast in the tropics and by the time they had kitted up in black combat gear and were waiting in the jungle beside the railway, it was pitch dark. The Panama Canal railway had been plying the short 65 kilometers up and down this narrow neck of land since 1855. The forest on each side of the track was old and thick, so hiding was easy.

They decided to each carry silenced dart pistols, now that they knew they may encounter guards again.

The containers were spread out, back from carriage 30, 35 and 37. Misha had come up with the brilliant idea of painting the tracking devices with the same battered jade green of the containers. They would place the trackers on the tops of the steel boxes.

Misha told them the train was five minutes out from their position and Alistair launched a small Parrot Drone fitted with a thermal camera towards the approaching train. Soon both powerful diesel engines glowed bright orange on his screen. Approaching the railway crossing, the train's huge exhausts and whistles masked the buzzing of the drone.

Alistair guided the UAV down the train, mentally counting off containers until he reached 30. No tale-tell signature of human heat showed, and he moved on to 35. There, crouched behind the container on the expanded metal platform, was a human figure.

35 was Tatiana's target.

"Vodka, this is Whisky. You have a guard at the rear of the container 35."

"Roger that."

The twin yellow and red engines screeched to a noisy halt at the crossing and the driver shouted at Dr. KV, who was under the bonnet of the white Toyota pickup that sat astride the steel tracks.

"I am sorry. I do not speak Spanish. Help me, please. I have a problem with my car." He said in exaggerated, slow English.

"Chuletta!" said the driver, using a favorite expletive in Panama which translates to 'pork chop'. He stepped down from his cab, muttering about useless gringos.

Alistair flew the drone to 37, Paloma's target.

"Bloody Mary, this is Whisky. All clear, but be careful because Vodka has a bogey two carriages down."

"Roger that."

As the carriages bumped each other to a halt, the guard on 35 jumped down on to the gravel beside the track to see why they had stopped. Tatiana silently stepped behind him and fired a little dart into his neck with an almost silent hiss from her pistol. Slapping his neck as if he had been bitten by a large insect, he crumpled in a heap on the floor.

"OK, 'nasty man' is down. I need some help loading him back on. You won't believe it, but it's the guy I put on the ground in Colon."

Paloma and Alistair had already installed their trackers and ran over. Alistair grabbed the guy's legs together as they dumped him back on the steel mesh on the back of the carriage.

"Wow, you're right, it is the same guy who grabbed you earlier, he's having a terrible day trying to guard these containers. You don't think he might roll off when he wakes up?"

"Actually, on second thoughts, he's going to wake up in about four hours and the train will arrive in Balboa in twenty minutes. If they find him, they are going to get very suspicious. Let's dump him off in the jungle between here and the stopping point. That way they'll think he fell asleep and rolled off. When he comes to, he probably won't remember anything."

Paloma scrambled up the container and set the tracker. The train was moving again, and they agreed she would pick them up at the bridge where the train crossed over the road. She jumped off, lightly running beside the slow train until it reached the railway crossing, then climbed into Dr. KV's waiting pickup.

Alistair and Tatiana stayed hidden on the carriage as they went through Gamboa and over the bridge that crossed the Chagres River.

Finding a wallet on the man, they photographed his driving license and sent it to Misha. The more information they could gather the better and they already knew simple desires rather than professionalism drove this man, so he might be useful to talk to later.

They had also collected the ID numbers on each of the three containers.

It turned out to be quite a task to get an unconscious person off a moving train in the night without doing serious damage to him. The dark shadows on the trees pressed into the sides of the train as it slowed on a slight incline. Tatiana and Alistair attempted to jump and run off the moving train but the problem was, Tatiana was much shorter than Alistair, and they ended up in a pile with the man underneath.

She howled with laughter as Alistair spat dirt out of his mouth. Sitting there, her phone vibrated. She looked at a message from Misha—they communicated in Russian, so Alistair didn't know what it said.

The train rumbled on.

"Alfonso Larata, a Spaniard." She picked up the man's limp right hand and bent his trigger finger all the way back until it made a sickening crack.

"Known hitman." She bent his thumb all the way back until it cracked.

"Thief and trafficker of underage girls." She stood up and kicked him with all her strength between his legs, her combat boot making a deep thud as it made contact.

Even in his unconscious state, he groaned.

"Wanted by INTERPOL." She spat at his face.

Alistair took her hand and gently guided her away.

"Let's find Paloma and have a nice cup of tea?"

Seeming to snap out of it, she suddenly noticed that Alistair was with her.

"Yes, thank you, that would be lovely."

The last carriage of the train clattered past, leaving Alfonso Larata uncomfortably sprawled on the side of the track.

They headed back to the road through the sweet-smelling forest, where

Paloma and Dr. KV were waiting. They handed back mugs of tea as Alistair and Tatiana jumped in. Paloma eyed them both—they looked shaken.

Paloma, however, looked back at her iPad and studied the three blinking dots almost at Balboa Port. "All the trackers are working nicely, let's see where they go. Do you think they will load them on a ship tonight?"

"If the ship is ready, they will load it straight away, but I think it normally takes 24 hours to load a container ship, depending on the size of the ship." Alistair didn't want to talk about what had just happened, and was happy to avoid the subject.

When they got back to the Ops room, Misha had got into the CCTV at Balboa Port and was watching containers being loaded onto a small 150 meter container ship.

"This is the '*Maxime Express*'. She has a capacity of 32 40ft containers and will fit into most ports. Her first port of call on leaving Balboa is Los Cabos, in the state of Baja California Sur, Mexico."

"This little seaside town was voted 'The Most Violent City in the World'. It is the playground for some of Mexico's most notorious drug lords and it is here, we think, that they will unload our three containers."

"Who feels like a pleasant trip to the beach?"

19

Sirene

Deirdre Shepherd was Alistair and Paloma's godmother. They adored her. As children, they had many joyous adventures on her sprawling estate in California and aboard her exquisite 1920s motor yacht *Sirene*.

Deirdre was one of the Extinct Company's senior members and benefactors. She had become an ardent fighter of wildlife crime since her husband, Pete, a world-renowned photographer of endangered animals, had been killed by poachers in Kenya.

Alistair, Paloma, Tatiana, Misha, Charlie and Dr. KV had joined Deidre at her estate, which included several miles of Pacific coastline and a private harbor with its own lighthouse.

After a day of preparation, they boarded Dierdre's yacht. *Sirene*'s bow cut its elegant wake out of Deirdre's stone walled harbor and the captain set his course south to Los Cabos, Mexico.

Charlie went below deck, happily admiring and tending to the yacht's engines, wearing a WW2 WREN's uniform.

The rest of the team sat around Misha's bank of computers which were open on the map table in the chart room behind the bridge.

On one screen they could see three blinking dots labeled, 'Maxime

Express'. She also was en route to Los Cabos carrying the three 20ft containers filled with what they believed to be several tons of poached ivory from Kenya.

Misha pointed to another screen. "The Earl and his crew at INTERPOL, along with me and Dr. KV, have been doing some digging." The screen showed a man's broad, flat, and very pockmarked, Asian face. One eyeball was milky white and his lips were slightly moist. "Henry Cheng, we believe, is a half-brother of Poppy. It seems Henry is actually older than Poppy. The result of a previous relationship of Poppy's father. But interestingly, it seems that Poppy was given command and control of all her father's assets when he died. Henry effectively works for Poppy and my guess is he doesn't like it. So that is worth exploring."

Misha clicked through a series of photographs and satellite images. "This is where Henry Cheng lives and works. It is 20 kilometers from Los Cabos." Images showed what looked remarkably like a contemporary version of Krak des Chevaliers, the crusaders' massive hilltop fort in Syria, rising out of the swirling seas.

"INTERPOL believes that underneath this fort is a series of factories where they manufacture drugs for the Mexican cartels. The workers are all Chinese and they live within the fort, also underground. Nobody ever leaves or enters. All exchanges happen here."

"We have given it the code name The Kraken after the mythological sea monster," Dr. KV added.

On the screen was a wide, gated bridge connected to a rocky island and then another bridge leading to the fort. At the land end was an open shelter with stone benches and at the other end was an enclosed bunker with gun slits that surrounded a gate big enough to take a large truck.

"They make deliveries like this..." on her screen was a stop motion film of a truck arriving, the driver getting out and sitting on the stone bench. Then, another driver, wearing a full-face mask, walking out from the bunker and boarding the truck.

"He gets in and drives it through the gate. The truck stays inside the gatehouse for 25 minutes, presumably while they search it. Then it is seen driving across this next bridge and through another gate into the bowels of the fort. It returns an hour later."

"We know that if the contents of the truck are not correct, they either shoot the driver or take him away and he is never seen again. Unmanned, armed boats patrol around the fort." A squat grey boat with a heavy machine gun on the deck appeared on the screen.

"There is a fully automated anti-aircraft system, cameras, motion detectors and sentries with dogs." Zooming into a picture, they could see several masked men with dogs patrolling the ramparts.

"Our information on Henry Cheng is very limited, but we know he operates as a sort of broker to the cartels for Poppy. He supplies them with everything they need for their operations: guns, missiles, boats and yes, very sophisticated drones."

"He seems to have one obsession, ivory. INTERPOL believe he is the biggest single buyer of elephant tusks in the world. We think that several of China's most famous ivory carvers have been kidnapped and work here. We think this because after he kidnaps the carvers, their families receive a generous and regular income. Tatiana and I tracked payments in Mexico. But those same families also sometimes all end up with their throats cut, presumably if the artist has not satisfied Mr. Cheng."

"So, here we have a man, obsessed with ivory, who sells sophisticated weaponry to drugs cartels. Can you image what would happen if those cartels could get hold of a device that captured and blocked GPS systems? Just to begin with they could open a border floodgate to let drugs into the US, they could cripple the already struggling Mexican police, they could destroy rivals by tracking and capturing all their goods. We think this is where your three containers are going. Henry Cheng is going to be 'renting' the Mengbi Weapon to the cartels on behalf of Poppy. Questions?"

A tall man walked in. He had the handsome features of a Maasai.

Deidre smiled. "Ladies and gentlemen, allow me to introduce Mingati Miterienanka. Mingati is completing his degree at Oxford. He is studying the effects of wildlife poaching on indigenous populations. He is going back to Kenya in two weeks so I asked if he would like to join us." Everyone introduced themselves and shook his hand, apart from Alistair and Paloma, who had known him from Kenya and already spent several hours with him exchanging news.

"You can trust Mingati implicitly and he is a wealth of information."

Dr. KV spoke up. His voice was a blend of command, knowledge, and sophistication. His words always counted. "Our mission has three goals. 1. stop and destroy the poachers and their ivory. 2. prevent the GPS blockers reaching anyone who can use them for harm. 3. if Henry Cheng's workshops prove to be the ivory processing factory and he is the one that traffics the finished goods, we destroy him."

"To do this, we will require all our combined skills, knowledge, and courage. As we have seen, this is going to be a challenging operation."

"I believe we need to compile as much information as we can on Fort Kraken. Can I suggest we start by creating a 3D digital model and going back into history to find any weak spots?"

20

P of A

"Did you know that when the Spaniards first arrived in Baja California area in 1539, they believed they had reached a mythical island of female warriors governed by Queen Califia?" Paloma was reading from Wikipedia.

"Thank you, Paloma, but I think we have to get a little deeper to find anything useful about The Kraken Fort. I have a good friend, Dr. Jose Garcia, from the University of Mexico who has spent his life studying the archaeology of the peninsula. If there is anything we can use, he will know," Dr. KV said as he picked up his phone and studied the contacts through the lower portion of his glasses.

They had less than 12 hours left before the containers reached Los Cabos Port and Kraken Fort was only 20 kilometers up the coast from there.

Alistair and Tatiana had built a fairly accurate digital model of Kraken Fort. The Earl had sent them thousands of drone pictures for reference. Apparently, the CIA had got the footage last year but lost twelve drones in the process. Any object flying near the fort was target practice for the guards.

They labeled their 3D model, including the location of a Phalanx

Sea-wiz close weapons system that could fire 4,500 rounds a minute.

"We think the only way to get in would be if there was some kind of underwater entrance, and even if we get in, it looks like it's built like the Maginot Line, which would basically trap us into a series of corridors of fire." Alistair was speculating.

"Are we to assume that the containers have both the elephant tusks and the GPS blocking system? In my mind you give the present, he pays the big bucks and then he gets the system?"

"Tatiana, you are correct, they would never put them together. We are not being so smart. If we focus on destroying the ivory, that only gets us part of one of the three goals that Dr. KV so elegantly outlined."

"From the information we found on the computers in the fish factory, the GPS blocking system would be small and would need a technician. I think they would bring that in by helicopter. After Henry's client has made the payment, maybe Poppy would bring it herself?" Misha was talking and walking over to the computer with the 3D model. "I assume this is where visiting helicopters land?" She was pointing towards the bridge where the truck had stopped.

"Could we fire a Javelin missile at the helicopter when it lands?" They had three on board.

"No. Sorry, Misha, that Sea-wiz system is specifically designed to take out incoming missiles." Alistair was shaking his head.

"How about we find out where it is coming from, park the yacht nearby and shoot it down before it reaches Kraken?" Paloma offered.

"First, their intelligence and radar systems would quickly tell them from where the attack launched and they would simply retaliate and sink us. Secondly, it doesn't get us Henry." Deidre said. She certainly did not want her yacht blasted out from under her. "And, you lot are being far too nice. We need to think like them. How can we make it look like Poppy got the money and then failed to deliver a correctly functioning GPS jamming system? What we really need to find out is the negotiation between Henry and Poppy and exploit that." Deidre looked at Misha. They were becoming great friends, spending happy evenings drinking and plotting the downfall of poachers.

Misha nodded. "If we could somehow spike the GPS jammer so it worked in reverse... so that every time it was turned on it revealed the location of the operator, and those operators were hit hard and fast by authorities, old Henry would immediately become suspicious of that Poppy was setting her up so he failed in front of the cartels or who ever is renting the weapon and go after her? We would have to do it once they loaded it onto Henry's drone, perhaps even allowing it to be used successfully once in case they test it on a soft target?"

Shaking his head, Alistair held both hands up. "The problem is, The Kraken is an impenetrable fortress. We just can't work out how to get in there to spike the system once it is on his drone."

But Misha held a finger up. "Wait, what you just said. We don't need to get in there, we just need to get them to get out of there and to somewhere that's easier for us to reach."

"B52 Bombing raid perhaps?" Paloma offered. Everyone laughed, and it was what they really wanted but they doubted even The Earl could pull enough strings for that.

They talked in circles for a few more minutes while watching the blinking red dots of the containers aboard the Maxime Express get closer and closer to Los Cabos.

Dr. KV gazed at his screen as the hand drawn images sent from the famous Dr. Jose Garcia popped into his email. He looked up and addressed everyone.

"Do you know the Poem by Alfred Lord Tennyson, *The Kraken*? Bear with me, Paloma, I have an idea." Paloma had loved being taught English Literature by Dr. KV, but he face showed she wasn't in the mood with the red dots approaching.

"I just received a fascinating 1920s study from Dr. Garcia. The study and the poem gave me an idea. Indulge me and let me walk you back in history.

"The Spanish settled the Las Cabos area first in around 1697. Fort Kraken was actually a monastery. We don't know its original name, but what we know is that it sits on top a high pressure, hot water geyser. The monks dug a tunnel all the way down from the top of the biggest island to just above an area where there is a natural tube known as an underwater vent. This vent is exposed only at the very lowest of tides. When everything was ready, they installed a huge, stone valve with a square rock counterweight. This meant they could direct the water up their tunnel or into the sea.

"Then they cut out a series of baths which they would fill by lifting the counterweight. The boiling water would surge up the tunnel, shoot into the air and fall back down into the baths. There was a grandstand where people could watch, protected from the spray of boiling water."

Dr. KV showed a sketch of the top of the island covered in carved out baths.

"Then they would shut the valve when the baths were full, wait for them to cool enough and—voila—you have hundreds of baths filled with hot sulfur water. Sick people would make pilgrimages to have a bath in the magic water and be cured. It made the monks very rich. This went on for hundreds of years until 1815, when the monasteries started to fail and the locals began using the sprays of boiling water as a torture, chaining people to posts and boiling them alive.

"Eventually the Mexican government stepped in and during a super low tide they cut the chain of the counterbalance forever. It now holds the entrance to the tunnel closed and the boiling water just goes into the sea.

"Let me show you the archaeologists' 1920s sketches of the monks' tunnel."

They all looked at his screen and looked at the grainy drawings. They could recognize some of the rock formations. Alistair took the sketches, pushed the contrast, made them transparent, and then overlaid them onto their 3D model.

"Allow me to quote at least the end of Tennyson's poem."

"The Kraken:
Unnumbered and enormous polypi
Winnow with giant arms the slumbering green
There hath he lain for ages, and will lie
Battening upon huge sea worms in his sleep
Until the latter fire shall heat the deep;
Then once by and angels be seen,
In roaring he shall rise and on the surface die."

"Splendid stuff, don't you think? Now look at Henry's fort and where it is."

"Good Grief, it is right on top of the tunnel where the boiling water used to shoot out." Alistair zoomed in.

"They probably do not know what they are sitting on."

"Exactly. If we can wake the Kraken, we can blast the fort full of scalding water. There is a roof and hundreds of interconnecting tunnels. It will be like pouring boiling water down a rat's nest—except the water will keep pouring." Dr. KV looked pleased with himself.

"I would love to find out which room the water will burst into first because that is likely to kill people. It will be just below boiling temperature when it comes in. The rest will escape as it seeps through the tunnels."

"You are right, Alistair. We don't want to pump boiling water into a room full of captive workers. Let's see if we can find anyone involved in the fort's construction. That looks like a lot of concrete and someone must have delivered it."

"So, when is the next super low tide?" Tatiana asked.

Misha checked the tide tables online. "In twenty-three hours and forty-seven minutes and then again in thirty days. So, we're looking at 10.30pm tomorrow night,"

"Brilliant, the water will just keep pouring through the fort until someone puts another rock on the counterbalance and there isn't another low tide for a month, so Henry will have to move!"

"Minor question. How big is the rock we have to move?" Paloma asked.

21

Poaching the Poachers

Sirene cut her elegant way through the enticingly clear water off Baja California Sur on the Eastern coast of Mexico. The team was assembled in the map room behind the bridge.

"Because of Henry Cheng and his known associations with ivory and cartels, The Earl had some assets posted in Las Cabos. They were able to obtain a sketch from the concrete contractor when he built the place, but sadly the contractor 'disappeared' when he finished the job." Misha put a very crude floor plan sketch up on the screen.

"We think this is where the monks' tunnel entrance is," she said, pointing to the center of a room showing on the screen. "It looks like this is the guard's room, which you must go through to get to Henry's private quarters. Supposedly, the guards throw weighted bodies down the tunnel and every now and again, a victim washes up on the beach at Los Cabos. Those bodies—I've seen the photos—look like they have been boiled."

Alistair said, "Great, we get to poach the poachers and maybe even trap Henry in his rooms. So how are we going to move that bloody great rock which, judging from our crude estimates, looks about three or four tonnes?"

"Alistair, YouTube? I have already learnt how to destroy a large boulder, and silently. It would surprise you how many people have posted step-by-step instructions on how to destroy a rock in the sea by drilling under water, waiting until the tide drops and then breaking it into hundreds of pieces. It's called Dexpan demolition grout. No explosions required. I have already given Charlie a shopping list." Paloma said.

They were now moored the *Sirene* 2 kilometers away from the Kraken Fort. Tiny islands with perfect beaches dotted the area, and the sight of a fancy 'gin palace' moored near one island was normal. Outside it was a sunny and clear day but the team was glued to their screen below deck.

They had watched the three blinking trackers aboard the 'Maxime Express' make port at Los Cabos, be unloaded and then Charlie, posing as a tourist in a convertible 66 Ford Mustang, had streamed live film of the trucks with their 20ft containers entering across the first bridge at the Kraken Fort. Luckily for them, it looked like they emptied the containers at the gatehouse and sent them back outside, empty trackers still attached. They worried if they had wanted to take the containers into the building, they would have searched the outsides and found the trackers triggering alarm.

An hour later, Charlie had filmed a Eurocopter EC175 land at the bridge to the fort as the team had expected. An elegant woman in a long black dress got out—Poppy Cheng . She had a tall bodyguard with her. Misha identified him using her database. "That is Singsong, her head of security."

The big helicopter had a large cargo area and Charlie recorded the unloading of ten bulky Pelican cases. The Mengbi Weapon.

"Looks like Henry's client paid for his toys then."

"At least they are in waterproof cases. We don't want to destroy the system before we set Poppy up. Right, Alistair?" Paloma was still concerned that Alistair continued to hold a flame for Poppy. She had seen his face when she got out of the helicopter. He ignored Paloma.

She kept pushing. "Who knows, we might even boil her pretty little face off?"

Alistair gave her a look that warned her she'd gone too far.

The Earl had sent them some equipment which was loaded onto the yacht in California. Tatiana's favorite was the Stidd Diver Propulsion device, similar to the mini subs the special forces had used in WW2. This was basically a torpedo that divers could drive. This one, though, could drive itself and could carry large amounts of equipment. The Earl had also sent three Nemo underwater drills and Cobham rebreathing gear. Developed for special forces—the Cobham gear would allow them to stay underwater for extend periods and without the telltale trail of bubbles.

At 6.30pm, the sun started its last leg to the ocean's horizon. Warm evening light filled *Sirene*'s saloon. Through the portholes, white beaches on the tiny island begged them to come for sundowners.

"Lovely evening for a little swim." Paloma was pulling a black drysuit over her rash guard.

Laid out and ready to go into water proof bags were a stubby Uzi submachine each, several bags of Dexpan demolition grout, plastic tubes, a funnel, a battery-operated mini pump, and fresh water.

They would keep the waterproof drills strapped to their drysuits along with their Argonaut Titanium diving knives.

Misha was watching the ship's radar. She could see the two unmanned patrol boats circling the sea around the fort. They followed a set routine which she had mapped. Although Tatiana, Alistair and Paloma were approaching the fort underwater, it was better not to take risks so that if they needed to surface unexpectedly, they wouldn't run into a patrol boat. Misha started her final briefing.

"You have a twenty-minute window to travel just under 2000 meters, then you will have another twenty minutes to drill the holes while they are still underwater. Start at the top of the rock and work downwards. It is a good forty meters up from your rock to the top of the wall of the fort. We can't tell if they will hear you drilling so better be safe and do all the work underwater."

"Remember, exploit the natural seams and cracks in the rocks, only drill existing seams if they are too small. Luckily it's a calm night so you shouldn't get battered by waves." Dr. KV had been teaching them about geology.

The crew had already lowered the Stidd into the water. This was the XT version which gave them more speed and carrying capacity than the standard one. They could see the LED navigation screen bobbing just below the surface as they climbed down the ladder to get on board. The sun had disappeared and a full moon was lifting out of the sea.

Stowing the rest of the gear, Tatiana took the controls. Paloma climbed on behind her and Alistair grabbed the strap at the rear.

"OK, all clear, go."

The Stidd motors were silent and they slipped beneath the dark water with hardly a ripple, the dim glow of the navigation console disappearing quickly.

Dropping to the sandy ocean floor, skimming along in the darkness at a depth of ten meters and then looking up through the inky water, they could see the rising moon. Paloma pulled Alistair's arm and pointed upwards just as an Olive Ridley turtle glided over them on its nightly hunt for jelly fish.

Fifteen minutes later they felt the warmer water coming out of the vents. Approaching the rock, they could see the marks of man on the walls of stone rising above them. 'Parking' the Stidd on the sandy floor, they finned up to the rock. It was an incredible piece of engineering, carried out nearly five hundred years ago in an area that would only be exposed for a few hours once a month.

A massive flat rock sat over the opening of the underwater vent and boiling water hit the rock and pushed into the surrounding sea.

The rock rested on two carved hinge rocks, set so that it balanced almost perfectly like a trapdoor. Sitting on the back of the flat rock was the block they were after, carved into an almost flawless square box. Set in the top were the rusted remains of what once must have been a massive chain. This would have gone up to the fort.

The chain was long gone and the trapdoor permanently open. But if they could remove the stone box, the trapdoor would shut and the water would channel into the neat, cut tunnel which they could now see.

Running their hands along the ancient square stone as Dr. KV had taught them, they quickly found the small fissures. Tatiana marked them with a waterproof marker and they set to work drilling holes.

Although the stone was remarkably easy to drill into, the drilling created clouds of 'dust' which meant they couldn't see what they were doing, so every few minutes they had to stop and wait for the clouds to clear before going on. It was also exceedingly hot working so near the vent.

As the tide dropped and the surface got closer to where they were working, they started taking it in turns to pop their heads up and gasp in some of the cool night air. After twenty minutes of drilling, most of the box rock was exposed to the air with the dropping tide.

Alistair made several journeys down to the Stidd to get the rest of their gear. As he loaded it on a ledge which was carved out of the cliff, he imagined the monks putting their own crude tools there five hundred years ago.

Once the box rock was fully out of the water, they gratefully took off their drysuits and laid them carefully out so they could put them back on in a hurry if needed. The hot water bubbled and hissed around the edges of the trapdoor with the falling tide.

Occasionally, they could hear Chinese instructions shouted out from the fort above them and once they heard what sounded like someone being beaten.

Drinking deeply from the fresh water they had brought, they admired their work while they caught their breath

Alistair used the tiny pump to suck the water and debris out of the holes they'd drilled underwater that formed a neat lattice across the tiny crevices in the rock.

Paloma mixed the fresh water with the expanding Dexpan grout using an attachment on one of their drills.

Tatiana held the funnel while she poured the grey slurry into each of the holes until it spilled out on the surface of the stone.

The cracks and holes filled slowly, and they realized they would need to mix many loads before they had finished.

Over the next few hours, the grout would expand, pushing the rock apart and cracking the ancient cube into many pieces.

They hoped that the sea would wash the pieces off the trapdoor, allowing it to close once more, thus forcing the boiling water up the ancient monk's tunnel in an unstoppable volcano that would overwhelm the fort above.

Working as silently as they could in the moonlit night, they interpreted the sounds above them, coming from the fort.

When they finished the last hole and stopped to listen more carefully, they came to realize that there were many people imprisoned in the lowest rooms of the fort. They could see the narrow, horizontal windows not far above the high tide line.

Tatiana strained to hear the voices through the windows. She understood Chinese. "It sounds like they are shackled to the floors." Her voice turned hard. "They are going to be trapped. When the top floors fill with water from the tunnel it will flood those rooms underneath—they will all drown."

"What can we do? We can't take the grout out. In about six hours this rock is going to fall into pieces. After that it won't be long before the trapdoor shuts, and hundreds and thousands of liters of boiling water will pour into the fort," Alistair said.

"We have to release them." Paloma was emphatic.

"You are crazy Paloma. The whole reason we are doing this is because the fort is impenetrable." Alistair was shaking his head.

"We can't let them drown."

"I agree with Paloma and the fort is not impenetrable; we have a tunnel that leads straight into the heart of it. That is a way in and a way out. We don't have to bring the prisoners out, just make sure they can reach the windows to breathe when their cells fill up with water," Tatiana said.

"OK, let's say we crawl up the tunnel or even part way up the tunnel; we are going straight into the lion's mouth, i.e., a room full of guards, and we'll be trapped. Have you ever heard the expression 'as easy as shooting rats in a barrel'?" Alistair could hear the prisoners' chains moving across the floors in the cells above them, and was deeply troubled. Take the very dangerous choice of going right into the lion's mouth or leave all those innocent people who may drown. "So, we need a distraction to get the guards out of the room. Tatiana, you're the distractions expert."

"Remember Dr. KV said the CIA lost twelve drones trying to get photographs of the fort because the guards used them for target practice. How about we give them some target practice?"

"Brilliant, let's call Misha. Deidre has drones. Remember the party she threw for us in California, she had a swarm of drones so let's see if we can use them? Charlie can fly them. She does drone racing in her spare time. I'm betting she'll drive the guards crazy."

A faint cracking sound came from the box rock.

They froze and stared at it, wide-eyed.

"I thought it would take four hours to crack? If that thing goes and we are in the tunnel, we're going to come out like lobsters in a pot." Paloma knelt and looked at the rock, running her hands over the surface. "It's only a couple of millimeters but it is going."

"OK, Tatiana call Misha and tell her to get Charlie to light up the fort with drones, Paloma help me take the rebreathing units back down to the Stidd, then I'm going to move it to the deepest part of the sea under the fort wall. There's no way we are coming back down this tunnel, we'll jump off the fort and swim down to our gear."

"Grab your UZIs and strap your knives on, let's go."

22

The Kraken Awakes

Alistair found a sandy depression at ten meters depth on the sea floor below the fort wall and settled the Stidd on the bottom. He hoped it was deep enough for them to jump off the wall without hitting the sand. When he resurfaced at the tunnel edge, he heard a noise like a swarm of angry wasps. The drones were coming.

By the time he climbed out, the guards were already running out onto the ramparts, futilely firing their weapons on fully automatic at the swirling drones. Charlie had disabled all of their lights, making them just a noise in the night sky.

Starting up the tunnel, they saw it was worn smooth by hundreds of years of gushing water, but the monks had created steps in the walls during construction. At only a meter wide and pitch black, it was going to be a hard climb. But by putting their backs against one side and their feet on the other, they could shimmy their way up.

There was a glow of light coming from the guards' room forty meters above them. Dressed in their black rash guards nobody would see them unless they shone a torch down the tunnel. Three times they froze as they heard the guards run back into the room above them. Hearing weapons being cocked, they feared the worst but doors slammed, and they were in silence again. At one point, a voice they decided must belong to Henry Cheng could be heard screaming at the guards. Tatiana said she couldn't translate into English, just Russian, but whatever he said was not polite.

She was the first one to the top, her light gymnast's body was perfectly designed for this kind of climbing, rolling out of the small wall at the top into the guards' room she tucked in behind it, Uzi at the ready while the other two climbed out gasping for breath. From the bowels of the tunnel came an ominous, deep crack.

"Keys, we need keys to get the prisoners out." Paloma began opening the gray metal cupboards attached to the walls. She found one full of neat rows of keys with Chinese labels under each one.

"Shit, Tatiana, throw me that bag." Paloma pulled all the keys off their hooks and dumped them in the bag. Grabbing another bag Alistair started filling it with the banana shaped magazines for AK 47s, and half a dozen fragmentation grenades, then he picked up three of the weapons from a rack on one wall and handed one to each of them. At 600 rounds per minute their Uzi ammunition wouldn't last long.

"Ready." Standing next to what they assumed was the exit, they prepared to attack. Just as they reached for the handle, the door opened, and two short Chinese guards stepped in. Before Paloma and Alistair could react, Tatiana's knife flashed and both men collapsed on the floor clutching their throats as bright red blood ran out between their fingers and across the cold stone floor.

Stepping out into the corridor, they fanned out tactically and moved towards a concrete stairwell which they hoped connected to the cells below. Above them, the sound of angry drones was studded with machine gun fire.

"Let's hope those buggers use up all their ammo blasting the night sky." As he spoke, boots clattered up the stairs they were heading towards. Darting behind columns, the three of them raised their weapons. Five guards' heads appeared above the concrete railings. Waiting until they walked off the last step, the team opened up with their Uzis. At a range of less than four meters, the guards looked as though an invisible 18-wheeler truck had hit them.

Stepping quickly over the still twitching bodies, they ran down the stairs, loading fresh magazines as they went.

Solid steel doors lined the corridor at the base of the stairs. Every five meters a bare lightbulb lit the raw concrete walls. There was an overpowering smell of human waste, sweat, and something rotting. Gagging, Tatiana opened the steel hatch on the first door and shouted something in Chinese. Tipping all the keys out on the floor, Paloma tried them on the door, Alistair stood, weapon ready.

Ten keys later, Paloma still hadn't found the right one.

"Paloma, we don't have time. That rock is going to crack any minute. Stand guard, I'm going to use the old-fashioned method. Tatiana, ask them to cover their faces with their arms."

Switching his weapon to single shot, he put the stubby barrel into the keyhole and squeezed the triggers. The sound echoed around the hard concrete surfaces and the door swung open. Running in, Tatiana found ten terrified faces staring up at them, their emaciated bodies on crude beds, each with a leg shackle through which a single steel cable ran, attaching them to the floor. It secured the cable with a very solid-looking padlock.

"Bring the key collection. If I fire a shot in here, it's going to bounce all over the place."

Tatiana dumped the keys in front of an elderly-looking man and asked him if he recognized the one for the padlock. With slow, deliberate movements his boney fingers shifted through the pile of keys. Finally bringing out a modern looking one he inserted it into the padlock, and it clicked open. Pulling the cable, Alistair released everyone.

They bowed in gratitude.

"Tatiana, can you explain that they must use the keys to help us release the rest of the prisoners and then they have to go to the top of the fort because it is going to flood? It has to be quick."

The prisoners, who had looked like flotsam on a beach, came to life as Tatiana spoke to them. The old man replied as he divided the keys among the other people.

"He says the guards will just shoot them as soon as they see that they have escaped. He's right, we need to take out as many guards as we can." She spoke to the old man again.

"Let's go hunting. I told him we are going to deal with the guards, and he needed to lead his people to hide somewhere as high as possible away from the boiling water."

Alistair, Paloma and Tatiana had been in enough battles together to move as a single, efficient weapon, covering, firing and moving without stopping. They returned to the next level leaving three more guards' corpses in their wake.

Switching to the AKs as they reached the upper levels, Charlie was performing a dance with the drones, a dance that was driving the remaining ten guards on the parapets insane. The drones would gather in a group high in the night sky, only their buzzing propeller blades giving a clue as to where they were. The guards searched the blackness with powerful torches clipped under the barrels of their weapons, firing randomly when they thought they saw something.

Charlie burst the group apart and sent them below the ramparts, so the guards ran to the walls to see where they had gone. Just as they stepped to the edge, she brought the drones straight at them. It was at this moment that Tatiana, Paloma, and Alistair opened fire.

Shooting fast, accurate double taps, three guards immediately dropped straight off the ramparts into the sea below. The others turned in surprise to face the new threat. Three more crumpled to the ground. The remaining four ran towards a concrete bunker with gun slits that sat in the center of the fort's flat roof. Alistair sprinted across the open compound and posted a frag grenade through the slit window, just as the guards closed the steel door. The grenade went off with a muffled crump and smoke poured out of the gun slits.

Ragged figures of prisoners appeared on the roof.

"Open the gates," Alistair shouted to Paloma.

Running into the guardhouse beside the vast gates, she pulled two levers and both gates across the bridges swung silently open. More and more prisoners appeared, some dragging others with them. Tatiana shouted to them and pointed at the open bridges. They needed no more information and soon they were disappearing into the darkness on the other side.

The whole fort shook and vibrated.

"The Kraken awakes!" Shouted Alistair, as steaming water began erupting from the windows at the sides of the fort. The last prisoner disappeared into the night and they were alone.

Screams came from below and more guards appeared at the top of the stairs, swollen hands held in front of them, faces blistering and peeling from the boiling water. Paloma looked away. Several guards jumped off the battlements into the water below. Others were less fortunate and made sickening thumping noises as they bounced off the rocks on their way down.

"They must be Henry's bodyguards. You have to be especially evil to get a job like that." Alistair was trying to give his sister justification for the spectacle.

"Company, here comes the cartel. It's time to go." They could see rows of headlights streaming towards the fort along the dirt road.

They moved to the battlements where forty meters below, waiting underwater, were the Stidd and rebreathing equipment.

"Feet together, arms tight by your sides, jump out as far as you can," fearless Paloma said, and went first. Seconds later, her head popped up above the surface.

"No problem, come on down," she shouted up at them.

Tatiana jumped. Just as Alistair was about to jump, a bedraggled figure in a black dress appeared at the top of the stairs. At first, he didn't recognize her—half her face looked like a blowtorch had been applied to it. Bits of raw cheek flapped, only partly attached.

Slowly raising his weapon, he pointed the muzzle at her.

"Poppy Cheng, the crimes you have committed against the world mean that you no longer have the right to be part of it."

Poppy walked towards him. She raised her eyes to him; they were full of pain. She put her hand on her heart, moving so close he could smell her perfume.

"Alistair, I still love you. I never stopped loving you. I can help you, I can get all those people for you, they trust me. I'll do anything for you. Let me go and I will become your agent." She said almost as a whisper.

Lowering his weapon, he saw the pleading in her eyes.

"Promise?"

"I promise, and I love you forever."

"Will you give me a list of all the poachers you control in Africa?"

"Anything you ask."

"Give me your cell phone." He said, pointing to the device in her hand.

Hesitating for a fraction of a second, she handed it to him.

"Passcode?" The cartel cars were rattling across the bridge. "Poppy. Passcode." He motioned with his barrel.

"One—two—three—four—eight—nine." He punch the numbers in as she said them. The phone unlocked.

He took a deep breath, tucked the phone into a waterproof pouch and said, "Go." She shuffled away, heading towards the gate. He heard the doors of cars opening near the entrance.

Alistair jumped up on the battlements, throwing down his weapon as he prepared to launch himself off.

Turning to get a last glance at Poppy as she walked out the gate, he found her standing facing him only five meters away, AK 47 aimed at his torso. She was laughing a vile, cruel laugh.

"You were always such a bloody sucker." And she squeezed the trigger.

23

Old Wounds

Alistair had jumped as Poppy had squeezed the trigger. One round had hit him in the shoulder. It had enough force to push him further away from the fort wall. Hitting the water with both arms out and feet apart had been painful, but not fatal. The girls were waiting on the surface with his rebreathing kit. After putting his mask on, they pulled him underwater like two mermaids, trailing blood from his wound as they swam down to the Stidd.

Through the water they felt the chop, *chop, chop* of Poppy's helicopter taking off, followed by several headlights, cutting blades of light through the night sky as the Cartel vehicles crossed the bridge and entered the main courtyard.

Keeping close to the ocean floor, with Paloma holding Alistair, they set off back to the yacht. Thirty minutes later, hands reached down to pull Alistair on board the *Sirene*. Dr. KV, with years of combat experience and having repaired many a bullet wound, treated Alistair, starting with a glass of Laphroaig.

"Paloma, I owe you an apology. You tried to warn me." Alistair explained what happened with Poppy.

"Well, at least we got to boil half her face off. Talking of ugly, what happened to Henry? Did we cook him?" Paloma asked.

"With that many drones flying, we have actually got a vast amount of imagery, including all the Cartel as they got out of their cars." Misha started swiping through the images on her laptop. "You're right Paloma, he is ugly, if this is him?" zooming into a squat man with a menacing face. They nodded. "Looks like Henry didn't get cooked, but he sure looks angry."

"Not surprised. We just flooded his entire operation, chased off all his prisoners and probably boiled his apartment. Let's see where he goes next." Tatiana folded her arms and looked like a woman satisfied with a day's work.

The Earl had assets around the area were feeding information back to him. They already knew that Henry Cheng had an old airstrip and hangers about 30 kilometers north of Fort Kraken. The team thought it likely that he would use this to launch drones loaded with The Mengbi Weapon.

"It's going to take him a while to set up his operation. We want to make sure we destroy everything, not just part of it, so I think we should wait before taking it out."

"Misha is right. I believe we need to concentrate on Poppy's Kenyan poaching operation. Even though we took out the fish factory and their planes, we know they still have the digital keys to every elephant that they flew over, so while they can't block them, they can find them. Let's start by looking at Poppy's phone." Dr. KV was finishing putting a dressing on Alistair's wounds.

"I already did—it was wiped remotely, plus it had a tracker on it I couldn't stop. It was a very sophisticated piece of equipment and I couldn't afford to spend the time hacking it. They would have found us." Misha said.

"So where is it?" Alistair asked.

"Charlie attached it to a drone, and it is on its way to Los Cabos."

Misha smiled.

"Deidre, whatever happens next, I think we need to head back to California. Those Cartels make me nervous and who knows, when they realize we are only anchored 2000 meters from the fort they might start putting two and two together and come and pay us a visit. Can we cast off immediately? If anybody asks, we are just tourists who got nervous from all the gunfire."

"Certainly, I agree. Let me ask the captain to get underway and I suggest the rest of you go to your cabins and get some sleep."

The rhythm of the ship's engines, along with the gentle swell of the waves, provided everyone with a deep sleep. Getting up later than usual, people headed for the stern deck for a buffet breakfast.

Misha and Deidre were having their usual morning kickoff Bloody Marys, made with a whole, crushed Scotch bonnet chili pepper.

Alistair's eyes watered as he sat down. Blood had seeped through his dressing in the night and he was in pain.

Dr. KV quietly put two pills beside his cup of coffee, which Alistair downed quickly.

"I'll give you a fresh dressing after breakfast."

Alistair pulled him closer and whispered in his ear, "it's not the bloody bullet wound. I hit the water with my legs apart." Alistair crossed his eyes and Dr. KV breathed in sharply between his teeth, "Ouch." Turning to face everybody, he said, "I talked to the Earl last night and he agrees that going after the poaching operation should come first."

"I think we should start by chopping off its head." Paloma was grinning "Poppy is going to be vulnerable right now. My guess is that she is going back to Hong Kong to get medical attention. If we get her and break into her system, we can hopefully find out everyone who is working for her in Kenya and pick them off one by one?"

"Misha, can we find out what flights left Los Cabos International

Airport last night? Probably looking for a long-range jet with a medical team on board—that would be hard to hide." Misha started tapping on her iPad while sipping her drink.

"Correct assumptions Dr. KV and Paloma. There was an emergency flight out of Los Cabos at 7am this morning. It is headed for Hawaii and then Hong Kong."

"Good, the Earl has lots of assets in Hong Kong and not just people; I believe he still has a safe house up on Victoria's Peak. Let me talk to him to see where she goes when she lands. Tatiana, we may need your skills to get into her apartment, hopefully she will be in hospital."

Dr. KV was looking at Alistair, who was waiting for his drugs to kick in.

"Well, Alistair, consider yourself lucky. Just think how much pain Poppy Cheng is going to have to endure, she's going to need half her face replacing."

"Yeah, you're right, and when they're done doing that, I might just finish the bitch off myself."

Paloma clapped her hands together, delighted that he was finally over her arch enemy.

"Hong Kong here we come. Tatiana how do you say 'Please may I have a large, cold beer' in Cantonese? I need to practice."

24

The Cullinan

The Earl joined them in California. He arrived in a new Citation Longitude jet which had the range to get them to Hong Kong with one stop in Hawaii. Misha stayed in California with Deidre; they were becoming a formidable team. Dr. KV and Charlie headed back to Panama, leaving Alistair, Tatiana and Paloma to carry on with The Earl.

The plane was quiet and comfortable, with eight plush leather seats. The Earl's last pilot had proved to be a traitor, feeding INTERPOL information straight back to one of the world's most notorious rhino poachers. Dave, the new pilot, an unflappable ginger haired man had retired from the Fleet Air Arm with countless hours' combat experience in Harrier jump jets. He was teaching Paloma how to fly the plane.

Seventeen hours later, the Citation swept over the orange glowing islands of Hong Kong and headed towards the airport, which had an island all to itself. They landed and immediately climbed into a helicopter, which took them through the brightly lit skyscrapers. Heading for the tallest one, the helicopter landed on the roof. It was the Ritz Carlton.

"I thought we should start here with dinner. There is a Cantonese restaurant which I think you might enjoy, it's called the Tin Lung Heen." He led the way out towards the lifts as staff unloaded the bags.

High, at the 102nd level, the restaurant had sweeping views across the pulsating city. The food was, as The Earl promised, exquisite.

"Actually, I didn't just bring us here for the food. Over there..." he pointed to a sleek black tower that was a series of twisting triangles about 200 meters from where they were sitting, "... is Poppy Cheng's penthouse. In fact she owns the whole tower known as 'The Cullinan'. I have got us a suite and rooms above the restaurant that look down on her place."

"The security is state-of-the art and tight. However, I can confirm that she is in the Gleneagles Hong Kong Hospital, which means we have two likely locations to explore."

"It sounds like she travels a lot, so she will need to access her files remotely. I expect someone like her would have her own, private server, that is most likely in her apartment. So, we either try to go after the server itself or we go after her passwords and try to hack it. The way to get her passwords would probably be through her laptop, which I expect she will have with her." Tatiana and Misha had been tracking Poppy and looking at the security systems in her apartment.

"You are right Tatiana, or we could just wait until she comes out of hospital and simply shoot her from our bedrooms?" Tatiana, the Earl, and Alistair looked at Paloma to see if she was joking. They weren't sure.

"More wine?"

It had been a long journey, Alistair's shoulder was throbbing, and after dinner they retired gratefully to their rooms and luxurious sheets. Their bags had been unpacked for them.

Misha had given them all new passports before they had left. Now that Poppy had seen Alistair, they needed to hide their tracks.

The following morning, they joined the Earl for breakfast in his rooms. He had set up a tripod with a Leica camera and 50 magnification digiscope that looked down on Poppy's apartment. Tatiana walked over to it.

"Looks like all the blinds are down, wow those are pretty gigantic windows. My guess is at some point today she'll have some staff come in. We need to get a floor plan."

"Already on it, my dear, architectural offices generally have pretty slack online security. I will see if I can get the floor plans today."

"I found out where the hospital staff uniforms are laundered. Tatiana, as you are the only one Poppy doesn't know, I thought you might like to pay an 'official' visit. We are organizing a uniform and Misha is sorting an ID for you. You'll have to be a cleaner. The nurses and doctors are a small team, and they would notice a new face, but nobody notices cleaners. Many of the staff, even the cleaners, are European, so you won't look out of place, and you speak Cantonese."

"Perfect, my cleaning skills are close to professional, my nursing skills not so much."

"Actually, you did a pretty good job of patching me up in Egypt when we both got hit by an M60 machine gun."

"True Paloma, but my plastic surgery skills may give me away."

They decided that Paloma and Alistair would keep watch on the apartment while The Earl met his various sources and Tatiana would go to the hospital as soon as her uniform arrived.

An hour later, a messenger appeared with a sealed box. Opening it, they found a grey and white uniform, white shoes, and an ID card bearing the name 'Natascha Gordon'. Tatiana tried it on, doing a swirl. She added a blonde wig and blue lenses to match the ID photo.

"Can you wash up my cups please?" Alistair was holding up a tray full of used coffee cups.

Tatiana gave him a look which made him put the tray down quickly.

The words 'Gleneagles Hong Kong Hospital' were written on her back.

The Earl gave Tatiana detailed instructions on which entrance to go into and where the changing rooms were for cleaners. She had changed into plain looking street clothes befitting a cleaner.

25

Gleneagles

Poppy lay in a darkened room in the private wing of Gleneagles hospital. She had just spent ten hours in surgery. It was to be the first of many. Her surgeon, considered the best facial reconstructive surgeon in the world, had flown in from Pakistan.

She moved in and out of a kind of grey haze of consciousness. She recalled the gaudy furniture of Henry Cheng's windowless apartment, water rushing towards her face, Alistair's blue eyes and then the recoil of the AK 47 in her hands.

As she lay there with one half of her face bandaged, she sensed another person moving around her room. She couldn't move. Lying on her back, she could only see slight shadows on the ceiling as the person walked in front of the blinking lights on the consul, monitoring her vitals. Unintentionally, she made a slight moaning noise.

"Do you need anything? I am just cleaning the room for you, but I can ask the nurse," Tatiana said in Cantonese.

Poppy made another slight groaning noise. Tatiana noted the small MacBook laptop in a drawer in the bedside table, which wasn't completely shut. She walked over and, picking up an empty glass, she wiped the table. As she did so, she opened the drawer a fraction more and mentally registered the model and color.

"I'll ask the nurse to come in. I'll be back later. We have a very high standard of cleanliness at Gleneagles. Thank you."

Tatiana went through the glass door of the room and spoke to the duty nurse.

"The patient is moaning. I am not sure what she wants, so I thought it best if I came back later to finish cleaning."

"Alright, I'll go in and see her. Poor thing had half her face boiled off. She must have been exquisite. What's your name, I haven't seen you before?"

"Natascha, I just started working at this level, it's a promotion, I hope one day to be a nurse."

"OK Natascha, come back in an hour, I am Nurse Mackenzie, I'll still be on duty."

Tatiana hastened to the cleaners' changing rooms, put her street clothes on and rushed out into the street, heading for the Mac store.

An hour later, she was wearing surgical gloves and pushing a small trolley filled with towels, between which she had a new MacBook Air. On the top shelf of the trolley, neatly organized cleaning products sat in small pockets. Tatiana trotted over to Nurse Mackenzie's desk.

"How is the patient? Shall I finish cleaning?"

"She was still moaning, I am afraid. Looks like her tongue was damaged but go ahead, she may be asleep now."

Tatiana, the picture of efficiency, went through the glass door and began methodically cleaning surfaces and picking up discarded medical packaging. Poppy was breathing with difficultly, a plastic tube around her nose. She appeared to be asleep. Glancing up at Mackenzie's desk, she knelt and pretended to pick something out from under the bed. With her other hand, she pulled open the drawer on the bedside table and extracted the laptop. Slipping it between two towels, she replaced it with the new one. She noticed a yellow post-it note with something written on it just under the bed. Shutting the drawer, she bent down to pick up the paper. Feeling a hand run up her back and then onto her bare neck, she stood up, whirling around, pushing the hand away as she did so.

Grinning in front of her was a stocky Chinese man wearing a leather jacket, tattoos running all the way up his neck.

"If you wait for me outside when you finish, I'll give you the best paid cleaning job you've ever had," he said in Cantonese.

Tatiana bit her lip and turned to go. His fat, sweaty, hand grabbed her hand and pulled her face towards his.

"Maybe we can do the cleaning right here." His breath smelled of fried pork and cheap cigarettes.

"Ying, give me my laptop," a raspy voice came from the bed.

Wheeling around in surprise, Ying replied, "Sorry Miss Cheng, I thought you were sleeping."

Tatiana used the opportunity to pull out of his grasp. Turning sharply, she marched her trolley out of the door.

"All done, see you later." Nurse McKenzie looked a bit surprised as Tatiana hurried off down the corridor, little trolley wheels spinning wildly.

Stepping into the elevator, she heard a shout in Cantonese. "Oi, come back here, you thieving bitch."

The door slid silently closed before the running footsteps reached her. As the lift descended to the next floor, she pulled out the MacBook and pushed it into her waistband under her cleaning smock, then picked up the bottle of spray bleach and aimed it at the gap between the two closed doors. The lift gently came to a halt on the next floor down and pinged as the doors opened.

Ying stood there, slightly out of breath, and grinned.

"Still need that cleaning?" Tatiana said as she fired the bleach into his eyes, pressing the close door button at the same time. She could still hear him screaming blue murder as the lift sped downwards to the service level.

Seconds after her lift door opened, she heard the one next to hers open too. She and Ying both stepped out together. His eyes were streaming, but in his hand, he had a Glock G17 and it was pointed at her chest.

"Come here little cleaning girl, you have got someth— " he never finished his sentence. Moving forward and grabbing his gun hand in one smooth movement, she twisted it around, pushed it into his chest and squeezed the trigger. He crashed to the ground like a fallen tree. Tatiana wiped the gun with a cloth and bleach from her trolley and then started walking. As she approached the rear loading bay, a British racing green Jaguar electric I-Pace appeared, all tires squealing as it slid neatly sideways towards her on the painted surface.

The passenger door opened. "Jump in, it's about to get hot around here." The Earl passed her a shawl and a pair of large sunglasses and Tatiana pulled off her blonde wig. They disappeared into the river of Hong Kong traffic.

Tatiana pulled the laptop from her waistband and opened it up.

There was a single icon, a poppy, in the center of the screen under which was a space for a username.

"Wow, that's original." She typed in the word *'Poppy'* and it gave her a password box. She knew if she got it wrong too many times, it would lock her out. Tatiana also knew the computer could be tracked right now.

There were two choices, crack open the case and try to take the hard drive out without damaging it or get the password right.

"Did she see your face?" The Earl asked. Tatiana processed the seconds she had spent in the room with Poppy, it reminded her why she had bent over, searching in her pocket she pulled out the post it and read it aloud as she typed it "*PLUSESTENVOUS*" and hit enter. The screen changed to a home screen.

Her fingers darted quickly across the keyboard as she disabled the tracking device.

"Do you know where 'PLUS EST EN VOUS or THERE IS MORE IN YOU' comes from?" The Earl asked.

"No idea. Is it a French proverb?"

"No, it comes from Gordonstoun, the school they expelled her from—it's the school motto."

"Interesting, seeing as she got kicked out for having sex with another student, maybe she misunderstood the motto!"

They both chuckled.

26

OP

Tatiana and the Earl walked into the room in the hotel carrying Poppy's MacBook. Paloma sat cross-legged on her vast bed. Her laptop was in front of her with a cable running to the Leica Digiscope, pointing at Poppy's apartment. A glass of freshly squeezed orange juice was on the bedside table.

"This is without doubt the most comfortable OP we have ever done. Wow, you got it. Any trouble?"

"Yeah, I had to do some cleaning." Alistair came in with a pot of tea and Marmite sandwiches and Tatiana explained what happened at the hospital.

They called Misha while Tatiana uploaded the entire contents of Poppy's laptop so Misha could access it.

Opening his laptop, The Earl looked up Ying whom Tatiana had just shot with his own gun and added him to their wall of players with a red line across his photo. He typed the word EXTINCT below the picture. It turned out that Ying was on INTERPOL's most wanted list. His list of crimes included an attack on young girls in Gabon in Central Africa along with the export of an entire shipload of illegally cut tropical hardwood. He was a distant cousin of Poppy's.

"Perfect," Tatiana said as she helped herself to Paloma's juice. "He got what he deserved."

Alistair and Paloma had cataloged who and when people came into Poppy's apartment.

"So far, the maid shows up at 8am and does some light dusting until ten. Her name is Angel Cha. She too is a distant cousin."

Misha was still on the line, "I am going to make a family tree of all Poppy's relatives. It looks like she only does business or employs people connected to her family."

"So, I guess we need to see what we can find on her laptop and then decide if we still need to go into her apartment? I am worried now she knows someone has got her computer she is going to look for us. Even if she didn't see my face, the CCTV in the hospital will have caught me disposing of Ying in the loading bay."

"You are correct, Granddaughter, but I am many streets ahead of you. Before you even went into the hospital, I accessed the cameras and I was watching your excellent work. Then I deleted the parts whenever you appeared. Don't worry Tatiana, as far as the hospital is concerned, you don't exist."

"Plus, you were a blue-eyed blonde," Alistair added.

"Paloma, I know you are enjoying the Ritz and Misha covered our tracks, but if Poppy so much as suspects it involves you and Alistair, she's going to send out your picture to her multitude of contacts across the city. I am sure she has people in this hotel. It's time to move to our place on the Peak, you'll love it. The British Secret Service and then INTERPOL have been using it since the First World War."

"Nasty Dragon Lady, maybe we should just take her out and go back to our nice green jungle? A chemical added to her drip while she is lying in hospital will do it." Paloma looked around for support.

Misha spoke up and shared her screen. "This is what her hospital room looks like now." The CCTV showed a man with a machine gun on each side of her bed and another one on the other side of the glass door.

"Nurse Mackenzie is going to love that."

"Misha, how much time do you need on the laptop until we can decide whether to go into Poppy's apartment?"

"Give me 24 hours,"

"OK, everyone needs to change before we walk out of here." The Earl pulled a suitcase onto the bed and opened it. Wigs, glasses, and boxes of makeup spilled out. They all laughed. "Oh, I love dressing up." Paloma said, putting on an enormous black wig and small glasses.

A van with tinted windows was waiting at the service entrance of the hotel. Getting in, they headed up a twisty road to Victoria Peak. In the 1800s, many of the British senior staff had built their homes there because it was the coolest, least disease-ridden part of Hong Kong. Some houses were still occupied, several abandoned, and many torn down and replaced with more modern structures. The INTERPOL house on 32 Severn Road was still cherished and in its original condition. It had sweeping views across the steep forest-covered slopes down towards the city. Tucked tightly against the hill behind, it felt like a safe refuge.

The resident staff stepped out to greet them. The Earl, speaking Cantonese, introduced everybody.

"You were wrong, you know Sir, I much prefer this to the hotel. You can breathe up here. What lovely tall rooms and views." Paloma said, spreading her arms and twirling.

Setting up their laptops, the staff brought in Lapsang Souchong tea.

"This is the real thing." Alistair said, tasting the smokey tea, "all the way from China."

By the following morning, Misha had examined the contents of Poppy's computer. They connected to her.

"First, from the CCTV at the hospital, we can see she is still there.

My information says she'll be there for a least a week, if not longer."

"The computer has emails, but very few actual files. It seems she has a server in her apartment and the only way to get to it is by using a dynamic key which is probably on her cell phone, or else we must physically steal the server drives."

"I think it is unlikely we'll get close enough to her to steal her phone, but we may be able to pay a visit to her penthouse."

Misha shared her screen. It pulled up a picture of two glass clad towers joined at the center labelled 'The Cullinan.'

"This is the apartment you have been watching," she said, zooming into a penthouse at the top of one tower. "It is considered some of the most expensive real estate in the world. The apartment is 270 meters up from the road on the 68th floor.

Here is the floor plan kindly provided by Wong and Ouyang the architects... although they don't know it," they could hear her chuckling.

"Any thoughts on how to get in?"

"OK excuse the crazy but we have to start somewhere," Alistair cleared his throat. "We know all the normal entry points are covered and landing a helicopter on the roof is just going to send up all kinds of alarms. How about we do HAHO parachute drop onto the top of her roof, abseil down the front of her building, cut through the glass, break into the server room and then parachute off into the water and get picked up by a boat?"

"Wow, Alistair, I think that bullet in your shoulder is affecting your head... and I like the bit about 'we.' I don't think you are capable of all those monkey antics with that hole through you." Paloma looked at Alistair, shaking her head.

"As soon as you cut through the glass, the alarms will go off, then you really only have a couple of minutes before the goons arrive. Unless you have a brilliant, old Russian super-agent who can hack into the system and disable it." Misha added, smiling to herself.

"Still crazy, remember our last HAHO? We lost Tatiana for a good couple of hours. This is not a big open desert; that looks like a 50m x 30m roof studded with sharp antennas." Paloma was not convinced. "I think we could get pretty close to the top by just using the lift. It is a residential tower after all, and then whack a few guards in front of her apartment."

"Those guards are probably highly trained killers. Up there she will have the best of the best. It is her fortress. Good as we are, it will only take one guard to hit an alarm and dozens will swarm the building. What do you think, Grandma Misha?"

"Tatiana is correct, I am looking at the floor below Poppy's. It has twenty-five bedrooms, communal showers, and a commercial kitchen. That means it is a barracks. I know some of those guys will be at the hospital, but even if only half of them are there, the risk is too high."

"Do we mind if some of them might die?" Tatiana looked at everyone.

"From the list we have so far, they are all on the INTERPOL most wanted. They are all probably part of Poppy's wildlife trafficking operation. They are all part of our mission to poach the poachers. So no, I have no objections. Anyone else?" The Earl looked at everyone nodding in agreement. He said to Tatiana, "What are you thinking?"

"Kolokol -1. Powerful sleeping gas. Fast acting, untraceable within 30 minutes. Add it to their HVAC system and they will drop like flies. They should wake up two hours later but it is strong and some people don't wake up, especially heavy smokers." Tatiana let her breath out.

"That's my girl. Now you are thinking like a Russian." Misha grinned.

They would need to go in disguised.

Alistair was too tall, too blonde, and too blue eyed to get away with playing the role of a Hong Kong maintenance guy, but they could make him into a wealthy old Brit, shuffling about his tower.

Tatiana was of the right stature, but it worried them that female building engineers were too rare. However, Tatiana was adamant she could pull off a stern looking Chinese engineer.

Paloma was to play the role of a slightly drugged out 'it' girl, which Alistair said was just her playing herself.

Paloma had asked The Earl to buy her a full theatre makeup kit. She spent several hours working on Alistair and Tatiana.

All of them would need to carry bags with weapons, the gas and equipment, plus, parachutes. They had agreed the safest and fastest exit would be to jump off the roof and then get whisked away in a fast boat. The Earl would be in charge of this.

"In case any of you have any doubts, I should remind you that Poppy Cheng runs one of the biggest poaching operations in the world. Getting the names and contacts of everyone connected to those operations will give us the means to destroy that operation and even reverse the mass extinction of some of Earth's most precious creatures."

"Think of it like this: every name you collect will probably represent the life of one living but critically endangered creature."

The Earl lifted his glass."The Extinct Company... and poaching the poachers."

27

Picking Poppies

They entered the building separately. They would break into an empty apartment well below Poppy's. Alistair and Paloma had chosen one that showed no evidence of occupation when they were watching the tower. They would wait there until 2.30am when things were at their quietest and then go into action.

Paloma worried about Alistair's wound, and he joked about getting older, doing a very convincing impression of a doddering old man. With his makeup and walking stick, nobody was going to doubt he was anything else. Although they were in costume, they had deliberately chosen dark clothes for their exit. Tatiana had a reflective waistcoat to go over her dark grey, fireproof overalls and then a white helmet on her head. She had an upright chest of work boxes on wheels that she could easily fit into the lift. Inside were two canisters of gas which, when combined, would create what the Russian agent called "Kolokol -1" the powerful sleeping gas.

They each had a gas mask in their bags.

They entered the chosen twentieth-floor apartment and, as usual, Tatiana, always cool under stress, lay down on the first flat surface she could find and instantly fell asleep. Alistair and Paloma drank tea and tried to calm each other's nerves. Misha had given a full briefing with descriptions of every guard, and she was right: they were a nasty, dangerous, and highly trained bunch.

At 2.15am they woke Tatiana. She popped up like it was a normal Monday and she was heading off to work.

Taking separate lifts, they had all assumed their roles by the time they reached the 66th floor. Misha had rigged them with hidden mikes and webcams so the teams could monitor their progress.

Paloma as an 'It Girl' trotted up the stairs wearing black boots, a short black dress with a high collar that fastened at the neck. She was carrying a large handbag.

She staggered slightly as she opened the fire door into the corridor, slurring her words as she said in English, "where's da party?" To a guard slouched on an expensive-looking chair outside the only door in the corridor.

"No, English." Then he added something in Cantonese which Paloma really didn't understand, but then he backed it up by standing and pointing a pistol at her.

"Oopsee-daisy. I surrender." She slightly raising her hands.

The guard smiled as if he was about to have some fun and walked towards her, allowing his gun to swing loosely at his side as he walked.

The lift opened, and Tatiana, pushing her toolboxes, walked out. She marched straight over to the guard, who turned in surprise the moment she brought her pistol butt down hard on his temple.

Paloma pulled a syringe from her bag and injected the guard. "Nighty nighty No English." Together, they dragged him to the service stairs and dumped him in a corner. Tatiana pulled a bottle of brandy from her toolbox and poured some around his mouth and down the top of his shirt, then placed it beside him. Paloma, grinning, picked it up as she poured the rest in his crotch, making a dark stain on his trousers. She pushed the empty bottle into his stubby hand.

"Perfect," Tatiana said.

Alistair bumbled out of one lift, mumbling to himself like a disoriented old man.

They headed towards the HVAC room for the barracks. It had a steel ventilated door and

Tatiana picked the lock in seconds. Once inside, the low droning from the machinery filled their eardrums. Pulling the engineering drawings from his tattered bag, Alistair spread them out on a worn stainless-steel table. Tubes, wires, pipes and conduit ran in well-ordered lines up the walls and turned 90 degrees into what they assumed was the 'barracks.'

The fattest insulated pipes marked HVAC ran into a large register that hummed happily. Opening a drawer from her toolbox, Tatiana handed Alistair a small impact screwdriver, and together they removed the cover from the register. They had come prepared. The box had a large inlet tube which fed cool air to the barracks and Tatiana pulled out a short pipe with two valves attached.

"Get ready." Paloma pulled her mask on and stepped out the door with a silenced MP5 machine gun. She presented an interesting sight: cute, short, black dress, boots, machine gun and gas mask.

Inside, the other two put on their masks.

Tatiana pulled out two small gas tanks. Both were green and marked OXYGEN, but one had an A and the other a B. They were the agents for the Kolokol -1.

"Ready?"

"Go." Alistair unscrewed the outlet pipe and dropped it on the floor. Cold air filled the room. Tatiana screwed in the attachment with the two valves and they each screwed in a green bottle.

"3-2-1-Go," they had practiced in the house both opened their valves in perfect timing, creating the exact blend. Tatiana was staring at her watch, "20-15-10-5 seconds and done."

Replacing the outlet pipe, they put the two tanks back in Tatiana's work box.

Outside, Paloma trained her weapon on the barrack door. If anyone tried to escape the gas, they would come out here. Nobody appeared.

"All Clear."

The other two packed up their equipment, reattached the AC, checked the room, and closed the door behind them.

"Nobody came out," Paloma whispered.

"Good, let's give them twenty seconds then check the room." Tatiana looked at her watch again.

"I'll stand guard. Try to find the keys or card to get into Poppy's floor, they must have them." He took off his gas mask and sniffed. "Seems OK."

"Time. Let's go." Paloma and Tatiana used the key from the guard they had immobilized before.

The hallway inside was dimly lit by a single, slightly broken lamp, boots and socks were scattered about the entry hall.

"Why are boys always so messy?" Paloma whispered through her mask.

Turning on their powerful torches, they swept through the rooms, moving tactically. Everyone was unconscious, sprawled out where they had stood as if somebody had cut their power switches. Six were in their bunks. With Paloma ready with her weapon, they checked each person, pulling out wallets and phones for information, 'mining' as Misha called it.

"Hey, this guy's got a huge bundle of $100 bills wrapped in plastic." Tatiana photographed him.

"So has this one, weird, let's check the rest."

They all had neat bundles of cash, even the ones in their bunks had them tucked under the pillows. They photographed each one, then collected the cash into their bags.

The main sitting room was a mess, weapons scattered over tables and sofas' old food cartons on the floor. Tatiana shoved a small blob of metal epoxy down each barrel, enough to make it explode when fired.

In the TV room, they found a laptop playing porn, which they added to their collection.

"OK Paloma, that's it, let's find the keys or card to Poppy's apartment, if they are here."

After five minutes of searching, they decided it would be better if Tatiana would break in.

Alistair was still 'patrolling' outside. They joined him.

"OK we finished, they are all out cold, can't find the keys, so Tatiana will break in."

They went back into the service stairwell. Stepping over the unconscious guard, they told Alistair about the cash.

Reaching the next floor, they got ready. Tatiana pulled open the door to the hallway and Paloma whipped around, weapon ready.

"Clear."

Working towards Poppy's front door, the three of them advanced.

"Wait, the door's open. I can hear voices inside."

Blood was pooling out under the partially open door, Tatiana pushed it further open, and Paloma stepped inside, followed by the other two.

Sprawled on the floor, mouth open and a neat hole in his forehead, was Singsong Poppy's head of security.

Avoiding the body and blood, they silently moved closer to the voices. Having memorized the floor plan, they had a good idea where it was coming from.

"Server room, two men. Paloma, you take the guy on the right. I'll take the one on the left. Tatiana, watch for more, they must have a lookout somewhere. And try to avoid rounds going through their bodies and smashing the server."

There was already a pile of hard drives on the floor, and Alistair could see them pulling out more.

"Now." two neat thunks from their silenced MP5s and both men crumpled to the floor. A third suppressed shot went off behind them and they heard another body thump to the floor. "That was the lookout." Tatiana reappeared.

Stepping forward, they pulled the bodies out of the tiny room, looking at their faces as they did so. "Shit, these are Henry's men, I recognize this one from the mugshots we got." Alistair took a photo and sent it to Misha.

"They must have paid off the guards below. Let's get this gear and get out of here fast. Tatiana, can you help me get the rest of the hard drives out? Misha, do you read me? What's the status of the alarms?"

"Someone already disabled them."

Paloma was taking in the apartment. Despite her bitter hatred of Poppy, she was impressed. The ceilings were twice the height of a normal house. Furnishings were sparse but comfortable, everything looked exquisite. The contrast with the noisy, messy colorful city 68 floors below was almost a shock. In one recessed wall was a subtlety lit display of what looked like ancient Asian swords.

"Hey, Alistair, look where dragon lady keeps her teeth." There was a library of very old books and manuscripts. The only thing out of place were themselves and the bodies.

"Paloma, head out to the verandah. My guess is they will send a heli to pick this lot up. Stay in the shadows and if you get a shot, hit something vital in the engine so that he has to land somewhere fast." Alistair snapped her out of it.

The veranda was too small to land a helicopter, so Alistair assumed they would use a winch and harness.

As Tatiana and Alistair loaded the last hard drive into two waterproof bags and headed out to join Paloma, they heard the high-pitched whine of a helicopter approaching. Getting louder, the engine note suddenly changed and started coughing like a lawnmower on the blink.

Paloma came over the radio. "Sweet—took out the fuel lines. He's going off to find a nice cozy patch of grass to crash land in." The noise cut off as the helicopter dropped below the window and around the back of the tower.

Joining her on the veranda, Alistair said, "nice shot Paloma, we are finished let's get the chutes ready," looking up to the sky for more helicopters.

They laid out the harnesses and strapped on their parachutes.

"This is Whisky to Brandy. We are leaving the building. See you in the drink."

"Roger that, ready and waiting."

Tatiana and Paloma would carry the bags with hard drives. They weren't heavy, but they were awkward. Jumping off a skyscraper was hard enough, and they worried about the extra strain on Alistair's wounded shoulder.

They spaced themselves out along Poppy's long veranda so that they wouldn't bump into each other as they jumped. Stepping up on the wide railing, the noise and smell of traffic from 68 floors below surprised them. Ahead of them was the inky water of Hong Kong Harbor. They hoped the Earl would be fast to collect them.

"3-2-1...Go." Flinging their lines out, they dropped over twenty floors before their chutes snapped opened. The rushing wind slowed and they could hear the sounds of the city again. The Earl was watching and sent out a brief, green pulsing strobe light from his boat as arranged. They all acknowledged on their radios and headed in his direction. Toggling their chutes, they could steer accurately enough—they just hoped there weren't any ferries around when they hit the waters.

Paloma and Alistair had perfected the technique of parachuting onto water with their dad, who had learnt it from his mate in the French

Foreign legion. The trick was to dump your chute just as you hit the water, so it didn't drag you down.

Paloma had once achieved barefoot kite surfing by flipping her chute around and getting it to pull her across the waves. But you needed a good wind and tonight they were just going to dump unceremoniously into the rather dubious waters of Hong Kong harbor.

"For goodness' sake, don't swallow the water," She announced over their radio, seconds before they smacked into the warm liquid.

The Earl was on the job, driving a neat RIB with a mesh platform on the rear for divers. The boat was jet powered so there was no prop to get tangled in. Presenting the stern to Tatiana, she rolled on to the platform and climbed to the seats in the center. Alistair was collected next, and he winced as Tatiana pulled him out of the water.

"The water in Majorka don't taste like what it oughta." Paloma spat out a mouthful of Hong Kong Harbor water as she nimbly flipped herself onto the stern.

"Gasping for a cup of tea."

"You are kidding, Alistair. Tatiana and I doing vodka, da Chica?" Paloma rolled her eyes at her brother as she mixed Russian and Spanish.

The girls smacked their hands together.

"Poaching was good tonight and we need to celebrate."

"Maybe a wee dram, Sir?"

"Aye Laddie, I have a 30-year-old Laphroaig that you might enjoy." The Earl curved the boat in a neat arc and headed towards a small jetty below the Peak.

28

Henry's not happy

"Wow, we created a storm, and they don't know it involved us." Alistair was reading the English newspaper delivered to the gates of 37 Severn Road, as it had been for the last 100 years.

"This is a sibling war. 68 gang members murdered before dawn. And from both sides."

"It looks like Poppy thinks Henry's people stole her laptop from the hospital and then raided her apartment. She must believe her half-brother is trying to take the throne. And Henry thinks Poppy had inside information and killed all his men, including his five top lieutenants who did not survive the helicopter crash in the big grassy park of the West Kowloon District... but no bystanders were injured. Excellent shooting Paloma."

"And we achieved our goal, which is to get these." The Earl swept his hand across the row of hard drives on the table. "For the sake of safety—both ours and the information on the —we are going to take these to my plane immediately and go straight back to the Magic Shop in Panama as soon as we can."

"Misha is on her way back there right now."

"I just hope Poppy's face really hurts right now, but I think she won't take too long to work out someone other than Henry is involved."

Poppy was, in fact, having one of the worst days she had ever experienced. Half of her perfect face was at this moment, covered in stitches. It was swollen, throbbing, and she realized she would never look the same again. Her beauty was one of her most powerful weapons, which she used ruthlessly and to significant effect. Her bad day was compounded because Henry's men had somehow got past all of her guards, killed her favorite and most loyal man Singsong, and had stolen all the contents of her server and her laptop, giving Henry access to all of her assets in Africa. She realized that, if she wasn't careful, Henry could take over as head of the whole organization. She knew he always felt like he, as the oldest male heir, should have been named head. She knew jealousy consumed him. He referred to Poppy as The Half-Blood woman because she wasn't pure Chinese.

So she, fearing a takeover by her half-brother, had declared war on Henry and all his people. He, in turn, had declared war on her organization. She had already lost thirty of her best and most loyal team in the last 24 hours. It was a tit for tat war that would destroy both their organizations.

But something made no sense. Who had killed Henry's men in her apartment? Who shot the helicopter down? It turned out all her men were dead or unconscious when this happened. There was someone else involved.

She steeled herself. Knowing what she had to do, she dialed Henry's number.

He answered in anger. One of his men had just been run over by a rubbish truck on the street. And the truck belonged to a company owned by Poppy.

Poppy explained, between his screaming at her, that it was impossible that her men could have killed his men in the apartment or shot down the helicopter.

Then she asked him what had happened to the hard drives. He told her he did not have them and they were not in the crashed heli.

Despite the bitterness between them, they quickly worked out that there was a third party involved. Then it dawned on her.

"The Stuarts, they have been after both of us." She explained how she saw Alistair at his fort and what happened to him.

"They must be in Hong Kong right now. They destroyed the fort in Mexico, they killed your men, they destroyed my face, and they have my hard drives. We must stop them."

"We must capture them and kill them slowly. Send me pictures."

And so, the manhunt began with Henry and Poppy's people teaming up in a frenzied search for the Stuarts—their combined hatred binding them back together.

Poppy imagined the fun she would have once she had the brother and sister in her hands.

Misha, who was monitoring communications from the two organizations, told the team to move immediately.

The Earl led Tatiana, Alistair, and Paloma out to the garage, carrying black canvas bags full of weapons. They were all dressed in dark combat gear and had taped the hard drives inside their Kevlar vests. Flipping on the lights revealed two Range Rover Sentinels.

"These come from Land Rover Special Vehicle Operations. They are armored and sealed. They also have roof hatches, so you can fire from those without opening the windows." A small, circular hatch opened above the passenger's seat. There was a 15cm protective steel plate all around the hatch. Opening the rear door, he pressed a button in the cab and what looked like an entire armory nestled into foam cut outs appeared.

The Rangys had full roll cages, racing seats and five-point harnesses. Windows were blacked out and they were fitted with run-flat tires.

"Nice kit Sir, you have all the best toys." Paloma was stroking the car like it was a cat.

"Can we call them Bill and Ben?"

"The Flower Pot Men? Really, Paloma?" Alistair was shaking his head.

"Tatiana and I will take the front car, code named Bill. You two take the rear car, code named Ben. Thank you, Paloma, good idea. If we get separated, just head for the airport. Don't stop for anything. Unlike the previous one, these have reinforced front, back and sides, so ram anything that gets in your way. Convoy procedure drive: as close as you can to my rear bumper. Let nothing get between us."

29

Chased by the Dragon

Pulling out of 37 Severn Road of the Peak, set on 'sport' mode, the pair of Rangys took the first corner with a mild complaint of rubber as the cars corrected their own differentials. Tatiana was reading the road like a rally navigator, using her headset. They were so close together, their bumpers kissed twice.

"Whisky, this is Vodka Two. Easy Right: one hundred into double caution sharp left. Steep down, 50... hello double bogey, 100, prepare to ram."

Rounding the corner, they saw two sedans parked in an arrow, pointing towards them. Instead of braking or hesitating, The Earl pushed his foot to the floor, and the V8 surged forward.

Four men with Type 79 machine guns behind the cars opened up, but their burst of fire was short, inaccurate, and panicked. With several tonnes of British steel hurtling towards them, they dropped their weapons and ran for it, but not fast enough. By the time Bill had blasted into the front of the cheap Chinese sedans, they were only meters away. On the right, the car cannoned straight down the steep slope of the forest, battering over two of the men. The other sedan slammed into the hillside on the left and crumpled on top of the other two men. The

Earl's Range Rover hardly slowed down.

"Excellent billiards Sir, I mean Brandy. I wonder how many more shots we are going to have to pocket before we get there."

"Team, this is Misha. I am tracking you and have you on the city CCTV. Whisky there is a silver Mercedes coming up behind you fast."

"Roger that Vodka One. Brandy, I am going to let him come up behind and slam it in reverse."

"Paloma, open the hatch. They will try to bump us off the road. After I push him, I want you to open fire."

"Got it, here he comes."

Tires squealing and barely in control, a big, old silver Mercedes slid sideways around the corner behind them then shot forwards towards them. The driver was trying to ram one corner of the Rangy and flip it into a spin, a standard maneuver in the US police, but on wide open roads, whereas they were on a narrow road with an almost vertical cliff on one side, a fatal consequence for the Rangy.

Alistair imperceptibly eased off the power, letting the big Merc catch up. Moments before it turned to hit one corner of the Rangy, Alistair put the anchors out. The brakes on the big car brought the beast to a fast halt without putting lines of black rubber on the road, the old Mercedes was less sophisticated and by the time the driver had realized and slammed his foot on the floor, all four wheels locked in an uncontrollable slide towards the rear of the Rangy. It crunched into the back of their car. Milliseconds after feeling the bump, Alistair flicked it in reverse and massive torque the Mercedes was now sliding backward under the sheer force of over two tonnes.

"Now."

Popping up, Paloma fired two double taps into the driver and rear passenger of the sideways, sliding car and then, for good measure, switched to auto fire and filled the roof of the car full of holes.

She slid back into her set and shouted, "Go!"

The Earl and Tatiana were waiting around the next corner.

"Brandy, this is Whisky. Bogey dealt with, carry on."

The front Range Rover pulled away fast as they caught up and the two cars dropped the final few hundred meters to the flat road below the Peak, within centimeters of each other, like a pair of tango dancers.

"Well, this is the most exciting journey to the airport I've ever had. I wonder what they will throw at us next?"

Paloma didn't have to wait long for her answer. Seconds later, a fat, ugly and heavily armed helicopter roared over the cars.

"Wow, that thing is an antique Mi_17, still packs a punch. Find me a tunnel. I can take it out with the Barrett."

The Range Rovers were armored, but the Mi-17 carried machine-guns with armor-piercing shells. It would tear them to shreds.

"Misha. Any tunnels? We need cover from an aerial attack, fast."

The big helicopter had swung around and was preparing to charge down towards them, but trees mostly obscured the road. He fired blindly, blasting the trees apart. Civilians ran for their lives. Several rounds tore ragged holes in the roof of their car.

"Next left, 50 meters."

In front, The Earl whipped into the tiny side road. Alistair followed as the helicopter over ran them and then banked into steep turn, rotors chopping the air, like a dog taking a corner on a parquet floor.

Paloma scrambled into the back and pulled out a sand-colored Barrett M82 sniper's rifle.

"Tunnel ahead."

Both cars pulled to a hard halt under the dark tunnel. Rifle in hand, Paloma ran back to the entrance road. "Alistair, tripod."

"Yeah, all the girls call me that."

"Alistair, stop buggering about, he's coming back."

Running in front of her and facing the oncoming helicopter, he stood feet apart, hands on his thighs, and held his breath. Paloma nestled the long rifle on his back, shoulder and bipod on his chest.

As a pilot, she had studied this aircraft and knew its weak spot. The Mi-17 belly had armor plating, but there was a gap and if her aim was true, she would take out the pilot and the main panel for the engine. The heavy 50 Cal rounds from the Barrett would drill straight through the lot.

Paloma drew back the bolt, snickering a round into the breach and tracked her sweet spot through the scope, feet wide apart. As she predicted, the pilot flared the blades back to provide a nice, steady platform for the gunner to fire into the tunnel. It was the last thing he would ever do.

Her weapon thumped and instantly the massive helicopter went into a gyrating spin, black smoke pouring from the engine. As the untamed beast wobbled towards the tunnel, Paloma and Alistair jumped back into their car, following The Earl who was already out the other side.

Looking back, Paloma watched in horror as the blades started tearing at the road, flipping the whole machine on its back where it burst into flames.

"You're actually a pretty good shot."

"Wow, thanks, Alistair. Did I just get a compliment from you?"

They had fifteen minutes of driving left before they reached the airport. The Earl called his pilot and warned that they would come in hot.

Police sirens wailed all around them. They had had a busy 24 hours: chaos had taken over and tribal warfare had left a trail of destruction on the streets of Hong Kong.

The Earl made a phone call. Speaking in Cantonese, he gave instructions. They had reached the big, six-lane motorway that led to the airport.

"We are going to be getting a police escort for the final bit but keep your eyes peeled."

As he spoke, a pair of police motorbikes streaked out of one of the slip roads, lights and sirens blaring. They pulled in front of 'Bill' the first Rangey and acted like a snow plough through the traffic. They settled down to 110kmh, then four police Land Rover Defenders pulled out from the next slip road and took up formation on either side of them.

"We need these boys in Panama City. I hate traffic." Paloma saluted and smiled at the uniformed police in the Land Rover on her side.

From behind, they heard the high-pitched scream of racing motorbikes.

Looking backwards, Paloma saw a pair of high-performance bikes coming at them like missiles.

"Incoming high-speed bikes and there are blokes on the back with H&K MP7 machine guns." They all knew these weapons would have armor-piercing rounds. The bikes weaved through the cars and both headed for the drivers' sides. Because the police Land Rovers were parallel with them, the team couldn't fire for fear of taking them out too.

"Whisky, brake and open door on my command."

"Aye, Aye Sir,"

In perfect choreography, the bikes whipped in between the police cars and the two Range Rovers. Alistair saw the pillion rider grin as he raised his stubby weapon to fire.

"Now!" Simultaneously, Alistair and the Earl each put his brake foot to the floor and opened their doors. The bikes never stopped, hitting the heavy armored doors at high speed so hard that the doors came straight off. All four riders and two doors smashed, spun, and rolled down the road in front of them. One rider came to a halt sitting up. By this time the Rangy had surged back to speed and Alistair went straight through the man, his helmet bouncing across the median.

They sped on down the motorway without driver's doors. The police

Land Rovers closed the gap to a bare meter, creating a protective shield.

As they pulled into the airport, their escort wheeled them over to the waiting jet. Police fanned out in a protective arc as the team rushed to the open cabin door.

Climbing in the aircraft, the Earl, Alistair, Tatiana, and Paloma hesitated to look back at the battle scarred Rangys.

"Looks like we need to rethink the doors, Sir?"

"Thanks Bill and Ben, our flowerpot men, you did an outstanding job."

"Paloma, think you had too much sun?"

30

Get Lost

"You lost them! You lost them—you had sixty men, a helicopter, enough firepower to stop an army, and you lost them." Poppy threw her phone on the bed in disgust. Now she really hated Henry, who had assured her the Stuarts would never leave Hong Kong alive. She had needed to make them feel pain. The whole side of her face felt like it was about to explode. Her doctor had told her she had to stay in bed and avoid stressing her skin.

Poppy's staff had set up her bedroom with all the equipment required to look after her while she recovered. Gone was her king-sized bed with carved ivory headboard (it had taken fourteen tusks to complete or, more accurately, the death of seven elephants.) In its place was a hi-tech medical bed. The normally minimal room was now full of hospital cabinets on wheels, beeping machines and almost always a nurse in a crisp white uniform and silent shoes.

Poppy missed Singsong; he was the only person she could truly trust. Singsong had been her protector and leader of all her staff since she was a teenager. Singsong wouldn't have let the Stuarts go.

She knew Henry must have ordered him executed when Singsong refused to take a bribe, unlike the rest of her useless men.

Without Singsong she was in real danger of loosing everything to her half-brother Henry.

Poppy realized she need to work out a plan to eliminate Henry. Her father had insisted that Henry run the Mexican operations, but she knew Henry was building a power-base across the world and she knew that right now she was vulnerable.

She needed a strategy.

"Get out, out, go, leave!" Poppy shouted at the nurse who had just stepped silently into the room.

Poppy stormed out of her bedroom after the fleeing nurse. She hated all the clutter in there. Walking into her main room, she sat down at her desk, carefully arranging her keyboard so it was perfectly parallel to the front of the polished wood.

Her apartment door closed as the nurse left.

Poppy shook her mouse and woke up her new computer. Her tech team had installed a complete replacement system. It would, they assured her, be impossible to hack and impossible to use to locate her.

Clicking on the icon of an airplane she watched a map of the earth. There was a blinking dot heading towards Hawaii.

Poppy pulled up her email and typed in a message. Then she attached two photographs. They were of Alistair and Paloma Stuart when they were at school.

She rang a tiny gold bell that was sitting on the side of her desk. Angel Cha, her silent maid, appeared almost immediately, dressed in simple Chinese clothes, barefoot and carrying a black lacquer tray covered in a cloth.

Angel Cha placed the tray on the desk, removed the cloth and stepped backwards, bowing.

On the tray were five perfect pieces of raw tuna or sashimi, a small bowl of rice and a tiny porcelain pot of soy sauce.

Poppy didn't acknowledge Angel Cha who disappeared back into the kitchen. Picking up one piece of tuna with ivory chopsticks she carefully put it in her mouth without touching her still swollen lips.

The tuna was so perfect it seemed to melt.

She watched the plane on her screen a notification popped up. '*Citation G—AMNU destination ATL*'.

Picking up her phone she scrolled through the contacts until she got to Wang.

"I have a job for you and your brother. Go to Atlanta. Wait there for further instructions."

Closing the call, she placed another piece of tuna in her mouth.

She made another call. "Get my plane ready. I'll be leaving tomorrow. No, I will give you the final destination when I am on board."

Poppy had decided to disappear for a bit, and she knew exactly where she was going. She needed to get lost.

31

Debriefing

Engulfed by the quiet peace of the Citation jet after the fury, speed, and noise of what the team had just experienced, they all fell into a deep and blissful sleep. Nobody stirred until they reached the island of O'ahu, Hawaii, where they stopped and switched planes. The Citation would continue to Atlanta in the United States. The team would continue in a FedEx plane that had a passenger module installed. They would effectively disappear.

After take-off, a meal of roast lamb was served with a robust Pinotage from South Africa. Work started as soon as they finished eating.

Tatiana made duplicates of each of the hard drives from Poppy's server. She put them into a waterproof Pelican case, each duplicate tucked into a neat slot in black foam inside the case. They would store this in a secure vault inside the INTERPOL HQ in Lyon, France.

They would need several days to study the hard drives, but two major items required their immediate attention:

The first was to stop all the poachers that they hoped the hard drives would reveal. They understood that many would have simply 'gone to ground' once Poppy inadvertently exposed them by compromising her server. If she revealed it, that is; she may just let them get caught. It seemed to the team that she may use it as a way of cleaning up her operation, as each poacher was a witness against her. Flushing them out would be tough. Local agencies and INTERPOL would carry out much of this work. This was good because as long as they were hiding, they weren't poaching.

Tatiana was keen on launching a hunting trip—it was time to follow their calling.

The second problem was more complex. 'The Mengbi Weapon' GPS blocking device. Based on the combination of the computers they rescued from destruction in the fish factory and the hard drives from Poppy's server, they hoped they had enough information to understand how it worked. If they knew how it worked, they could develop a countermeasure. At least that was the theory. Simply chasing after buyers of the system wouldn't stop it getting into other people's hands, it would just delay it. In the wrong hands, it would be a deadly weapon.

They realized they did not have the capabilities to develop a countermeasure and they would need to find someone to help them.

Landing at the bustling little airport at Albrook in Panama gave them a feeling of sanctity. The suburb of Panama City felt small and parochial compared to the heaving beast of Hong Kong.

As they stepped out of the main doors of the airport, the warm tropical air washed over them. Dr Kitts-Vincent was waiting in Alistair's Defender.

"Hello campers, welcome home. I hear you had an exciting trip?"

"Rather." The Earl was going to stay with them for a few days for debriefing and then fly back to INTERPOL HQ in France.

"I hope the trip from this airport is a little more peaceful than the one to the airport in Hong Kong. I presume those are your men, Sir?" Paloma noticed a black Range Rover sitting protectively just across the street.

"It's unlikely we were tracked here, I had our pilot file multiple flight plans and none of them ended in Panama, plus the plane they think we are on is heading to Atlanta. but it's good to be cautious, so you are right. I asked my security team to keep us company on the way back to Gamboa."

"You probably won't notice him, but Alistair's friend Miguel will be discretely shadowing us on his new motorbike. We gave him an upgrade. It turns out Miguel is a very savvy and streetwise chap—seems to see everything. He is a kind of urban Maasai. He knows where the lions are crouching." Dr. KV pulled out from the front of the airport and they started on the 21 kilometers back to Gamboa. All the windows were open so that when they reached the final stretch through Soberania National Park, they would be able to smell the forest.

Jeeves came running out to greet them as soon as the car stopped in the car park at the G57 pub.

The pub and apartments above, on the bank of the canal in the ex-Canal Zone town of Gamboa, belonged to Dr. KV and the Stuarts. It was home. Gamboa only had one proper road in and was bordered by thick jungle, the Chagres River, and the Panama Canal. After quickly changing and dumping their bags, they continued the last bumpy stretch of track to their hidden bunker in the jungle: the Magic Shop.

Apart from the fact that the bunker was so well hidden that nobody had stumbled across it since it was closed in the early 70s, the bunker was what the label said, a military bunker that could withstand a frontal attack from a tank. It also had three well concealed exits, one for vehicles, one for their PBR their patrol boat and an opening hanger which housed a Huey gunship.

The Land Rover turned off the main track, through a pebble stream and approach what looked like an impregnable wall of jungle. Just as they were about to hit the wall, it hissed up, revealing a long, well-lit, domed tunnel. At the end of the tunnel, another door opened, and they drove into the garage full of military vehicles and jumped out. Unusually, nobody else was around.

They walked on through to the Ops room. Everyone was huddled around one screen.

On the screen was the image of a powerful and perfectly camouflaged animal caught in the cameras that were monitoring the Magic Shop environs. The elusive and endangered jaguar. The four joined the watchers. Staring in silence and awe, they followed him on the monitors until he had settled in a tree right next to the bunker. It was a big male, Paloma decided to call him His Royal Highness, or HRH.

As a critically endangered animal, he was a reminder of why they were risking their lives. He would become their talisman and symbol.

Delighted with the cache of hard drives Tatiana was carefully spreading out across the steel table, Misha immediately began hooking everything up.

While she was working, they told her everything they had discussed on the plane. McDonnell, delighted to have a good crowd to feed again, came in with a tray of scones, clotted cream, jam, and tea. Pausing in her work with the drives, Misha started walking and talking. Cup of tea and saucer in one hand.

"I believe I might have someone who could help with our second problem, creating a countermeasure for the GPS blocker.

I have never met him. He was my opposite number in the CIA. We had a healthy rivalry. He sort of disappeared in the late seventies and I recently discovered that he started working under Gladys West. You may remember her—she was a brilliant mathematician who developed the satellite geodesy models that became incorporated into what we know as Global Positioning System or GPS.

In the KGB his codename was The Machete because he could hack into anything, but we think his actual name is Stan Smith. He officially 'retired' a few years ago and moved to a cabin in Tennessee in the Smokey Mountains, but I know he still works on GPS systems as a consultant for the government."

"Excellent, thank you Misha, I think you and Alistair should pay him a visit once we have processed all this data.

Tatiana, Paloma, and Jeeves, when we are ready, I think you all should go hunting in East Africa, you take Moggy. May need some upgrades." Dr. KV said.

"Yes, Sir." They replied. Paloma was smiling at the prospect of 'upgrades.'

They spent the next ten days filling their big screens with the cast of characters and maps with dots marking locations.

Paloma and Tatiana created a matrix from the cast of characters, from which they could decide who were the most critical players they needed to eliminate to collapse Poppy's Kenyan poaching operation. At the top of the list was Poppy herself.

The Earl had set up a secret jail in Kenya, manned by trusted INTERPOL staff. They had done it by making a series of cells out of 20ft shipping containers, which they put inside the now burnt-out fish canning factory in Turkana.

"Brings a whole new meaning to the phrase 'thrown in the can.' Let's hope we can throw Dragon lady in there at the end." Aiming to collect enough people who could give evidence, they would catch her last.

Instructions were clear, if they couldn't capture their targets, they would eliminate them.

Misha connected with Stan Smith by email, who was amused and intrigued to be contacted by his former rival in the KGB. She didn't explain why she wanted to meet, but he agreed to a rendezvous in a neutral space.

32

The Machete

Alistair and Misha decided they would play Grandson and Grandmother as cover for their trip to Tennessee.

Although in her 70s, Misha was fitter and more active than most middle-aged people.

"My granny needs a blanket, please?" Alistair smiled at the young Delta air flight attendant when they settled into their first-class seats on route to Atlanta. She gave him a very sweet smile.

"Stop using your granny to go exploring the knickers of girls in uniform. I need vodka, not blankets." Misha hissed at him.

It was going to be a fun trip.

After passing through Atlanta, they finally landed in Knoxville, Tennessee. The summer was on its last legs and dark storm clouds rolled overhead.

"No, no, we need something bigger, stronger. We are going to be smoking mountains."

The man behind the counter of the car rental center looked at Alistair with a pleading expression on his face. He was holding up a picture of a small hatchback.

"Granny means the Smokey Mountains—we may have to drive on

dirt roads, so we need something with four-wheel drive."

"Oh, sorry Ma'am, how 'bout this little beauty?" He had a rich Tennessee accent and Misha couldn't understand a word. He was holding up a picture of a massive black Chevy Suburban.

"Is that armored? I have heard the people here have more guns than the mujahideen?"

"Granny, I will handle this. Thank you, we will take that one."

She was laughing.

Getting on the road, they headed southeast and soon they were driving along the Little River that led into the Smokey Mountains National Park.

Just before reaching the mountains, Alistair pulled into a gravel parking lot beside a tired and beaten building with the words 'The Dive Inn Bar' written on a creaking sign outside.

"Lovely. Shall we go in Granny?"

"Alistair, there is a limit, you know that?"

The inside of The Dive Inn Bar smelled of old beer, cigarettes, tired coffee and fly spray. The windows were covered in broken shades, excluding most of the natural light. Freezing air blasted from window mounted AC units that shook like a child's rattle. The owners had nailed random memorabilia to the walls, most of it broken, as if they somehow couldn't bear to part with it once it broke. Strangely, this combination made it cozy, and it felt like you could happily spend a long afternoon drinking there.

Three baseball caps swiveled in their direction as the locals checked out the tourists.

Alistair gave his winning smile. "Good afternoon gentlemen, we are looking for Stan Smith." he hadn't meant to sound so British, but it just came out.

The three men didn't move or smile.

A voice came from beyond the pool table. "In the back."

They headed over, nodding to the locals as they passed.

"Good job they don't know I am a communist agent!" Misha stage whispered in her strong Russian accent as they walked.

A solid-looking man sat in the corner of an orange vinyl booth. He had one hand under the table. Attached to the ceiling above his head was an old wooden tennis racket with no strings. His bald head reflected the florescent lights on the ceiling. Peering over the top of his glasses, he asked, "Where's Misha?"

Misha immediately slid into the booth beside him and held out her hand. Stan flinched slightly. "I am Misha."

"But you're a woman?"

"This is true, it has always been true."

"But..."

"Do you think they would allow a woman to be head of KGB cyber security in USSR? Most people never actually saw me. I used a man's name, which I like and still use. Both Russians and Americans thought I was a man."

Stan visibly relaxed.

"Hello Misha, it is a pleasure to meet you after all these years, Stan Smith."

"Hello Stan, this is Alistair, my unofficial British grandson."

Shaking his head, Stan called the barman, "Bob, one more Budweiser, one vodka and one... hmm Guinness please. Sorry Alistair, I think that's as close as we get to British here."

Stan pushed something into his waistband and pulled his jacket over it, then put both hands on the table.

"Stan, the world is facing a serious threat, something that is bigger than both our pasts. We need your help to tackle it. Before I tell you about the threat, I want Alistair to explain who we are and what we do. After that, if you want to help us, we will tell you about our problem."

"Go ahead, Alistair. Thanks Bob, better keep them coming." Drinks were placed in front of them on the table.

Alistair told their story, a story of blood, beasts, extinction, greed and finally, of hope. He recounted what they had done and how they would continue. He told Stan about a secret base in the depths of the Panama rainforest, of people from all walks of life and resources, and how they could do what no official government agency or organization could ever even think of doing. When he finished, Stan was visibly moved.

"It sounds like the CIA in the 70s except with a genuine cause." He said, chuckling bitterly. "I am in. I will give you all the help I can. You know, living out in the woods, alone as I am, I have surprised myself. Today, the thing that I value more than anything is the natural world that surrounds me. Nothing gives me greater peace or pleasure than sitting quietly on my deck and watching the simple, ancient, pantomime of the wild unfold peacefully before me. And as Misha knows, I will do anything to protect that what I hold dear. So, what is the problem that I might be able to help you with?"

Misha explained the Askari System and how Poppy had used 'The Mengbi Weapon' to hijack the GPS locations and then block the signals. She told him how they had gained almost all the information required to duplicate the weapon and how they needed to create a countermeasure.

Stan was incredulous. "You realize that we have teams working on exactly that problem for decades and while we could produce localized GPS blocking, just like the ones you can buy online but we have managed nothing wider than 30 meters. Plus, we have never done a mass harvest of GPS data like that. I presume you have realized the catastrophic consequences if this goes on the market?"

"It was on its way to a drug dealer in Mexico, but we intercepted it. That's how we have the files."

"Can I see them?"

"You can. We don't think you could develop a countermeasure without them. But be aware that several people have died trying to get them and by being involved you put your life in danger." Misha looked into his eyes to see if he understood.

"I should probably tell you the reason I stopped work and moved out to the woods is because I have cancer. The docs give me one more year, if I am lucky. Since I moved out here, I have realized I must do one decent thing before I die. You have just given me a gift. If I get bumped off as a result, I'll be delighted. I don't want to spend my last days lying in a sad pool of my own waste."

Misha's old KGB guard dropped for a fraction of second and her face expressed a look of sympathy, then her mouth quickly tightened back into a straight line, and she said, "Understood."

"Good, can I suggest we go to my cabin where I can look at the data you collected in my studio? It's only half an hour away, we can pick up barbecue on the way; there's a place a mile away from here."

"Now we are talking, I'm starving."

Outside, Stan admired the huge suburban.

"Wow, is it armored?" Misha looked at Alistair, raised her eyebrows, and raised a palm.

"I'll follow you. Misha, why don't you travel with Stan so you can talk about the good old days in the Cold War?"

33

The Bat Cave

Stan had an old but beautifully cared for Jeep Wagoneer, complete with 'wood' panels, chrome roof rack and white walled tires. Charlie would have loved it.

Misha climbed in the passenger seat beside Stan and they all pulled out of the gravel lot.

The smell of wood smoke, sweet, sticky cooked meat and fried food greeted them long before they saw the signs for the 'Piggy in the Middle BBQ'.

Pulling off the road, they saw seven fat Harley-Davidson motorbikes lined up outside the cabin-like restaurant. There was a group of middle-aged men and women seated on tables on the veranda on each side of the front doors, wearing black leather jackets and American flag headscarves. Dozens of empty beer bottles and jugs were on the surrounding tables.

"Alistair, you wait here. Misha and I will go in and order."

He parked so he could watch the entrance and leave if needed, a recent habit he'd developed.

The Earl had arranged with the US authorities that they could bring in their weapons in their checked luggage. Alistair had his MP5, and Misha had borrowed Tatiana's favorite Vintorez silence assault weapon. "We are old friends," she had said. Both were in cases behind the front seats.

Misha and Stan appeared in the front entrance after about ten minutes, loaded up with steaming boxes that Alistair could smell from his open car window.

Two of the biggest leather jacketed bikers crossed their boots in front of the door, blocking Misha and Stan's exit. The men were laughing.

"Tax is a pulled pork sandwich for passing." They took swigs from their beer and wagged their gloved fingers at the pair. One of them pulled out a pistol.

Alistair sat up, and as he got out of the car he saw a look pass between the old secret agents.

Inclining their heads slightly, keeping eye contact with the bikers, they smiled and carefully placed their boxes of food on the tables, one on each side.

The same hands that placed the boxes so carefully each grabbed a heavy, plastic beer jug in a swift movement, bringing them up in swinging arcs so they smashed into the faces of the black booted men. Without waiting for the men to finish their backwards fall to the floor, the two stepped forward, bringing the now broken jugs down hard onto the faces of the next two men who screamed as blood streamed through their up thrown hands.

The remaining three jumped to their feet, one of them with a stubby dagger in her hand. As she tried to punch it into Misha's stomach, Misha caught it and there was the dull snapping sound of a bone cracking as the knife clattered to the floor. The remaining two dragged their wounded comrades away down the veranda while Misha and Stan quietly picked up their pulled pork sandwiches and grinned at each other.

"Maybe, it will be time for my afternoon vodka when we get to Stan's dacha?"

Stan roared with laughter.

"This, is going to be fun."

Soon they had left the main road and were driving down a narrow gravel track. There were no houses anywhere to be seen. The tree-covered slopes of the mountain reached up, blocking out the sky. A serious-looking gate opened as they approached it, closing behind the Chevy as Alistair followed the dust of the Wagoneer.

The track followed the river until they came to a rambling cabin perched on the banks, a large deck hanging over the water. There were two spaces for cars under a roof to the side of the building, they both reversed into them.

Stan pressed some buttons on the screen of his phone and showed them the front door. A sign screwed to one side said 'Watergate'.

"The joke is getting old, I have to admit," Stan said as he held the door open for them. Inside was unexpectedly neat, clean, and completely devoid of the folksy nick knacks found in so many mountain cabins. In the center there was a cast iron wood-burning stove that filled the space with the welcoming smell of hickory smoke.

Stan added to this by getting plates and passing out barbecued pork sandwiches and ice-cold beer. He poured Misha a large vodka from a bottle in the freezer.

Walking out to the deck, the sound of water greeted them along with three German shepherds, who sat neatly waiting until they were invited to meet the guests.

"I see what you mean by enjoying the pantomime of nature," Alistair said, sinking down in a chair and watching a pair of eagles soaring around the mountains in front of the cabin.

When they had finished their meal and a couple more beers, Stan spoke up.

"Shall we look at what you've got?" Nodding to the Pelican case

Alistair had brought in.

"I have my own bunker here."

Getting up, they followed him into the house. He pressed another button on his phone and the cast-iron stove swung neatly aside, revealing concrete stairs that disappeared underneath them.

"I built this myself. You are the first people to see it."

On the first step, the lights flicked on, revealing a deep passage.

"Welcome to the Bat Cave." The stove slide back into its place as they descended.

Stan put his palm on a pad beside a door and it hissed open.

Walking in, the lights snapped on and revealed a room big enough to park their Suburban and run around it. One wall was covered in photographs, mostly of Stan and his old mates. Alistair noted Stan in full uniform hanging out of a Huey in Vietnam, in a fighter jet, drinking beer with some general; lots of wonderful stories by the look of it.

One wall was a highly organized bank of computers and screens.

Another wall was just a huge whiteboard, nothing was on it.

The last wall, apart from the stairs and presumably the loo was Alistair's favorite: it was a wall of weapons, guns, spears, throwing knives, axes, maces—everything from the history of war was there.

Looking closer and reading a label, he asked, "Stan, is that really Wellington's sword from the Battle of Waterloo?"

"Ahh yes, that is actually one of my favorites it took me two decades to find. Pick it up, it's a thing of beauty."

Alistair, whose father had given him swords and taught him how to use them since he was seven, picked it up and sliced the air into several small pieces, sword hissing as it cut. Stan was enjoying the demonstration.

"You should try the 17th century Samurai sword up there."

"Gentlemen, I hate to take boys from their toys, but we have a little work to do?"

"A yes, sorry Granny. OK, here are the hard drives." Alistair popped the clasps on the Pelican case and pulling out the hard drives, he placed each one on the table.

She narrowed her eyes at him.

"Stan, this is not really my area of expertise. May I take your dogs for a run?" Alistair asked.

He laughed, "Of course, they would love it. Let me introduce you properly and show you a good loop to follow."

As they went back upstairs, Stan showed him how to move the stove so he could come back down when he returned.

"Meet Winston, Joseph, and Franklin. Actually, they are brothers. Boys, this is Alistair." He knelt and rubbed their muzzles.

"Look after him and show him our route." Their intelligent eyes looked up at Alistair, who also knelt.

"Hello chaps, can you boys show me your mountains?"

All their tails were wagging. They trotted off, looking back at him as if asking him to follow.

"Thanks Stan, they'll be great. You need to feed Misha vodka on the hour, every hour." Stan hooted with laughter and pulled a bottle from the freezer.

"Got it."

34

Smoking the Mountain

When Alistair returned from his run, he found Misha and Stan staring at the huge whiteboard like a couple of mathematicians trying to solve the unsolvable. They had covered it in scribbles that seemed unintelligible. Alistair attempted to get the gist of what they were talking about, but it came across like a foreign language, punctuated by cracks of laughter from Misha.

They were still at it after midnight when Alistair retired to bed. They had intended to go to a motel, but Stan wouldn't hear of it—he had plenty of spare rooms.

Upstairs, in his room the dogs positioned themselves around Alistair's bed like sentinels, then lay down, muzzles on paws. He fell into a deep sleep to the sounds of the river, trees and three large dogs snoring.

The morning sun gently pouring through the windows woke him. The dogs were gone. Padding downstairs in bare feet, Alistair made himself a coffee and then slid the doors open and walked out onto the cool deck. Then he understood how the smokey mountains got their name. Shafts of light pierced the swirling mists as the sun rose beyond the distant peaks.

The deck was still in the deep shadow of the tree-covered slopes when Misha and Stan emerged. Misha looked like she had just awoken from a light afternoon nap. Stan looked like he'd been on an all-night bender with the boys.

"Something you Russians would always beat us at, drinking. I don't understand how you guys do it, and all of you have the same ability?" Stan rubbed his head and stared blackly through slits of eyes.

"Ahh, they train us from childhood. Vodka mixed with the mother's milk makes the strong Russian children."

Stan wasn't sure if she was joking.

"So, Alistair, I have an important mission for you. Come over here." He gestured to the front of the deck. Looking down into the dark shadows among the rocks under the lazy river, Stan pointed out an enormous catfish.

"That, Sir, is Jesus." Stan may have still been a little squiffy.

"Your mission is to catch him and we will have him for supper."

"I have caught him no less than five times, but he always escapes. Once, I even got him on the deck, on the chopping board and he was for all intents and purposes, dead. I turned around to get my knife and when I turned back all I saw was his tail flipping over the deck back into the river."

"Excellent. Do you have a fishing rod?"

"Actually, they call it a fishing pole in these parts. It's there on the wall, ready for action."

"There's eggs and bacon in the fridge, help yourself. Misha and I are going back to work."

With that, they disappeared under the black stove.

Alistair ran upstairs and grabbed his pot of Marmite, made a one pan fry up of bacon and eggs, filled his cup with steaming coffee and sat down at a small table on the edge of the deck, eyeing the catfish whose whiskers were exploring the muddy bottom of the river below.

"Ready to party Mr. Jesus?" Gesturing with his hand, he knocked his coffee cup off the table.

As he bent down to pick it up, something slashed through the air over his head and turned three deck boards into a line of splinters. Knowing exactly what it was, Alistair acted on instinct. Diving behind a large wooden planter, he heard another round thwack into its side, making the earth jump. He was trapped—the planter was barely wide or tall enough to cover his crouched body, and it was too far from the door to make a run for it.

Another round hit the front of the box, peppering him with splinters of wood and dirt.

Whoever was shooting knew what they were doing, and they were using a heavy caliber weapon to do it. A few more rounds and the planter would be matchsticks and a pile of earth.

He heard the dogs barking around the other side of the house; an urgent warning bark.

"Alistair, when I say 'go,' run for the veranda door. Misha will open it, it's armored glass."

Stan's voice came from above him.

The sound of a heavy caliber machine gun shook the air.

"Go."

Alistair went through the open door in a flat sprint. It closed behind him.

Metal shutters descended on all the doors and windows, plunging them into momentary darkness before the lights came on.

Stan walked down the stairs, looking like he was enjoying himself.

"Battle stations. Boys, come." The dogs appeared at his side as he reached the bottom.

"Let's go into the bunker and see if we can find him."

Once inside, Stan hit some buttons on the computer and the screens filled with images of forest trails and tracks. Each one labeled with a name and location. One set showed a line of graphs, which Alistair studied. One had lines jumping all over the place, another had a sharp jump and then barely a wobble.

"Motion sensors, this is a deer. He is running like crazy because of my gunfire. This was a human firing a weapon, and now he is hardly moving. I guess he didn't expect return fire."

"He's about a thousand meters out. If he moves again, we'll probably see him on the cameras."

Pulling up a highly detailed 3D model, Stan clicked a point and inserted skull and crossbones at the location of the movement.

"I didn't spend my life on GPS equipment not to install some for myself."

"My guess is he is a trained sniper, and he will be very well camouflaged. You could work your way around behind him by going up here and then climbing down here. It looks impossible to climb, which is probably why he chose that position, but I installed some handy grips. For someone like you it will be a cinch,"

"How do I get him out of his bolt hole? Ideally, we'd capture and question him rather than just drill a hole in him."

"A good question, I have created a little device from a grenade launcher which now fires tear gas 'grenades.' It has a range of over 1000 yards. You will go out with a gas mask and when you get close enough, I will pop some smoke on top of him. I added some chili power to the mix and some extra chemicals that I can't tell you about... but he should come squealing out."

"Brilliant. I'll need to borrow some kit. You don't want to join me?"

"I do, but I can't move as fast as I used to, and I'll end up a liability. From what Misha tells me, you can handle yourself well enough alone. What I will do is let the dogs help once the smoke has cleared."

Alistair kitted up, gas mask, Kevlar, camo jacket, zip ties for the prisoner, GPS and comms system. He kept his own HKMP 5 machine pistol.

"Ready?"

"Ready. I'll tell you when to smoke the mountain. One click, affirmative, two clicks negative, three clicks send the smoke, my code name is Whisky,"

"Ha, well I guess I'll use the one these guys gave me: Machete."

Alistair headed out to the forest from the back of the house. He was an expert at moving through woods without being seen, a skill honed through hours and hours of games with Paloma when they were growing up in Panama.

Reaching the cliff, he realized that Stan had been right about it looking unscalable, but he found a deep crevice with almost polished rock sides and, as promised, he located a series of neat hand holds that had been carved into the rocks.

Dropping to the base of the rock, he tiptoed to the back of a tree on a steep bank.

"Whisky, this is Machete, are you in position?" He clicked his mike once as speaking risked giving his location away.

"I estimate you are 150 yards northeast of the bogey. Can you see him?" Two clicks.

"Want me to get him to fire a shot, I have a good dummy I could move onto the deck." Two clicks.

Alistair had good eyes, trained to spot things hidden in nature by the experts, the Maasai. He decided to sit, watch and wait. Far better to know where his quarry was. However good someone was, they always moved at some point.

"Misha says you will sit and wait, correct?" One click.

Alistair was well tucked into the shadows and the sun was behind him so he could use his Leica 10x50 range binoculars without fear of the glass flashing in the sun.

He studied the forest in front of him, deciding where he would set up a position as a sniper. Then he saw it, the barely perceptible underside of some leaves. The sniper must have cut some branches to cover himself, but the topmost branch was upside down.

Staring through his binos, he gradually made out the shape of a man and his gun, making a mental note of the spot he put on his gas mask and picked up his MP5. Giving three clicks on his mike, he estimated the escape route for the sniper.

From the house came a series of hollow whomps, like someone banging an empty pipe. Around the sniper, he heard small objects dropping into the forest, followed by a series of pops. Dense white smoke billowed up from the ground, creating a thick fog.

From within the white blanket came the sound of swearing, coughing, and then running. Alistair was wrong about the escape route. The guy was running blindly towards him, hands in front, no rifle. The first attempt to escape the smoke had him running straight into a tree. Alistair stifled a laugh.

The man was wearing a Ghillie suit, a full body suit covered in a thousand strips of natural colored fabric: classic sniper's camouflage. Difficult to run in on the best of days but almost impossible when you are trying to run through thick undergrowth and your eyes and throat are full of tear gas and chili pepper.

He ran straight past Alistair's hiding place. Alistair had been in the first 15 rugby team, both at Prep school and at Gordonstoun. Taking out a blinded man who looked like a Yeti was easy, and within seconds the man was face down, Alistair's knee in his back as he zipped tied his hands together.

"Prisoner is secured."

"Hello, you were trying to kill me?" Ripping off the man's hood revealed a heavily scarred face and mean little brown eyes. Searching him, he found a stiletto knife, Glock pistol, cell phone, car keys and wallet.

The man said nothing.

Alistair took a photo of the man and his ID and sent it to Misha

The three dogs arrived, surrounding the sniper.

"If you move, they will tear you apart."

The smoke was nearly gone, cleared by the mountain breeze. Alistair walked over to the sniper's hide and found a suppressed subsonic.308 snipers rifle complete with bag. He packed it up and climbed back to the man, who hadn't moved a muscle. Forcing him to his feet, Alistair guided him by pushing his back.

"OK, let's go for a little walk." the dogs kept careful guard.

As they got closer to the house, Stan told him to blindfold the prisoner.

Stan and Misha came out to meet them. The sniper was still wearing his Ghillie suit as they followed to a door under the house. Through the thick door was a dark concrete corridor, at the end of which was a cell with the padded door. Stan pushed the man in, removed his Ghillie suit and shut the door, turning off the lights as he did so.

35

The Bounty Hunter

"He's a bounty hunter. Alistair, it looks you might have a price on your head, probably Paloma too. Word must be out." Misha said.

"Really, how much? That must be Henry or Poppy, or both. What should we do?" Alistair asked.

"I'm just guessing, but we can probably ask our yeti. If there is a bounty, I think we should collect it." Misha looked at their surprised faces. "First, let's warn the rest of the team so they stay low and know about the threat. Then we stage Alistair's assassination and collect the bounty. Hopefully that will lead us to the person who set it and we can then take them out. Simple?" She held her hands up in a question.

"Very good." Stan looked at Alistair. "You only live twice?"

"OK, let's do it. It means we need our friend downstairs to give us some information pretty quick."

"I have a solution for that." Stan tapped his nose.

Stan hit the light switch before they went back into the cell. The prisoner was lying on his side, hands tied behind him, eyes covered.

They put a steel chair in the room and lifted him onto it, then attached his already bound hands to the back of the chair.

"Water, give me a drink."

Stan had done this many times and they decided he would lead the questioning.

"Sure, but you need to earn it. Is Hank Jones your actual name?" Misha had already checked: it was.

"Yes,"

"Good, open your mouth." Hank desperately drank the water that Stan poured in.

"So, Hank, just so you know, you can answer the questions correctly and this will be easy for everyone but if you lie things will get nasty."

"Got it."

"How did you know Alistair was here?"

"A friend told me."

"I see. Who and where was your friend? How did he know who Alistair was and track him here?"

"I dunno, he didn't say."

Stan walked behind Hank and whispered something in his ear. Hank urgently attempted to get up without success.

Misha remained silent, standing there like an umpire, clipboard in one hand, pen poised in the other. She clicked the pen and the blindfolded Hank spun his head around in her direction.

"I think we need a little something to jog your memory." Stan marched out of the cell. They heard another metal door open and, to Alistair's surprise and horror, he came back holding a chainsaw. He smiled and winked at Alistair, then walked behind Hank's chair.

Slowly and deliberately, he put the machine on the floor and opened the fuel cap. The smell of fuel filled the room. Hank moved his head from side to side, moaning slightly.

Stan put the cap back on, put his foot through the handle, and pulled the toggle. The machine coughed and was silent. He fiddled with the choke and pulled toggle again. This time it fired, filling the room with a deafening noise and white acrid smoke. Picking it up, he revved it, keeping the chain near Hank's head.

"Stopppp, I'll tell you!"

"Good." The machine went silent.

"It was a friend at Atlanta airport. He works for the TSA. I gave him a couple of photos and he was on the lookout for them. All he had to do was see where Stuart was going next and tell me which flight. I got on the same plane."

"I see, good, open." Stan poured some more water into his mouth.

"Your friend's name?" Stan flicked a switch on the chainsaw.

"OK, OK, just keep that thing away from me, Mike Powell."

Misha made a note.

"Who was the other person you were looking out for?"

"Paloma Stuart, a real cutie." Misha held her hand up to Alistair, who had moved forward.

"And how did you get those photos?"

"On my phone. I am a well-respected bounty hunter. Plenty of people have my number."

"Actually, you are a murderer. Password for your phone?"

"CASH4ME."

"Where is your vehicle?"

Hank described where the vehicle was.

"How do you arrange the exchange?"

"I just send a picture and they tell me a location and I deliver the target—they give the cash."

They walked out, locking the door, and turning off the lights.

"Hey. I told you everything, untie me."

They went back to Stan's bunker. Misha hooked the phone to a laptop and downloaded all the data.

On Hank's phone, there was a WhatsApp message that showed a picture of Alistair and Paloma with the words 'D or A $3m pp'.

"Brilliant, Alistair we don't have to kill you, it says D or A Dead or Alive, and $3m per person isn't too bad for someone as young as you." Misha was plotting.

"Problem is, they will set the rendezvous in a place that is at a serious disadvantage to Hank. Do you think they know what Hank looks like?"

Alistair was searching on a laptop

"Yup, he's got his own website 'Hank Bounty Hunter Services.' Nice, there's even a picture of him holding a felon around the neck."

"So, Hank obviously decided that it would be easier to deliver you dead than try to capture you... nice man, but I think we can use him." Misha was looking at Stan in a funny way.

After an hour, they went back downstairs. They assumed Hank had already seen all of them, so they didn't hide when pulling off his blindfold.

"Hank, we have a little job for you. Don't try anything. My lady friend here is a crack shot." Misha pointed a silenced pistol at his head as they cut off his hand ties.

Alistair had a black eye. Blood was running from his nose—his shirt was dirty and ripped. Misha had done some makeup work. Sitting in the chair, he put his hands behind his back. Stan handed Hank a pair of sunglasses and an orange baseball cap that said VOLS and told him to put them on.

"Stand behind Alistair and take a selfie of both of you, you are going to collect your fee after all."

"Take several, look triumphant."

"Look what?"

"Pleased that you have captured your victim."

Hank did as he was told.

They removed the chair and put a plastic bottle of water and half a loaf of bread on the floor. They left the light on after locking the door.

"That money's mine." He shouted through the door as they left.

"I actually think Hank is a couple of sandwiches short of a full picnic basket, not that I feel sorry for him but worth knowing if you are going to play him, Stan."

Stan had put on the baseball cap and sunglasses.

Misha selected a slightly fuzzy picture from the ones they had taken, attached Hank's phone to a laptop where Stan changed the location to several miles North of Knoxville and sent the image to the sender of the original message.

"I think I should enlist the help of a couple of friends of mine. I suspect we will be outgunned when they set up the meeting." Stan looked at Alistair and Misha.

"I am going to talk to the Earl. I think it is also time for INTERPOL to get involved."

36

Upgrades

Back in the jungles of Panama, Paloma and Charlie were looking at Moggy. They were in the main garage amongst their formidable collection of vehicles.

Moggy was the armored and armed Mercedes Unimog four-wheel-drive truck they had used on their last mission in Kenya. The truck had come under heavy fire and saved their lives. Charlie, vermillion lipped, dressed in her favorite Khaki Word War Two British army overalls, a beret, and a red scarf, was taking account of where bullets had pitted the windows and pockmarked the bodywork.

"Charlie, you spend your life working with engines, grease, oil. How do you remain so immaculate? One look at a plane engine and I'm streaked with black all over." Paloma smiled at her.

"My secret, my dear, is an endless supply of clean rags!".

Charlie's father, Charles Patel owned a series of very successful garages across Central America. They were efficient, reasonably priced, clean had a reputation for being able to fix any motor. They even had a branch in Albrook airport where they fixed planes. Charlie had grown up as the eldest son of six siblings. The rest were all girls. Mr. Patel had been teaching young Charlie everything he could ever know about engines since he could first hold a spanner. Mr. Patel had already added 'Patel & Son Garages' when Charlie junior, at the tender age of seventeen, had understood he was in the wrong body.

She realized that her father and mother who, had already lined up a young wife, would not take this news easily. So, Charlie, who loved them dearly, went away for a while. And with the money she saved up, along with paying her way by working odd mechanic jobs, she travelled the world. At 22 she returned to Panama, having faithfully written to her parents every week from far-flung locations. Charlie had decided to come home.

Sadly, her parents flatly refused to even talk to her, let alone see her.

Alistair, who had known her long before she came out, invited her to join The Extinct Company as their engineer and mechanic, and so she adopted a new family. Charlie had quickly become an invaluable member of the team, rebuilding their 1970s Huey helicopter gunship, an armed Patrol Boat River from the Vietnam war and her latest mission was to convert each one of their collection of vehicles into high performance electric ones.

Paloma was testing the new weapons command system on the Unimog when Dr. KV came to find them to explain what he had just heard from Misha.

"Dr. KV, you have to check this out. The weapon moves with your eyes. It is sort of virtual reality except it's not virtual. Dr. KV what's wrong? Is Alistair ok?" Paloma saw the look on Dr. KV's face. She had known him long enough to know when Alistair was in trouble.

"Alistair is fine, but he was very lucky. A sniper tried to shoot him. Alistair ducked by sheer chance and the round missed. He then went and captured the sniper." Dr. KV put his powerful arms around Paloma and squeezed her.

"Aren't they with Stan in Tennessee? How did anybody find them?" She asked. Charlie handed her a clean rag and pointed at Paloma's forehead where there was a long streak of grease.

"It seems that either Henry or Poppy or both of them put a bounty on both your and Alistair's head. It was sent out to bounty hunters across the US."

"Really, how much am I worth?" Paloma looked incredulous.

"Well, you will be amused to know you that your price is seventy thousand dollars and Alistair sixty thousand." Dr. KV knew what Paloma's reaction would be.

"Ha, I always knew I was worth more than him. I can't wait to see him to remind him." Paloma was smiling until she realized what a bounty like that really meant. "What's going to happen? I am about as safe as I could possibly be here, but how is Alistair going to hide?"

"He's not. They are going on the attack. The only way to stop a bounty like that is to destroy the people who set it. They have a plan, and it don't worry, Alistair won't put himself at risk."

Paloma looked at Dr. KV knowing Alistair frequently put himself at risk.

"Charlie, sorry to abandon you, but I need to go into the Ops Center to watch the show." Paloma handed the rag back to Charlie.

37

Quarry

Alistair and Stan went to collect Hank's car. It was an old, black, two-door Chevy Blazer. Filling the inside of the back end was a steel box. When they opened the rear tailgate, they found it had a metal door stenciled with a shield and the letters HBHS. It was padlocked shut.

"This is perfect Stan, that steel even looks thick enough to stop a bullet."

Stan tapped on the insides of the passenger door. Instead of soft foam, it was solid steel. The side windows and windscreen were thick glass.

"It's like a bloody armored car."

Stan drove the Chevy back down the mountain road to his cabin, with Alistair following in Stan's big Suburban.

When they got back, Misha had got a message on Hank's phone. It simply read: '*Vehicle. Picture.*'

Going outside, Misha took a picture of the old Chevy... far enough away so you couldn't see too much detail. Misha sent it, but fiddled the GPS to the same distant location.

A message came back with GPS position and time 18:00 and the instructions for the meeting: *'Come alone. Do not tell anyone where you are going.'*

Then the contact showed number unavailable. It was a burner phone, which the caller had obviously destroyed. Misha pulled the SIM card from Hank's phone to make sure it couldn't be tracked.

"I guess Jesus will have to wait another day." They both looked at Alistair.

"Saved by Jesus! The catfish. If I hadn't been talking to him, I wouldn't have knocked my coffee over and if I didn't duck down to pick it up, Hank wouldn't have missed. Actually, maybe we should let him live in peace. How about we get one for supper further down river?"

"Paloma is right, you are always thinking about the next meal." Misha handed him an apple.

The meeting location was a disused stone quarry with one entry point. They studied the layout using high resolution satellite images Stan downloaded from the CIA secure site. The entry was a narrow gorge with a dirt road. Trees lined the top of the great hole and in the center there was a flat gravel area with a slightly dilapidated office trailer. An ominous grey lake filled with murky water occupied one corner.

"It is a perfect trap—they'll have snipers positioned around the rim and men behind every bolder down below. Any ideas?" Alistair looked at the other two.

"I think this is a job for our friend Hank. A small, remotely detonated explosive under his seat should help to persuade him to drive in." Misha explained. "He can park his truck in the center, then hand over the key to the prisoner's box in the car when he gets to the gate and the money."

"We can put a blindfolded dummy in the back. I have a good one from the CIA that we used to use for hostage exchanges. It has a cavity for remote detonation explosives. It will be dark back there, so it will be hard to see it's not actually Alistair." Stan clapped his hands together.

"And the snipers around the rim?" Alistair asked.

"You, Sir, are going hunting. We need to get moving." Stan got up and cracked his knuckles.

Going down to the cell, they dragged Hank up and got him into the driver's seat of his own car.

Alistair made a great show of climbing into the steel box in the back, which already had the dummy inside. Then he rolled out quietly and snuck back to the house while Stan stood in front of Hank's rear view mirror.

Hank wasn't keen, even though they said he could keep the money. They told him they had gagged Alistair's mouth, so he wouldn't be able to talk.

Once they got him in the driver's seat and told him he was sitting on a small explosive device big enough to blow his testicles off but not big enough to harm Alistair in the back, he agreed to drive to the quarry.

They showed him the remote detonator for his seat. "It has sensors. If you try to leave the seat it will explode, just like the one they use to make that dinging sound when you don't put your seat belt on, it knows you are sitting there. Except this will be more than a dinging sound. Plus, this." Stan handcuffed one hand to the wheel.

"But how will I get out?"

"Alistair has the keys to your cuffs and the remote. He can pass the keys through the vent holes behind your head when it's time. He will disconnect the explosives with the remote."

"I don't trust you at all."

"That's pretty rich coming from someone who just tried to assassinate one of us. Do as you are told and you won't get hurt." Stan fixed a tracker to the Chevy and explained the directions.

Alistair stayed out of sight, loading the Suburban with an assortment of weapons, including Hank's silenced sniper rifle and his Ghillie suit

Giving Hank and the dummy five minutes, they started following in the big car.

After half an hour of driving through the mountain, they pulled up at a roadside café. Drawing into the parking lot, two sallow-looking young lads carrying four black backpacks got out of a battered Honda Civic car and walked towards them. Stan pulled to a halt and opened the rear door.

"Alistair and Misha, this is Carlos and Phil. They are part of my team. You can trust them with your lives."

"Hello Carlos and Phil. I hope you are looking forward to a little excitement this evening."

"We sure are—since Stan last called us, the most exciting thing we've had to do is play video games."

Carlos and Phil were quickly updated with the situation and shown detailed images of the quarry.

It was 16:00; they had two hours. Judging by the signal from Hank's car, it looked like he was nearly there, but he had just he stopped at a drive-thru liquor store. They hoped he would not get too drunk before completing the mission.

Pulling up on a quiet side road near the quarry, Alistair put on Hank's Ghillie suit, picked up the silenced .308 rifle and disappeared into the forest, heading for the rim of the quarry.

Moving with infinite care, he worked his way to the edge of the stone hole. Birds were beginning their evening song and the sun was receding towards the mountains. He was hoping the enemy snipers wouldn't be in position yet—they were just expecting Hank—and they knew Hank wasn't too concerned about his prisoner surviving. Sitting quietly hidden for half an hour, he watched for any signs of movement and for a suitable site for him to set up.

Alistair needed to find a spot that covered both the rim and the quarry but it had to be somewhere that nobody else would choose. Finally, he settled on a neat rock shelf ten meters up a cliff at the back of the quarry.

Shouldering his weapon, he easily worked his way up the cliff face.

Reaching the shelf and pulling himself up, he realized they had mined it out hundreds of years ago. There was even a small cave with a rusty lantern. The rocks around the entrance created defenses as good as a bunker.

After being so close to death this morning, he had no doubts about what he was going to do: as soon as he could, he would simply eliminate the enemy. As far as he was concerned, they were now at war with these people.

He didn't need to wait long. Almost immediately after tucking himself into his neat position, he heard voices across the big hole. The rock walls made them echo, so it felt like they were right next to him. They were speaking Cantonese.

"Vodka, do you read me?" Alistair whispered in his radio mike.

"Loud and clear Whisky, go ahead."

"I have at least two bogeys at around 12 o'clock on my position. They are on the other side of the rim." He knew they would have his location on their tracker. "They are talking in Cantonese and carrying sniper's rifles. They look like.50 Cal Barretts."

"Roger that, standing by."

Splitting at the edge of rim, the men walked away from each other in opposite directions. They were circling towards Alistair.

Each one stopped at the halfway point, got a blanket out of their backpack, and laid it carefully on the ground, right on the edge of the cliff. Putting their rifles on the fabric, they got out a small thermos and put it on the front corner.

He could now see their faces. They looked identical. Attaching his phone to the Leica, he took pictures and sent them to Misha.

"Vodka, I think I have a pair of twins on a hunting picnic. I've got one at my ten o'clock, range 325m and one at my two o'clock, range 320m." His Leica range-finding binoculars gave him incredible accuracy. He adjusted the scope on this rifle to match the distance. "Pretty good idea actually," he said to himself and he rummaged in his own pack to bring out a matt green thermos and pulled out a small steel box. He poured himself a cup of hot tea and extracted a Marmite sandwich from the box.

"Vodka to Whisky. You are right, they are twins. The Wang brothers. They are Poppy's men, a nasty pair of killers. Wanted pretty much all over the world. They always work together. I think that once Henry has the prisoner, she is going to try to take out all of Henry's men."

A pair of eagles swooped past Alistair at eye height, giving him a momentary fright.

The sound of approaching vehicles reverberated around the hard stone walls of the surrounding cliffs.

The line of sunlight moved off the dilapidated building in the middle and started climbing the cliff opposite Alistair.

38

Delivery

A pair of twin cab Ford F150 pickups, lights blazing, tore into the flat gorge floor below him, carving semicircles and filling the air with plumes of gray dust. The sun slashed daggers of light through the rising clouds.

The trucks slid to a halt, facing the entryway. Doors opened, and seven dark-haired men climbed out and positioned themselves behind the biggest boulders. Two approached the dilapidated office, kicked the door in, and disappeared inside.

All of them were armed with AK 47s.

Finally, a man dressed in an immaculate but slightly shimmering dark suit emerged from one of the pickups. Stepping carefully around the puddles, he walked to the office and went inside.

Alistair finished photographing everyone from his hideout on the cliff face. He pulled back and sent the photos to Misha.

The twin snipers moved right, to the edge, settling their rifles into their shoulders.

Alistair could hear the V8 of Hank's Chevy Blazer reverberating off the narrow walls of the quarry entryway and, in an instant, it was barreling down the track in a decidedly wobbly line, heading straight towards the office. Instead of slowing, it was speeding up. The men hidden behind the rocks rushed out, weapons forward.

"Whisky, those men who got out of the pickups, they are Poppy's men too."

Poppy's twin snipers moved closer to the edge, aiming their weapons at the Chevy Blazer below, waiting for it to stop.

Alistair aimed and squeezed the trigger. The 2 o'clock Wang brother crumpled onto his rifle and then rolled off the edge, bouncing off the rocks, before slamming into the ground in a cloud of dust. His twin at ten o'clock stood up and shouted to his brother, causing the men below to look up in surprise. Alistair drilled him straight through the center of his forehead with a neat, almost imperceptible 'poff' from his rifle. The man staggered and then pitched backwards onto his blanket, knocking over his thermos as he went down. Alistair watched the tea spill out, mixing with the man's spreading blood from the back of his head where the bullet had exited.

Hank's Chevy was now doing donuts around the two parked pickups, creating a bigger and bigger dust cloud. The men who had walked forward from behind their rocks were now standing in a semicircle outside the truck's donut cloud, slowly disappearing in the storm of gray powder.

Something inside their brains registered that opening fire would probably kill their own comrades on the other side of the semicircle.

Alistair went to work.

Now that the men had come out from their hiding places, partly blinded by the dust, they were, in the language of his forefathers, sitting ducks.

Alistair knew his aim improved under extreme pressure.

Under pressure, the world seemed to slow down.

He worked methodically, single head shots, starting with those closest to cover.

The men below panicked, the silent killer above them, the roar of the V8 going around and around, the clouds of dust, twilight. Opening fire on fully automatic, they filled the vast stone cauldron with ricocheting lead and shrapnel, firing blindly at their unseen hunter. Barrels appeared in the windows of the office and they, too, opened up.

Each gun fell silent as their ammunition ran out, and the remaining two men turned towards cover. The first one dropped before his forward step was complete.

Alistair finished up his grim work as the last man fell in a futile attempt to reach the cover of a boulder. There were five bodies in undignified poses scattered around the empty quarry floor.

Three men remained inside the office.

The Chevy, ending its last donut, came to an abrupt halt. The gray dust fell to the ground and there was silence in the fading light of the day.

The door of the car opened and a muscular southeast Asian man stepped out. He was carrying a large canvas work bag, the kind you would fill with power tools.

"That's not Hank," Alistair said over his mike.

"Vodka, shall I take him?"

"Negative. Whisky let him finish the job. That's one of Henry's men."

"What the bloody hell is going on?"

"Hang on, all will be revealed."

"I wish you had told me—this wasn't the plan."

"We know, things changed unexpectedly."

The man reached the office with his tool bag. He dropped it in front of the door and walked back to Hank's Chevy. Getting in, he drove it behind a bus-sized bolder at the far end of the quarry.

Then a mushroom cloud of powder rolled into the sky. The bag, the office and the whole of the quarry floor appeared to vaporize for a second. The sound shook the whole quarry and large rocks crashed down from the cliffs.

"Bloody... Hell... fire," Alistair said, quoting his old rugby coach.

The office was gone. The bodies of the men he had shot looked like they had been blown aside by a giant leaf blower.

The two pickups had flipped over like dinky toys, and one was partly submerged in the lake.

In the distance, Alistair could hear the distinct buzz of a helicopter. The sun had set, and the last vestiges of light disappeared. Below, the quarry floor was completely black, but from behind the bolder near the entrance, he could see a lighter flare up and the pinprick glow of a cigarette.

The ominous noise of the heli was growing louder as it crept closer. Alistair tucked himself deeper between his rock as it flared its rotors and came to an aerial halt above the rocky hole. Power lights burst on from the underside of the hovering machine, flooding the scene below.

Doing a neat 180 rotation, the helicopter lowered itself to the quarry floor. As it did so, Hank's old Chevy reappeared from its protective rock and pulled to a halt, rear end facing the aircraft.

Alistair checked his remaining .308 ammo. He only had one round left.

Raising the weapon, he trained it on the door of the machine. He wished he could grab one of the Barretts from the other snipers he'd taken out.

A man stepped out of the helicopter.

"Henry, bloody Cheng is here. That was why Poppy sent her snipers"

But he didn't have a clear shot. Two men had come out with him, shielding him. They were all wearing bullet-proof vests.

He waited, putting down his rifle as he picked up the remote detonator for the explosives in the dummy. Henry walked to the back of Hank's van and one of his men produced bolt cutters. They severed the padlock, and the man climbed in, dragging out the body.

The dummy flopped on the floor between them like a sleeping bag full of water balloons.

As Henry lifted his boot to kick the dummy in fury, Alistair pressed the button on the detonator.

Nothing happened. He pressed again and again, throwing it aside as he grabbed his rifle.

Alistair could sense their panic as they realized they had been tricked.

Turning and running, all three headed for the helicopter.

Henry getting in first, shielded by his men. He sat in the seat next to the pilot. Alistair could see him pulling on his headset and shouting at the man. The driver of the Chevy stood in shock until one of Henry's men, leaning out of the helicopter door, shot him in the chest with what looked like a .44 magnum. The man was thrown against the truck and slid down, leaving wet streaks of blood.

Punishment for his stupidity.

The helicopter went into take off before they shut the doors.

Alistair took aim at Henry, but just as he squeezed the trigger, the helicopter swung around. His round only made a neat hole in the Perspex.

"Bugger."

The heli rose vertically, rotors reverberating on the rocky cliffs, lights still streaming downwards, like some midnight cabaret.

Separate from the noise of the lifting helicopter, Alistair heard the familiar, high-pitched swarm of drones.

Then he saw them, four sets of green and red blinking lights neatly rising 10 meters up from the spinning blades.

The helicopter reached 20 meters above the lip of the quarry and dipped its nose to race off.

Alistair watched as the drones did kamikaze drops into the blades, milliseconds between each one.

One blade shared off immediately, sending the aircraft into a sideways, lopsided death spiral.

The body of the craft reverted into what it was without the blades to keep it aloft, a very heavy lump of metal. For a millisecond, it stayed suspended in midair before gravity took over. It plummeted down, smashing into the lake, and burst into orange flames, lighting up the cliffs, then sunk beneath the black water, leaving just a smell of burnt avgas and a small pool of debris floating on the surface.

Henry and his men were certainly dead. Henry was one of the world's most wanted wildlife traffickers. Until this moment, he had been able to avoid the law. But the law of The Extinct Company followed no rules. Today they had scored a major victory.

Alistair pulled off his Ghillie suit and scrambled back down the cliff, running around the rim until he reached his entry point. He peeled off through the forest, back to where he had been dropped off.

In the distance, dozens of headlights pierced the darkness, and the air filled with the wail of sirens. INTERPOL and the local police were finally arriving.

39

Cracking Codes

"Let me get this straight. Henry's men accosted Hank when he stopped at the drive-thru liquor store, right? But how did they know where to find him?" They had decided they needed fortification and stopped at the Dive Inn Bar. Alistair was on his second Guinness.

"Actually, there are only two roads heading towards the quarry. They just had to cover both. His car is easy to spot. Plus, they knew he was a heavy drinker. Henry's guys were double crossing Poppy using 'Alistair' as bait. So that Henry could take control of the organization. Hank must have told them about the bomb under his seat. They disabled it, gave him $500 and told him to get lost. The police found Hank half an hour ago with $375 in his pocket, round the back of the liquor store, drunk out of his mind." Misha sipped her frozen vodka. "We didn't realize until his car arrived at the quarry. They did the switch quickly, and we were hanging back. The new driver even did a drunk driving impression."

"So, Henry sent his man in place of Hank, but they failed to check if the person in the back was actually me, not a dummy? Poppy sent her snipers to the quarry to take out Henry and his men when they came to get me. Poppy wanted to get me and destroy Henry's team because the only reason they had a truce was their common hatred of me. Henry was aiming to take out Poppy's team and capture me. He probably thought I could lead him to Poppy's hard drives. Wow, those guys really weren't playing cricket."

"To tell the truth, Alistair, I have no idea how to play cricket." Stan waved for another round with a circular movement of his hand to the barman. "But you, Alistair, ruined everyone's plans by taking out Poppy's snipers and then five of Poppy's boys when they arrived in the pickups. The man in Hank's car then finished the job. That guy in the shiny suit who was in the office was Poppy's new number two. Thanks, Bob," Stan said to the barman as he handed out a tray of drinks.

"Sure. You guys look like you've been at war." Bob was an ex Green Beret from Vietnam, so his statement wasn't a flippant one. He recognized the look in someone's eyes after a firefight.

Alistair nodded at him gratefully. Words were not required. Bob returned to his bar. Everyone from thirty miles around would have heard the explosions and gunfire.

"Then, bloody Henry showed up in his chopper. You should have seen his face when your dummy flopped out on the ground, Stan."

"I guess when the office blew up, it disconnected the wires in the dummy? I should have made them more secure."

"Not your fault, Stan. That was a gigantic explosion. Nearly shook the teeth out of my head. Then I missed, put a hole in the heli's Perspex and I was out of ammo. Thank goodness for Carlos and Phil and their amazing exploding circus."

"Yeah, right, forget cricket. Henry's last game will be playing fish food in the quarry lake!"

Sitting in silence, they soaked up the warm camaraderie of having fought a battle together and won, relaxing more with each drink.

"I think I'll go back to Panama tonight, unless you two need me?

Calculating how to unblock a GPS blocker is probably beyond my skill set, plus I would be nervous about going out on your deck."

"Sure, man, you did an amazing piece of work this evening. Misha and I can handle the unblocking the blockers."

"Thank you. By the way, did somebody arrest Mike Powell, the TSA guy in Atlanta who tipped off Hank—not that I'm nervous or anything."

"Oh yes sir, we did some digging and found out all sorts of nasty stuff, he's going to be wearing an orange jumpsuit for a very long time."

Later that night, Alistair returned the Suburban at the airport rental agency. He was glad it was still in one piece—recently, every car he got into was turned into a wreck by the time it reached the airport.

Clearing customs and security, he finally flopped into his first-class seat on the Delta plane.

"Good evening, Sir, did you forget your Granny?" Recognizing him, the young air flight attendant smiled sweetly, straightening her uniform.

Alistair went bright red.

She looked at his tickets.

"I see you have a long layover in Atlanta, Mr. Stuart. Can I do anything to make your journey more comfortable?"

"Em... cup of tea?"

40

The Hunting Guide

Alistair was happy to be back in Panama, driving his Defender Land Rover with Paloma in the passenger seat, her feet on the dash. They headed down Pipeline Road towards the Magic Shop. He was pleased to see dry season had arrived.

With nearly two meters of rain a year, humidity up in the 80% range and over 30 degrees Celsius most of the time, it was a challenging place for most people to live in, but Alistair and Paloma had grown up in it and this was their natural habitat.

They considered the arrival of the dry season in January the start of 'summer' in Panama.

As children, they had spent every Christmas at their grandparents' estate, *Wynards,* on the island of Mull in Scotland. The contrast of travelling from the depths of the Scottish winter, with its layers of clothing, cracking log fires and deep snow to hot, green tropical Panama where shorts or swimming trunks were the order of the day, was thrilling to the young Stuarts. In the dry season in Panama, the mud turned into dust, leaves fell from the trees in the forest and everyone went to the beach. Alistair and Paloma's favorite beach was actually a sandy bank on one of the deep rivers crossed by the very track they were now driving on.

"Hey, we need to have a BBQ on Rio Frijoles. I brought some great sausages back from Tennessee. I bet McDonnell could put together a terrific spread for us."

"Alistair, does constantly thinking about food help you deal with a thing like nearly getting your head blown off by an assassin with a .308?"

"Gosh, I'd never thought of that, maybe?"

They were both still chuckling when they drove off the main track towards the hidden entrance of the bunker.

"Open Sesame," Paloma swept her arm. The door silently disappeared, revealing a long corrugated tunnel strung with industrial looking cables and lights in little cages.

"Welcome to my cave, young man. You have nothing to fear except fear itself."

"Paloma, that was funny until about the fifth time and you are getting your quotes mixed up."

"Really? Actually, it continues to amuse me. A rolling stone has a silver lining." She shouted the last sentence, so it echoed around the cavernous garage as they parked. Surrounded by so many military vehicles, the Land Rover looked positively tame. Moggy presently occupied the largest workspace, which included the biggest concentration of tools and equipment. Charlie referred to this as the Operating Theater. Alistair smiled when he saw the Unimog. She was a great battle comrade and her being parked in the Operating Theater meant Charlie and Paloma had been making upgrades for an imminent mission.

McDonnell was bringing in things for afternoon tea as Alistair and Paloma walked into the mess hall.

Alistair helped himself to tea, grabbed a Marmite sandwich, and then settled down in one of the cozy chairs and joined Dr KV, Paloma,

Tatiana, Charlie, and McDonnell.

"Thanks for coming so fast, Alistair. We heard you had a fairly exciting time in Tennessee. I hope you relaxed in your layover in Atlanta?"

Alistair reddened and nodded enthusiastically.

"Lords, ladies and gentlemen, I present to you..." Dr Kitts-Vincent held up a large bound book. The black letters on the front read 'The Hunting Guide'. "Printed on waterproof paper and designed for the field. It comes in this canvas cover. Digital version available on restricted sites."

This was the team meeting everyone had been working towards.

Misha and Stan were on a box on a screen, and Deidre and the Earl were on two more.

"Our mission is to capture or destroy all the unsavory characters in this book. Together, they represent the most deadly, efficient, prolific, and ruthless poaching organization in the whole of Africa. The damage they have done and will do to endangered wildlife in the region is incalculable. They must be stopped. We must make them extinct. Alistair, please continue."

"Thanks, Dr. KV. You have all been working on this, but I want to do a quick review before we move onto the next stage: Please open your guides. On each double page you will see a complete history, description, possible crimes committed and analysis of each poacher. Everyone has a code name. They are in order of importance. There are fifty in total. Thirty are still alive. You will see the first one, is Poppy Cheng. The photos show her before her face was boiled. Her code name is Dragon."

"Yeah, she got too close to her own fire."

"Thank you, Paloma. We know she is very dangerous. The second one is Henry Cheng, has a big red line through the middle of his face. This means we have eliminated him. He has been made extinct.

We believe we must take down the first five to make the rest easier. Right now, everyone is terrified of these remaining four, so until we remove them nobody will talk." Dr. KV concluded.

"The Big Five." The Earl was speaking from somewhere tropical by the look of the shutters in the room he was in.

"Exactly, and that's where we will start, but we must all learn every target by heart. We need to recognize these people in the street."

"No problem with Poppy Boiled Face Dragon there."

"Well actually Paloma, sorry to disappoint as I know you are proud of the work you did. She has been in plastic surgery for over three weeks and we may not recognize her."

"Thanks Misha. And, actually Misha, can you continue from here?"

"Yes, so we have this guide, but we need to work out individual and up-to-date locations. The Earl has his contacts looking all over the world, but what is going to help loosen people's tongues is the money. If you look at the book, each person has a number. You have permission to offer that amount if it leads you to the successful capture or elimination. You will see Poppy has $3 million. We think this is enough to loosen the tongue of even her most ardent supporter."

"Thank you, Misha." Dr Kitts-Vincent took the reins again. "I should point out that the funds that are paying for this were donated posthumously by Van Olenburgh, although he never knew that he was going to make the donation."

"Excellent, I can see all the rhinos in Africa raise their horns in approval." Alistair said, smiling. Van Olenburgh had created a global network that sold illegal Rhino horn-based pills. He was making millions until The Extinct Company and two very angry lions caught up with him.

"You will see there are two distinct groups. One is the poachers who are mostly Africa-based. The others are gangs from Hong Kong. The Hong group does all the international logistics and seems to handle all the money."

"The plan is for Alistair, Tatiana and Paloma to go to East Africa with Moggy."

"Charlie and Paloma have been adapting the rear module so it can also carry prisoners."

"The rest of us will be your trackers, scouring the world for these people."

"The ideal scenario would be for us to get as many of each group in the same place at the same time."

"Deidre, event planner of extraordinary talents, has come up with a rather brilliant plan. Deidre?"

"Thank you, Dr. KV, you make me blush. I know from experience the best way to attract the rich and famous, or in our case the rich and nasty, is to offer them an event that they can't afford to miss. Sort of like the Oscars. I want to do the same thing for our poachers. The bait will be the biggest and best collection of unguarded animals in the world... plus cash."

The image of an extensive building surrounded by lush green forests on three sides came on the screen. In front of the structure was a large watering hole. Large groups of elephant, rhino, and buffalo wallowed in the mud around its edge.

"This is the Ark, in the Aberdare National Park, Kenya."

The Ark was a famous lodge built in the late 60s, a funny-looking building clearly designed to do an imitation of a version of Noah's famous ship. At the front of the Ark was a solid bunker, so that guests could be eye level with the animals' feet.

On Deidre's presentation, moving infrared cameras tracked across the screen, it was teeming with animals.

"This is their live cam."

"This is Misha's 'live' cam. The landscape remained the same, but the number of animals quadrupled in size and all their tusks and horns grew bigger. Actually, that one is not live yet, but you get the idea."

"The Ark is under renovation at the moment. The head of wildlife security is very sick. Most of the rangers are on their annual leave, and the gates appear to be frequently unmanned. If I were a poacher, this would seem like a great opportunity, all those animals, all those massive tusks."

"Wow, Deirdre, that is a brilliant idea. That would be quite a party not to miss. If I were a poacher of poachers, I would see this a super time to go hunting poachers."

"Exactly, Alistair. You might expect an excellent bag of notorious criminals."

"We may even get some poacher species not in our guide! But there will be a tricky moment when everyone arrives, and they realize that the actual scene isn't as busy as the one on the live cam."

"Yes, but I know you three will come up with something brilliant!"

41

Steak and Kidney Pudding

Charlie explained Moggy's upgrades. They had installed a foldout 'prison' on the rear of the command module that reminded Alistair of a Murphy bed, except four steel walls popped out.

"Think of it as additional armor, except that it may be a little uncomfortable for the prisoners if you come under fire."

They had also added storage for the Javelin missile and repaired all the bullet damage from their last battle.

"Oh yes, and Paloma loves this. The mini-gun is now controlled from inside using the same sighting system as they have in fighter jets. You move your head and the gun moves. It's called a Helmet Mounted Sight or HMS."

"We call it HMS Mini."

When they were ready, the team spread their equipment across the workshop floor in front of Moggy while Tatiana checked each item and they loaded them in.

They would fly in the Airbus A400M Atlas to Kenya, landing at the British army base as before. The Atlas had a 4m height inside the cargo bay and easily fitted the Unimog.

Taking the canal sidetrack to a small pebble beach on the side of the Panama Canal, Tatiana, Alistair, Paloma, and Jeeves enjoyed the night sounds and smells of the jungle and water. It was a quiet in the cabin. Everyone was thinking of the battle ahead.

Carlouchi and his band of men arrived bang on time with their flat-bottomed landing craft to ferry them across the canal to the old US military base, Fort Sherman, where they would get picked up by the huge plane.

They loved going on a boat at night on the canal. It always felt slightly naughty because at night only official Panama Canal vessels were supposed to use the water.

Alistair and Paloma had, of course, spent many nights with friends camping and exploring all the hidden islands inside the canal zone. Avoiding canal security was part of the adventure.

Once they reached the other bank, drove to Fort Sherman and tucked themselves between two rusting hangers, they sat and waited. They were twenty minutes early.

Paloma took Jeeves around the back of a hangar.

"We need to pee like racehorses," she said as she disappeared.

Tatiana laughed and Alistair poured them each a cup of tea from his battered green thermos.

Twenty-one minutes later, the roar of the Atlas split the sky in half. Alistair looked at his watch and shouted, "one minute late!"

"You want to tell Taboga that?" Paloma winked at her brother. Taboga was the senior pilot and stood for no nonsense.

Getting picked up by the monstrous gray plane was always exciting. Its arrival alone was an event.

Once Moggy was secured inside and they had settled themselves in the separate passenger compartment, the Atlas took off almost vertically. It could easily perform a barrel roll... not that Taboga would do that; they might spill their tea.

Reaching cruising altitude, Taboga handed over to her copilot and came back to see them all. They had become an inseparable team. Tobago and her crew had rescued them more than once. She headed straight for Alistair and sat next to him, looking into his eyes.

"Alistair, I think you get better looking every time I see you." She stroked his blonde mop, knowing she was making him squirm. "Did you do something different with your hair?"

The two other girls giggled at Alistair, who didn't own a comb, was turning red.

Taboga turned to Jeeves, who was waiting to be greeted, his big tail sweeping the floor. "And you, Sir Jeeves Stuart, are the most handsome and bravest of them all."

He licked her face.

"So, usual routine: we'll refuel at St. Kitts, Ascension, Gib and Alex. We should be at Nanyuki Airfield at 18.00 hours, Kenyan time, tomorrow."

"My crew will overnight at the British army barracks there. You can too if you wish. The CO there, Major Taylor, says there's room for everyone and there will be steak and kidney pie for supper. Actually, I do not know what that is, but he said you lot would know."

"You'll love it, Taboga, but it's hard to explain so as to make it sound nice. Major Taylor was desperately trying to get me to join him for dinner last time. He wanted to sit down to a pint of stout and play chess."

"Don't worry, my pretty Paloma, I Tatiana, the great Russian chess player, will do battle with the major and his stout. He will be a defeated Britisher by the time I am finished."

"Thanks Tati, I'm sure there are some more fun people there, isn't it an SAS training base? Maybe some of Daddy's old mates are still around."

"Paloma, you do realize that any of dad's contemporaries would be the same age as Dr. KV, which means they wouldn't be on active service anymore. Plus, Dad was in the SBS...Special BOAT Squadron. So near water."

"Yeah, you're right, I suppose. Pity, I've always wanted to know more about Dad's days in the army. They based him in Kenya for a while, that's why we got sent to boarding school there, right? Dr. KV will never tell us much."

"It's all classified, and you know what those guys are like about talking."

"Maybe Tatiana will find herself a nice SAS officer."

"I think I have tried many special forces officers in Russia, my grandmother kept on fixing me up 'O Tatiana my little doll, I have a charming boy for you, special forces, good family, excellent shot, you will have much to talk about.' But they trained those men to kill, rather than make good boyfriends. Plus, when they are not on duty, they go crazy, crazy like bears off their chains."

"You are right, but we are biased. People like our father, Dr. KV, right back to David Stirling, brilliant, sophisticated men in the British Special Forces, lovely people—who are also expert killers."

"You are right. Dr. KV is an extraordinary man. He feels like a father to me too now. But I am not hunting. Maybe just a quiet game of chess with Major Taylor.... and steak and kidney pie."

They came into land at the Nanyuki Airport just as the sun was turning the sky into a deep gold. Landing the Atlas, Taboga pulled across to the taxiway and stopped. The team left Moggy on board. They would get her out in the morning. Having an overlanders' truck parked at a military barracks overnight was not a good idea.

Taboga's team was eight strong. They were all fit, highly trained women from a mixture of backgrounds. Half of them came from the islands around the Caribbean, the rest came from Panama, Belize, Colombia, and Venezuela. Between them they spoke several languages.

They operated as a single unit on duty and—as they were often deployed in strange and wild places—they operated the same way when they went out. Once they secured the plane, they marched across to the mess at the British base. Dressed in black combat fatigues, sidearms strapped to their legs, they were the picture of confidence. And with their heads up and chests out, they pushed open the doors of the mess and headed straight to the bar. The locals were awestruck. Battle-hardened soldiers stood with their mouths agape. A squadron of exotic birds of prey had descended upon the bar.

The rest of the team dropped their kit in the barracks. Major Taylor was very efficient and clearly delighted to see Paloma return. Her green eyes, lithe body, perfectly behaved dog and collection of serious weaponry had caused him many sleepless nights as he thought up a million ways to make a good impression the next time he saw her.

He mentioned steak and kidney pudding on several occasions.

Paloma introduced him to Tatiana—black-haired and gray-eyed, highly intelligent with an exotic Russian accent. Major Taylor suddenly imagined himself as 007.

After weeks of dreaming of Paloma, he was rather torn when Tatiana suggested chess, but she nailed it when she produced two shot glasses, a bottle of frozen vodka and said, "The British and The Russians to battle." Honor was at stake.

Tatiana winked at Paloma and licked her lips while the major carefully arranged the chess pieces before them.

Paloma mouthed 'thank you' and turned in relief back to the growing crowd at the bar.

News got around the base fast. Visitors were rare and this alluring bunch of fresh faces attracted everyone to the bar, both British and Kenyan. The base was too small to have the usual separate bars for officers and ranks, so all and sundry piled in. It was a good, cheerful crowd, an honest mix of SAS officers, low-ranking mechanics, Kenyan pilots, and auxiliary staff. The crowd was deeply connected to the military and they knew these people who just showed up at their base were going off to battle so there was a profound sense of respect: do your duty, you might not come back, we drink to you.

42

Aberdare Country Club

The team left just before dawn. The good thing about being on the equator was that dawn was pretty consistent. In fact, the Kenyans used a much more sensible clock. 0 o'clock was dawn, 1 o'clock was one hour after sunrise, sundown was 12. It didn't change, and it made sense.

"Sooo Tatiana, you and Major Taylor seemed pretty tight all evening. Did you have fun?"

"Thank you, Paloma, for introducing us. I enjoyed his company, at least until he had too much vodka and I needed to take him to his bed."

"Do tell, Tati, do tell." Alistair and Jeeves were fast asleep, splayed across the back seats of the Unimog.

"He beat me at the chess. Four times destroyed me completely. And he speaks perfect Russian with a Moscow accent. I was surprised. We had fun, he quoted Russian poetry, I am laughing, he is not special forces, he says he comes from a county regiment which I don't understand."

"And?"

"Well, he was not Russian and the vodka it makes him sleeping, but no problem, I put him in his room, take off his clothes, put on his night sleeping clothes with stripes, put him in bed. He seemed happy, sleeping, and smiling. This is better than the usual battle with the men. I write him a nice note on his chest, with the sharp pen."

"Sharpie."

"Yes, a black one, in Russian."

"What did it say?"

"Maybe you can read it when we come back. I don't think the major will be washing it off!"

They both roared with laughter, waking up both Alistair and Jeeves.

They were going to set up their first base at the Aberdare Country Club, Alistair and Paloma had gone to school with the owner's children, and they had often visited. It was only an hour's drive from the British base.

From there they would go into the Aberdare National Park and set up operations at the Ark. At least that was the plan so far.

The Aberdare Country Club was a rambling set of stone buildings that dotted around the landscape, connected by a series of walkways, steps and arches, giving the impression that it was an ancient village from the Cotswolds.

The three drove in through the service entrance and tucked Moggy behind the manager's house beside an old VW camper van.

"They can talk German together, maybe Moggy can cheer this old frau up. Let's find Tanga." Paloma patted the rather forlorn looking VW who had four flat tires. Tanga was one of the owner's daughters who was now the manager. Her full name was Tangawizi, which means 'ginger' in Kiswahili.

Four rather feral looking children with orange hair and freckles spilled out of the back door of the house as they got down from the Unimog. They all ran over to Jeeves and started talking to him, ignoring the humans.

"Hey, you hooligans, where's your mum?" Paloma asked the milling children.

One of them looked under Jeeves and replied, "What's his name?"

"His name is Jeeves. Where is your mum?"

"She's on the veranda doing 'The numbers'," answered the largest of the four children.

Tanga was sitting at a large table covered in stacks of paper. Each one had a colored stone on top. She was very tall with messy ginger hair and freckles—she looked tired.

"Paloma, Alistair, brilliant timing... bloody hate maths. Paloma, you were always so good at it. Let me get some tea. Hello, I'm Tanga," she said, noticing Tatiana. "Paloma always helped me with my maths homework, then my husband did it, but he ran off with some American tourist, so now I have to do it myself, have a seat."

"Hello Tanga, this is Tatiana."

"And this is Jeeves. He's a boy, I checked." one child piped up.

"Thank you, Sebastian. You are a clever chap. Can you four ask Miriam to get tea things?"

They sat down while the children ran off to find Miriam.

"How are you doing, Tanga?" Asked Paloma.

"Super, I am running the Country Club, The Ark construction Project. I have four children who run wild. Like I said, Malcolm, the bastard, ran off with some woman from Texas with lots of makeup and huge tits.... and we desperately need cash to keep the place going. Sorry guys, it's been a tough month. How are you? What on earth are you doing here?" Tanga seemed to suddenly realize the unexpected nature of their arrival.

"Tanga, Tatiana, and I are going to help you with your book-keeping. In fact, we will put the lot on a laptop so you can just add the numbers and it will do the rest for you."

Paloma, Tatiana, and Alistair were looking at the ledger Tanga had open, not only were parts of it rubbed out so many times that it actually made a hole in the paper but there was also a large, crayon drawing of what appeared to be an elephant over one whole set of numbers.

"Alistair will entertain the children with something educational. Won't you, Alistair?"

"Yes, right. On the job. Sebastian, Peach, Melba, Michael, I've got a surprise for you." Alistair shouted as Miriam arrived with a tray piled with cups, teapot, bits of cake, milk, and sugar.

The children came skidding around the corner with expectant looks on their faces.

"Right, you lot, have a cup of tea and some cake and then we have a glorious mission to complete."

Tanga explained her filing system to the girls.

"The paper pile with the red stone on top is outstanding bills." It was the biggest one.

"The blue stone is staff wages."

She went on as everyone drank their tea. After a few minutes, Alistair took the excited children away, accompanied by Jeeves.

As the girls started working with Tanga on the accounts, they explained part of what they were doing. They explained they needed to capture the poachers and if she could help, she would get the rewards.

"Oh my, this sounds fun. I have been stuck out here for so long I confess I am craving a little excitement AND it would solve all my financial problems. I could even send the kids to school. How are you going to get them and how can I help?"

Paloma, who had known Tanga since she was six, trusted her completely. They showed her the 'live' feed from the Ark. The actual feed was off because of construction.

"I can't believe it. There must be fifty elephants out there. Look at the tusks on that one. I have never seen so many elephants at the Ark. Typical just when there are no tourists."

Tatiana explained it was computer generated and how they were using it as bait to lure in the poachers.

Tanga's eyes grew as wide as saucers.

"Bloody hell! But what happens when they show up and there are only two old bulls with broken tusks?"

"Well, that is what we need you to help us with, actually we are bit stuck with ideas. Paloma told me you were an original thinker and probably knew the area better than any person alive. We're hoping you might come up with something," Tatiana explained.

Tanga hooted with laughter and pushed Paloma off the bench they were sharing.

"Original Thinker. Cheeky cow!"

"I remember what you did to that nasty boy Nigel McGuinness when you caught him taking photos up your skirt!" Paloma said, getting off the floor.

They both laughed at the memory. "Tatiana, you'll have to get Tanga to tell you over drinks later."

"I am going to need some help from the staff. They are the ones who know the Ark better than anyone. They would probably appreciate the rewards too. There are so few tourists at the moment they are short on cash. "

Tatiana was neatly stacking all the papers from the table.

They worked solidly at the accounts for three hours. Between them, they become very efficient.

"Thanks for setting up the accounts for me. I was looking at two days of misery until you guys showed up. Shall we see what Alistair and the children are doing? I've never known them so quiet."

Rounding the back of the house, they caught sight of the children running to stand to attention in a line. Jeeves sat at the end of the line, tail wagging.

"Mummy, start your engine." Sebastian, the eldest, handed Tanga the keys to the VW van. They were all bursting with pride.

The van was cleanish, inside and out. It had four fully inflated tires, and the doors were open.

Everyone piled in. The children all crossed their fingers on the instruction of Alistair, and Tanga turned the key. The comfortable rattle-rattle-pop-pop of a VW engine started instantly. They drove off to the staff lines to great cheers from the passengers. Tanga was laughing like she hadn't done for months.

43

The Ark

Steven, Simon and Blessed were Kikuyus. They and their extended families were as much part of the Aberdare Country Club and Ark as the buildings themselves. They had a deep knowledge of wildlife. The animals around the club and Ark were like members of their family: who was having babies and who was arguing with who were all part of mealtime conversations.

They remembered Alistair and Paloma visiting as children. The team explained what they were trying to do, showed them the 'live' feed and finally explained the problem of all the poachers showing up and then having nothing to shoot.

Steven, who was the most senior of the three, spoke first after contemplating the information and asking several questions.

"Do you think you can get everyone to arrive on the same day?"

Alistair answered. "I think we could. The plan is for Deidre, who is pretending to be someone else, to send out an invitation. She could make it so that they had to arrive at a set time."

"Many years ago we made the water hole bigger. To do that, we had to build an elephant proof fence around the whole Ark to keep the animals out while we worked. We took the fence down, but the posts are still there."

"Gosh, Steven, you are right. I remember it too. I was a teenager, and I was cross that all the animals were being kept away from their water hole. We actually do want to keep the animals away when those people arrive, but we could make it look like we are 'holding' them outside the fence. Tatiana, if we built the fence, could you and Misha make it look like there were loads of animals waiting to come in?" Tanga looked at Tatiana.

"Sure, easy, if you give me a fence, I give you the animals."

"Great, I can't believe I am saying this. You could make it like a fairground shooting game. Let the animals in and pay to shoot the ones they want. They won't actually shoot anything because there are no animals to let in. Then you guys have the poachers trapped inside the fence."

"Brilliant Tanga! See? The original thinker." Paloma clapped her hands together.

"We will need to disarm them. If that lot comes in, and there may be thirty of them, fully armed, we will have a huge gun battle. Actually, at the fairground, the guns are chained to the tables. Could we claim that to make it 'fair', we set up shooting stands and we supply the rifles? That would give us a chance to ask each person to hand in their weapons as they enter?"

"Good Alistair, maybe we should offer an orange teddy bear to the best shot?"

"Well, actually the orange teddy could be a million-dollar prize.... but then we would need judges."

Paloma spoke up, "you guys are over thinking it. Once they are inside the Ark and unarmed, we've got them. We can pretend to have judges on the invitation. The key thing is to get them inside the Ark surrounded by a fence that will keep any actual wildlife out and them inside. Personally, I would like to let them loose and then we have a competition to see how many we can hit, picking them off from the roof... I bag HMS Mini."

"Paloma, we need to capture them so we can interrogate them. Remember the big five—the one we have to poach first."

"Yeah, Dragon Bitch, I'm going to remove the rest of her fingers."

Tatiana high fived Paloma.

"Who's Dragon Bitch?" Tanga looked confused.

"Paloma will explain later, it's complicated." Alistair offered. "But you are right. We just need to get them inside. Can we go to the Ark after lunch and have a look?"

"Alistair remembers the buffet at the Aberdare Country Club... I can see it in his eyes, he is imagining lunch." Steven, Simon, and Blessing were smiling proudly. They could remember betting on the quantity of food the twelve-year-old Alistair could eat.

"I have a very fast constitution." He said in his own defense, much to the delight of the girls.

After lunch, which was suitably legendary, they took a Land Cruiser and Moggy and headed out into the Aberdare Forest. Alistair, who had done the buffet proud, fell into a deep sleep with his head resting on Jeeves in the back bench seat of Moggy.

They reached the gate of the park, which was closed but unguarded. Tanga jumped out and pushed it open while the two vehicles drove through.

Driving on into the park felt like another world. Here the animals were the bosses and humans, only the tolerated guests. Fresh elephant dung littered the road and trees closed over them in a green tunnel. They could hear the calls of Colobus monkeys. It felt like they were entering a monastery of nature. Ten minutes down the track they stopped to allow a family of elephants to pass, the massive beasts appeared out of the forest and swung their easy gait across the road, ignoring the two vehicles until they slipped between the trees on the other side and disappeared without a trace.

"That was Mama Chombo and her family," Steven said over the walkie talkie. "Did you see the little one? That is her sister's fourth child."

Rounding the last bend, the Ark came into view. It truly looked like an ark that might have come from Noah's biblical rescue. With its slightly curving roof, bow and stern, if there was a big enough storm, the animals could climb aboard and sail off for forty days and forty nights.

As they pulled into the parking area near the back of the Ark, the contractor, Francis Chege, in construction helmet and high visibility jacket, approached them. He was a big Kikuyu with iron-cast forearms. He wasn't smiling.

"Tanga, I am sorry. I have asked the crew to clear up. We cannot keep working unless we get paid. These men have to eat."

Tanga had been dreading this moment. The accounting they had done in the morning had confirmed what she knew in her heart. They had run out of money and the bank's loan upon loan had simply evaporated.

"Mr. Chege, I would like to introduce some old friends of mine who have a solution. Alistair, Paloma and Tatiana, this is Francis Chege, our contractor."

He smiled politely and shook their hands.

Alistair invited him for a stroll, and the others went to look at the old fence.

"Francis, I want to be very honest with you, but first, I need you to tell me something. What do you think of the animals that visit here and live in the National Parks?" Alistair was speaking Kiswahili, the common language of the tribes in East Africa.

Francis took his helmet off and scratched his head.

"I don't understand what you mean?"

"Do you enjoy watching the animals, do you think they are an important part of your heritage, your country?" They sat down on one bench overlooking the salt lick in front of the lodge. Five muddy elephants were muscling their way through some buffalos to get at the lick.

"Alistair, they are our heritage. They are like the mountains, rivers, the forests, and the people. There are many tribes in Kenya, but we all share the elephants, they are what makes us whole and united."

"Thank you, that was elegantly put. We both know Kenya is in crisis and that there are some people who are killing those animals and taking their tusks to Asia."

"I know this, and it makes me angry, it makes me angry because these arms," he held up his massive fists, "are not strong enough to stop them.

My eldest son has just joined the Kenya Wildlife Service. He hopes he can reach the Rapid Response unit so he can hit back. His mother is afraid, but I am very proud."

"Good. I understand you are a business owner and your crew needs to be paid, but please understand that we are are here to stop those poachers and we need your powerful arms, your skill and that of your men to help us do it."

"I am ready." Standing up quickly, he spoke in English.

Alistair also stood up, smiled, and shook his massive hand. He recognized the straight back and air of confidence.

"Francis, were you in the Kenya Army before becoming a building contractor?"

Francis came to attention and executed a perfect salute. Alistair did the same in return.

"Sergeant Major, Kenya Army Paratroopers, Ranger D Company. Eighteen years."

"Wow, that was the unit trained by US special forces to fight terrorists, correct?"

"Yes, we had some interesting missions that I cannot discuss."

"I believe you and I are going to get on well, Sergeant Major. We may call upon your military expertise as well?"

"Don't tell my wife, but to be honest, I am rather bored being a building contractor."

"What I am about to explain will change everything but first I have the funds that they owe you for the work you have done here, and then, on your agreement to carry out further works I will give you a full advance on that too."

Alistair judged Francis Chege to be an honest man and gave him the full story of what they wanted to do and how they were going to do it.

Francis changed visibly from a tired contractor who never got paid properly into a Sergeant Major on an urgent mission. Most of his work crew were ex-servicemen who had served with Francis, and they too instantly recognized their NCO was back and they had a mission.

Within an hour, the whole site changed from a lackluster refurbishment job to an army base that was under imminent attack.

Francis's firm voice could be heard giving commands across the whole compound.

"Bloody hell Alistair, what did you say to Francis? That man is on fire."

Tanga was impressed.

"You're not looking for a wife and four kids, are you? They come with a country club and a big boat in the middle of the forest."

Alistair laughed, but then he realized that Tanga was looking at him, and although she was smiling, she wasn't laughing. The smallest girl, Melba, ran over to him and took his hand.

"Right. Let's get to work. Tatiana, you need to find excellent sniper's positions to take out any of the blighters if they make a run for it," Alistair said after clearing his throat.

44

Baiting The Traps

Two weeks later, The Ark was ready.

The electric fence encircled the compound, 800 meters from the building, and invisible from the building. It was definitely up to the task of keeping the animals out. It had two sets of large gates: one remotely operated, the other manned, with what they called a 'dingly dangly' electrified wire that hung down from a series of lintels across the road. Any animals trying to go through would get an electric shock, whereas cars with their rubber tires could drive through with impunity.

Paloma had installed new salt licks and large water troughs all around the outside of the fence, so the animals were not missing anything. They just couldn't walk up to the buildings anymore.

Tatiana had installed several sniper nests, enough to cover almost the entire open area around the lodge, including several near the car park. Francis's men had shown great expertise in positioning and camouflaging these posts. They were comfortable, dry and, importantly, bulletproof in the right places using piled sandbags. Most were at least five meters off the ground. They even had a zip line to the terra firma for a fast escape.

The area around The Ark now had massive flood lights, essential for the snipers.

The Sergeant Major's men had insisted that they would help Tatiana in manning the nests. The Earl had shipped them ten British army L129A1 sniper rifles and Tatiana had done some testing by setting up targets. By the end of the day, the men were completely in awe of her. None of them could match her ability with the rifle.

Building together and target practice had made them into a tight team.

Alistair, Paloma, Francis and five of his men would work on capturing the poachers. Much to Paloma's amusement, they had built a series of cages in which they would store the prisoners.

Part of Francis's work was to install automatic locks on each room inside The Ark.

The 'guests' would be invited to freshen up in their rooms, doors would lock and then the sleeping agent added to the forced air heating system. Hopefully, most guests would be trapped in their rooms, but the team realized it was going to be impossible to get everyone into their rooms at the same time. They would have to flood the whole building with gas. Luckily nights in the Aberdares were bitterly cold, so they hoped people would be inside. The windows were all screwed shut. Staff would need to put on gas masks or leave the building seconds before the gas was released.

The gas was the same sleeping agent they had used in Hong Kong, the Russian Kolkol-1.

The snipers would stop escapees and Tatiana's team had been practicing shooting at the legs of their full-size human targets. Set at 800 meters, this was a tough shot even when the targets were stationary. But their aim was to capture. They had even flown in a combat medic to make repairs to their prisoners.

This was the plan, but they all understood it was perilous, given the number and nature of their quarry.

Meanwhile, the party invitations were going out. Misha and Deidre had created a new character who would be organizing the event. Centaine De Montfort, an avid hunter with a predilection for indulging in leather and whips.

The invitation promised a once in a lifetime opportunity, combining shooting endangered species, gambling and sex, with the added bonus that guests could take home their wildlife trophies. The invitation linked to the 'live' feed at The Ark, where the number of animals appeared to be increasing daily.

Misha and Deirdre were doing a series of tantalizing digital invites that disappeared seconds after they were opened. Some just had the date, some had pictures of animals, others pictured girls, guns, money, and short recorded videos from Centaine De Montfort.

The message was simple: come if you are brave enough. The rewards will be great.

Because the team had stolen Poppy's hard drive, they could monitor both her and Henry's team communications. Poppy was clearly conscious of online security and Misha struggled to keep up with her constantly changing passwords and VPNs, but the teams were less careful. Most of their passwords were 12345678.

The remains of Henry's men were now in Poppy's team. Poppy had simply disposed of those who refused to join.

Misha could see no one was telling Poppy of the event at The Ark, which was what they had hoped for. They had pitched it as a grand party rather than a poaching operation. This simple act of disloyalty would make their interrogations easier.

It looked like Poppy had also taken over Henry's operation in Mexico. There was a new factory producing drugs, selling arms, and selling carved ivory using Henry's old network. The drugs cartels themselves protected the factory, even the Mexican army wouldn't go within 100 kilometers of it.

By taking out Henry, The Extinct Company had unwittingly removed the middleman for Poppy. Building a case against her, crashing her organization, and capturing her had become their focus.

But she was like a ghost. They did not know what she looked like or where she was. They hoped capturing thirty of her henchmen would give them some answers.

Importantly, they needed to get hold of the GPS blocking system Poppy's team had developed in Turkana: The Mengbi Weapon. It would be devastating in the hands of a terrorist, drug lord, or as they had already seen—poaching syndicate.

Tatiana would play the role of Centaine De Montfort, supported by Taboga's team who would be suitably dressed in leather, high boots and carrying whips and sidearms. The guests would arrive in six hours, just as night fell on the Aberdares. This was a highly risky gamble they were taking. The guests, probably already on their way, probably already starting to party, were all highly trained and ruthless. The team would be outnumbered and outgunned but they had their wits and their teamwork. Everything was ready and planned with meticulous detail. Not one of them could say they weren't nervous.

45

Unsavory Guests

Tatiana stood with her back to the great stone fireplace in the main hall of The Ark. Several large gum tree logs were roaring in flames behind her. She was wearing a studded leather jacket, her combat boots laced to just below her knees, her black hair stood out in a wild tangle, and her eyes were made up with shades of gray. She had a mask over her mouth and nose. On her hip was a stubby Smith & Wesson Machine pistol. In her hand was a riding whip. Standing, feet apart, she looked defiantly at the gathering crowd of unsavory guests.

Flanking her were six of Taboga's team, similarly dressed and armed.

At the back of the room was a table laden with what Tanga had referred to as 'man snacks'. Men were piling plates of sweet BBQ ribs, diabolically spicy hot wings, and chunks of fire roasted 'nyama choma'. Most of the men felt entitled to spit filthy abuse from meat filled mouths. "Come on girl, I got a plate full of meat for you right here." Shards of ice appeared at a popped tops of beer bottles. The vodka, whisky and South African brandy were flowing. The men represented all corners of the world.

Misha was monitoring hidden cameras and matching faces to their

Hunting Guide. She had already identified two of the 'Big Five.'

The screen on Tatiana's left showed crowds of animals milling about near the gates of the great fence 800 meters from The Ark. Underneath were the words:

'We will release the animals at 20:00,' in several languages.

"Let us get this party started!" Tatiana bellowed above the noise of the crowd. "First, some basic rules of the games."

She waited for the assembled men to hush. She was deliberately taking on the role of a strict school mistress. One man, a short bald bloke with a broken nose, ignored her and continued to talk in loud Cantonese to the person next to him.

Tatiana slapped her whip on the table beside him, making a sharp crack.

"Pay attention." She commanded in Cantonese. The man sat smartly upright and gave her a slightly sheepish salute. She knew this was one of Poppy's men, and she knew Poppy treated him like a doormat, despite his bravado.

"The Game begins in one hour."

"You must wait in your rooms until then, while the shooting stands on the front veranda are being prepared. You will find drinks and food in your rooms. My girls or other entertainment are at your disposal. Simply use the phone in your rooms. A buzzer will sound three times when it is time to come down to the veranda for The Game to begin.

"I will give each one of you a .375 hunting rifle and fifty rounds of ammunition. You may only use these to shoot the animals. No other weapons are allowed. This makes it a fair competition." She held up a rifle.

"You must hand in your own weapons before you go to your rooms. We will label them and secure them.

"Using the range finding scopes provided at your shooting stand, you must nominate your animal, then state the range and bearing before firing. Hunters will keep their own tusks.

Judges will award points for distance and cleanest kill.

There is a $300,000 prize for the winner. $200,000 for second and $100,000 for third.

Please take a card from the hat to determine the number of your shooting stand. One of my team will pass the hat."

Taboga walked around with a hat and the men each took one. Several tried to grab her as she walked, realizing too late that her tight leather trousers were covered in tiny, sharp studs, and they came away blowing on their red fingers.

"Questions?"

"Yeah, do we get to choose which girls we have?"

Tatiana pointed to a camera and pressed some buttons on an iPad. The big screen changed images from the animals and showed a room that had the same decor as The Ark—it was full of girls all dressed in leather knickers and bras which were covered in studs. Several were carrying whips.

The girls were beckoning the men from the screen. One stepped forward, put her hand on her hips and said, "Go to your room, you naughty boy."

"The girls choose which men they will have. They will arrive once everyone is in their rooms," Tatiana said.

There were catcalls and whistles.

"Our team," Tatiana pointed at Taboga's crew, "will come around and put labels on your personal weapons. Please do not retain any. That will be an immediate disqualification. They will be secured in the gun room."

Reluctantly, the men began placing their weapons on the tables in front of them. Taboga and her team spread out and started clearing the breaches, removing the magazines, and then attaching labels with owners' names.

Remarks such as "watch out love you could have your eye out with that" faded fast as Taboga's team cleared the weapons with swift, neat movements.

The men's minds clearly on the excitement a

head and soon the room was empty.

Tatiana put on her Kevlar jacket and went out to see her sniper team.

Taboga's team collected all the weapons and locked them in a storeroom.

There were no girls to send up to the rooms. They had all been in the barn at Deidre's ranch, which had been decorated to look like The Ark.

The girls were being live streamed to the TVs in the rooms.

One girl stepped in front of the camera and said, "Mickey Robinson, room 25, I chose you, I'm coming right up, you had better be ready." She licked her lips seductively and pointed at the camera.

They knew they had only minutes before the men started to go berserk.

46

The Big Sleep

Taboga's team moved outside and drove to the main gates of The Ark to join the combat medic in the makeshift operating theater she had set up in the old manger's cottage just beyond the gate. The girls had a couple of army ambulances full of stretchers and a gurney where they would load the sleeping or wounded men and put them in the cages, which were also beyond the gate.

Alistair and Paloma put on their gas masks and went down into the service room. They could already hear some of their captives upstairs shouting and banging when they realized their room doors were locked.

Alistair turned off the furnace and disconnected the main air pipe. Attaching a funnel-like valve, he connected the two cylinders of Kolokol -1 gas which, when mixed, would create a powerful sleeping gas that the Russians had used so effectively in the Moscow Theatre Hostage Crisis.

"Hurry Alistair, I can hear them banging on the doors. Oh shit, that sounded like a window breaking." Her gas mask muffled her voice. The gas wouldn't work if the windows were open.

He opened the valves—there was a satisfying hissing noise as the gasses entered the main pipes.

Above them, they could hear chaos erupt as the men tried to escape the gas. Several shots rang out.

"I guess we didn't get all their guns," said Alistair grimly.

"Let's get back to Moggy and block the main gates. You may get to use your mini-gun after all."

Running outside, they sprinted towards the parked Unimog, climbed aboard, and headed towards the gate.

"Now the party is starting!" Paloma put on the weapons helmet and activated the mini-gun control system.

"Vodka 2, this is Bloody Mary. Can you give us a SITREP?"

"We can see several broken windows; looks like they are smashing the front door."

"Vodka 1 do you have the cameras inside online? What is happening? We are in Moggy. Can you patch us in?"

Misha connected the screens inside the Unimog to the cameras inside The Ark.

The screens lit up, and Paloma toggled through the rooms. Only about half of them contained unconscious poachers. A few figures were draped over the stairs. The rest were smashing open the doors to the outside with their hands or shirts over their mouths. Several had handguns.

They could hear Tatiana's calm voice over the radio.

"Hold fire until most of them are in the open or they will run back into cover. Open fire on my command."

"Alistair, what are you doing?" They had tucked the Unimog into the deep shadow under the trees near the entrance gate, which was as bright as daylight with several large floodlights.

"Eating a marmite sandwich, you hungry? We should have saved some of that poachers' buffet for ourselves, it looked yummy."

Paloma shook her head and scanned the screens. It was feeling like a video game, with bodies lying everywhere. She even had the mini gun moving in the direction of her sight.

The poachers had burst out of the doors and were tearing across the open ground in front of the lodge—they were clearly disoriented by the gas, several tripped and went sprawling in the muck.

"Open fire." They heard Tatiana give the command.

Six men crumpled to the mud on Paloma's videos, followed by the echoing sound of six rifles firing almost simultaneously more than a thousand meters away.

Even inside the Unimog, they could hear the screams of men who had been hit.

"Fire at will." Several more men crumpled, followed by the delayed sound of the weapons.

The Ark was equipped with an elephant-proof bunker which sat in front of the main building so that the guests could safely watch the animals from ground height. Just like a military bunker, it had slits for windows. It was from one of those that a familiar hiss, followed by a trail of blue smoke, now emitted.

"Get down. RPG." The voice came over the radio just as the rocket-propelled grenade exploded in the first sniper's tower that the team had built next to the fence. The tower erupted in an orange ball of fire, throwing bits of sandbag, wood, and what looked like two men into the air.

The remaining snipers immediately opened fire on the bunker, knowing that they could be the next target. Rounds zinged off the concrete structure and ricocheted away. The bunker was in the shadow of the powerful floodlights, so it was impossible to even see the narrow slits, let alone hit them.

Tatiana's voice came over the radio. "Emergency evac. Abandon posts."

Within seconds, zip lines whined overhead as pairs of snipers clung to the handles and launched themselves from their nests.

The first two were only five meters out when the next RPG ripped through their tower, severing their line, and throwing them into the air. They crashed through the trees to the ground, bruised but otherwise unhurt.

They jumped into the parked Land Rover and raced to help the men from the first tower.

An RPG blew the third tower to pieces—it seemed to hesitate before crashing down to earth, bringing down an entire section of fence with it. Blue sparks and flashes lit up the trees as the electric fence shorted itself out and then also crashed down.

Tatiana had remained in one tower, providing continuous cover fire with her silenced assault rifle. The person operating the RPG had been aiming at muzzle flashes to elect his targets, but Tatiana's silent weapon was also designed not to be seen, so his next shot went wildly off target, exploding harmlessly in the trees behind.

Tatiana's fire meant he could only pop up, aim, and fire quickly before seeking the refuge of the solid concrete walls again.

The destruction of the towers had created three gaping holes in the fence and the panicked elephants and buffalo who were the normal residents around The Ark surged in. They had learnt from over fifty years of persecution that The Ark represented safety, so on hearing the explosions and gunfire, they were doing what they always did: head to The Ark.

Except now The Ark was full of the very people they were running from, invited there by the Extinct Company.

Half a dozen buffalo appeared on the scene, their stiff-legged scampering now blocking Tatiana's fire towards The Ark.

The people inside the bunker had no such qualms about shooting animals, and the stucco fire of an AK47 filled the night air. Three buffalo sank to their knees, blood streaming from their flanks and legs.

At that moment, Alistair realized what had happened. Some men had escaped the gas unharmed and got back to their vehicles, which must have been loaded with weapons. Alistair grabbed some fragmentation and white phosphorus grenades, along with an MP 5 and some magazines of ammunition.

"Paloma, stay in Moggy and shoot anything that comes down that road that isn't one of us. I'm going to nail those buggers in the bunker." They could see where the fire was coming from on their video feed.

Taboga, ever watchful of Alistair, opened the gate and sprinted through. Rounding the side of the manager's house, he saw a Series One Land Rover, faded light green and without roof doors or windscreen. It coughed into life on the first turn of the key. It may have been over fifty years old, but it had been well maintained.

"Taboga, help woman the Moggy with Paloma. I'm going on a mission." Before she could say anything, he flew through the gate in the little car. The first Land Rovers were British versions of the famous Willys Jeep, exactly what Alistair needed.

He disappeared in a cloud of dust just as Taboga climbed into the Unimog.

"I hope Alistair ate something. You know what he's like when he's hungry," she said as she climbed in.

They were joking about him, but it was to cover the fear that they had. They knew he was about to put his head into the lion's mouth.

Alistair drove down the track like the rally driver he was, neatly reading the holes and ruts and placing the car so it took the corners perfectly. He approached the car park behind the Ark flat out. Surprise was essential. The car park was well above the water hole where the animals were. A five-meter wall stopped the animals from mixing with the humans, but he was headed towards the deep ramp and solid gate that allowed maintenance crews access. Problem was, there were so many cars that the ramp was blocked. Alistair had no choice.

"Sorry, Tanga," he shouted as he drove straight across the beautifully manicured flower beds to reach the access ramp.

Hitting the gate flat out, the tough little car punched through it like a charging rhino.

He slid the car sideways across the muddy salt licks, sending animals scattering everywhere.

The men in the bunker suddenly realized what was happening and opened fire at the wild, sliding Land Rover, sending showers of mud over Alistair.

They understood his plan too late to stop him. He drove right along the front of the bunker. The Series One, without a roof, doors or windscreen, was below the slits and the men inside couldn't get their weapons to fire low enough. As he drove, he posted grenades through the openings. Panicked howls and three men erupted from the back door of the bunker just as the grenades went off in a triumphant salute of explosions. Flashes of light burst from the slits, followed by deeper booms as the RPG rounds went off. The men that had got out collapsed at once, victims of Tatiana's deadly aim.

Alistair stopped the brave little car in front of the bunker and stood on the seat to check through the opening, the torch on his weapon cutting a bright hole through the smoke-filled room. The barely recognizable forms of three men were plastered against the walls.

"All clear inside."

He walked around to the doorway, pushing the weapons away from the figures sprawled on the ground. Each one had a black hole in their forehead.

"Nice shooting there, Vodka 2. They are all dead."

He heard a vehicle starting in the car park.

47

Goldilocks

"Incoming vehicle." Using her helmet, Paloma swiveled the mini-gun to the pair of headlights bouncing towards them.

"They must have hot-wired a car—we got all the keys."

The vehicle stopped 800 meters away. Paloma could have hit it, but at 6000 rounds per minute, several of the bullets would continue on to the lodge. She wasn't sure where Alistair was.

"They can't see us up here. Why did they stop?"

They soon found out. Four poachers moved forward, tactically keeping to the shadows. Each one had a machine pistol mounted and ready to use. The Unimog was tucked deep into the darkness near the gate.

"We have four armed men approaching the gate." Taboga was updating her crew.

One poacher gave a command and all four simultaneously lifted their weapons and blasted the flood lights to pieces. The noise of the gunfire reverberated off the valley, followed by the patter of glass on the road.

"Huh, guess they don't know we have night sights," Taboga whispered.

"They don't even know we exist—but they will soon."

With that, Paloma, who never played video games but could land a helicopter on a moving ship, opened fire using her helmet.

She fired four short bursts, each one like a hammer drill making holes in concrete. The men's legs simply disappeared from under them, as if they had stepped into a manhole without a cover.

Four of Taboga's team ran out from the partially opened gate, kicked the guns away from the moaning men, grabbed them by their collars and dragged them through the gate, leaving four streaks of blood in the road. Boots remained behind.

"Wow," was all Taboga could say.

"Four in the bag. Guess they won't be running away." Paloma looked at the screens.

The empty ground in front of The Ark had eight writhing figures on it. Two were trying to drag themselves back to the building. There was no other movement.

"We need to get back there before Goldilocks wakes up."

Alistair clicked his mike.

"OK everyone, let's make our collection."

Almost immediately, the main gate by the cottage opened and an army ambulance drove through, followed by another. Taboga's team were driving, everyone was wearing gas masks. The gate shut behind them.

Paloma and Tatiana followed in the Unimog.

Alistair, Paloma, and Tatiana ran upstairs wearing gas masks, carefully securing each unconscious body they came across. They zip-tied hands and feet, searched for weapons and photographed each one.

The combat medic and two of Taboga's team tended to the wounded while the rest worked behind the three Extinct Commandos, loading the unconscious figures unceremoniously onto baggage trolleys and putting them in the back of a pickup. Nobody was being too gentle with the unconscious poachers as they pushed them into the animal cages by the manager's cottage. The blasts of the bunker and Tatiana's shots had killed six poachers.

There were ten more with serious leg injuries from the mini-gun and from the snipers, who were loaded into the ambulances and taken to the operating theatre that they had set up in the cottage.

"How are your men, Sergeant?" Alistair had heard the RPG hit the hide the men were in.

"They have sustained multiple shrapnel wounds. Both have temporarily lost their hearing from the blast, and one has broken a leg on landing. They look a mess, but they will survive. They are tough men."

By the time the sun was rising, the men in the animal cages were waking up, seething with anger at having been tricked, but also afraid. Afraid of what Poppy might do if she found out they had deceived her.

They kept each man in careful isolation. The team gave the poachers water and bread and kept their faces covered when dealing with them. They gave the poachers water and bread.

"I borrowed a bus as requested. It belongs to my cousin. He is driving. I trust him." Francis nodded his head at the approaching coach, which was painted in the colors of the Kenyan flag, red, black, and green. The windows were covered with thick curtains.

"Excellent, let's put the hoods on the prisoners and get them on the bus. Taboga can four of your crew can drive the ambulances and then get the Atlas ready to fly to Turkana? We will go in convey with the bus. Francis, please can your men stand guard on the bus?"

"Sure Alistair, I am very happy to be back in action with my team."

"Well, I am afraid you have quite a lot of damage to repair at The Ark, but these poachers will pay you well for that, if you know what I mean. And don't forget each one of these guys has a price on their head, so you and your team should be well looked after."

"Thank you, we didn't do it for the reward, but my share will help pay for the education of my children."

The prisoners were shuffling onto the bus and being cuffed onto their seats.

"Francis, do you know a good Land Rover mechanic?" Alistair walked him over to the Series One, which was dripping water from its broken radiator. Both headlights were gone and the front wings were completely squashed.

"That I do. My father, he is retired and he needs a project. He was the chief mechanic for the British army back in the colonial days. They had hundreds of these puppies. What he doesn't know about Land Rovers isn't worth knowing."

"Brilliant, please tell Tanga that I will return to talk to her, but we will sort everything out."

"OK, let's move out."

The odd convey of a large bus, two ambulances, the Unimog and—for the bodies of the dead men —a refrigerated pickup, set off for the airport in Nanyuki. The prisoners would be loaded onto the Atlas and flown to Turkana where Misha and Stan were waiting to interrogate them.

They had created a prison by stacking refrigerated containers inside the damaged factory

and had renovated several of the staff houses and the clubhouse with its pool.

Stan and Misha both said it reminded them of the old soviet bases in Afghanistan, just a lot hotter.

Once the interrogations were complete, they would inform INTERPOL of the location and leave the prisoners, each with carefully documented evidence for trial. Once the prisoners had gone, The Extinct Company would maintain the facility for future operations.

Next, they had to deal with the GPS blocking system: 'The Mengbi Weapon'.

48

Border Patrol

From the air, the contrast between the Mexican side of the border and the US side felt like someone had taken a jug full of tiny houses, scattered them on the ground and then pushed a ruler up against them.

The US side was a flat, undulating desert where the only sign of life was the white numbered roofs of the border patrol vehicles. The Mexican side was a hive of activity.

The DEA helicopter plotted its course down the steel fence that divided the two nations.

The officers inside had got a tip-off that there would be a big drugs shipment coming over the fence tonight and they wanted to see if they could identify potential places where it would happen before darkness fell. They had been flying for nearly an hour.

Sánchez, the DEA officer sitting next to the pilot, pointed to a pair of tracks leading straight up to the fence, which then appeared to continue on the US side.

Steve marked it with his GPS, and then they traced it back until it hit I90.

"This looks promising. They have a mile to go before they get back on the road." They knew once a truck got onto the highway, they would lose it in the general traffic of the road. Alone in the desert, it would be easy to spot.

This was Officer Steve Williams' first flight to this part of Texas. Most of his work was hovering over buildings and traffic, in and around Dallas.

"DEA Base, this is Oscar Tango Five Five. We have identified what looks like a potential location where they might move the merchandise through the fence. Officer Sánchez will send you the coordinates now."

They would set up an ambush as soon as darkness fell.

"OK, returning to base."

"Roger that."

"Oscar Tango Five, Five, this is air traffic control. I have what looks like a small plane circling you at around 7000 feet. Please confirm if you can see it."

"Negative, air traffic control. We are at 1000 feet, and we cannot see anything above us."

"That's strange, wonder what it is?" Steve scanned the sky above him as he talked on the internal intercom with Sánchez.

"Probably just a joy rider?" She was also scanning the sky.

Landing at the local airport where the DEA had a tiny office, Sánchez and Williams went into the small town and stopped in at a local diner while the ground crew refueled their helicopter.

Sánchez had a salad and Williams ordered a chili. "No-Moy-Pick-Kante," he said with a Texas accent to the Mexican-looking server. Sánchez rolled her eyes. "'Muy Picante' you don't need to make it four words."

Maria Sánchez was his senior officer. They had been working together for nearly four months now, and he still had almost no idea about her. She used an English vocabulary far more sophisticated than his own and often had him completely lost—she seemed to have a sixth sense about how drugs were moved across the border but most of all she looked so beautiful in her flight suit that he desperately wanted to touch her face and pull down the zip that sat temptingly on her chest.

Instead, he laughed and looked longingly at the four beers on the table next to theirs. The beads of water running down the glass and making small tracks on the plastic floor tiles.

Officer Sánchez read his mind, "I'll buy you six cold ones when we get back, if we nail these guys."

He smiled and shook the sad cubes of ice in his plastic 24-ounce cup full of flat Coca-Cola.

"I wonder what was flying above us at 7000 feet, seems strange to me."

"Yeah, me too. I checked with air traffic when we got back, and they had no flight plans registered."

Their food arrived. Williams' tacos were so spicy they made his eyes bulge. He went red and started to sweat even in the super air-conditioned restaurant. He tried to hide it, but Sánchez had seen too many gringos taken out by a chili pepper.

"Looks like you really need those beers? I think she missed the 'no' part and just went for the picante?"

Williams slugged his flat Coke down and waved to the server for a refill, fruitlessly wafting air in his mouth as he did so.

Sánchez looked at Williams with her dark eyes. She had thick black hair and the body of a ballet dancer, which, in fact, she was and had been since the age of six.

She smiled at him. She liked Williams and trusted him, especially as a pilot. They had been involved in several pretty hairy incidents, and he had responded calmly and professionally. It was times like those when he took command and she discovered she liked it.

She knew they had both had hard childhoods.

"Listo? Let's go." She picked up the bill and laid some dollars on the table.

"Thanks, maybe I'll have a salad like you next time."

When they got to the airfield, the helicopter was fueled and ready. Williams checked the aircraft in the floodlit DEA hangar.

Sánchez disappeared into the office and came out moments later carrying an M16 assault rifle and several magazines of ammo. "You never know," she said in reply to Williams' quizzical look.

They strapped in and he started flipping switches and writing in the flight log.

"Tell you what, you teach me to speak Spanish properly and I'll teach you how to fly a helicopter. They both seem about as tough as the other?"

"All right, it's a deal. How about one hour of Spanish for one hour of piloting?"

They shook hands. Williams was feeling better. The blades of the helicopter started their slow wind up, and they put their Peltors over their ears.

The pilot requested permission to move to the runway and they set off.

"Lt. Sánchez to ground units, do you read me?"

"Affirmative."

"Are you in position?"

"Negative, our GPS units are giving us a strange reading ten clicks from the border. You must have made an error when you reported it."

They didn't want to send the coordinates over the radio. Williams rechecked it and sent it again using WhatsApp.

"That's what you sent before, it's still ten miles out from the border."

"Ground units, do you have a paper map? I want you to check the coordinates against that and see where it is."

There was a long silence. By this time, they were airborne and heading straight to the location they had picked out before.

"Boss, we have a paper map."

"And?"

There was another silence.

"And?"

"We are not sure how to use all those numbers to give us a position on the map."

The officer blurted it, like he had to get it out, but didn't want to.

"Amazing," she said to herself. "Stay where you are. Do not move."

"Something strange is going on." Williams was looking at his GPS screen.

"We just jumped over ten miles."

"Stop moving forward and land as soon as you can." Lt. Sánchez clicked her radio button.

"Control, this is Lt. Sánchez in Oscar Tango Five, Five. We are landing immediately. Our GPS has gone crazy and we need to re-establish our location."

Williams switched on the powerful searchlights under the helicopter and selected an open patch of land. He put the aircraft down neatly.

Pulling a paper map out of his flight bag, he drew a line from the airfield they had taken off from to the coordinates of the point they had marked before. He had written the coordinates down before they had left.

He then calculated their speed and flight time, including a slight head wind.

"So, we need to fly on a bearing of 177 degrees south, at a speed of 100 knots to hit our target, do you agree?" he said, showing her his calculations.

Lt. Sánchez was impressed. "Wow you really know your map reading."

"My grandfather was a bomber navigator during World War Two, and he taught me map reading when I was six. If he could find a factory in the middle of Germany at night while under heavy fire, I should be able to find a point on a fence that runs right across the state. Ready to go?"

"Roger that, let's do it."

He prepared to take off.

"Do you have any idea why the GPS has gone off? I am hearing the radio traffic and it seems to have gone down over a wide part of the state." Sánchez continued.

"No idea at all. The only thing I know is most people can't read a map, so our chance of getting backup is slim."

He reached his altitude, rotated the aircraft around until the compass on his control panel read 177 degrees, and punched a stopwatch.

"Estimated time to target ten minutes. Maybe we should be careful what we say over the radio to base?"

The helicopter dropped its nose and sped to their target.

Lt. Sánchez cocked the M16 in her lap and took a deep breath.

She'd done this before, as a Sergeant in the Rangers in Somalia.

49

On Target

"I'm going to hold 1000ft from the target so we can assess the situation." Williams flared back the blades of the machine to bring them to an aerial standstill.

Suddenly the cabin was chaos, holes stitched through the floor and up through the Plexiglass, and thick, toxic smoke poured in and half of the control panel shattered

"Mayday, Mayday, we are coming under heavy fire." Williams gave the position from his notepad, 100ft from their actual position. He looked across at Lt. Sánchez just as she slumped against her harness. Red was seeping across her flight suit like an oil slick. The M16 had dropped from her hands.

Williams fought the spinning machine and tried to pull away from the gunfire, into the dark night and hopefully to the ground safely.

He felt several more rounds pepper the outside of the helicopter.

None of the landing lights worked, they didn't even have switches anymore. The only way he could see the ground coming up towards them was because it was illuminated by the flames now bursting from the engine. It would only be seconds before the fuel tank went up.

They hit the sand hard, screaming forward like a toboggan as the machine inexorably slid sideways and, just as it was about to reach a tipping point, came to a stop.

Williams tore off his harness, flames were already filling the headliner. Kicking open his buckled door, he scrambled around the nose of the wreck to Lt. Sánchez. Pulling the quick release, the door fell away, he pressed the clasp of her straps and dragged her out. Luckily, she was light, and Williams was tall and fit. He hoisted her over his shoulder. She made no sound. He ripped the first aid kit from its Velcro mount, and grabbing the M16, he ran as fast as his load would allow him. But he only got thirty feet before the tanks exploded.

He felt the heat smash into his back. A wall of fire like dragon's breath rolled over them.

He could smell his own burnt hair. Barely able to stand, he grabbed Sánchez by putting his hand under her armpits and dragged her backwards, away from the searing heat.

His flight suit was fireproof, but he could feel the hot air coming through the ragged holes caused by the explosion.

He got them behind a rock, put the M16 where he could reach it, and then pulled out the knife that was attached to his calf.

Cutting away Sánchez's flight suit, he realized they had hit her multiple times. The blood was running between his fingers as he tried to stop it. His wet, shaking hands could not open the trauma kit. Her skin was turning gray.

She opened her eyes and smiled at him distantly. His right hand was pressing a deep hole under her left breast. He had cut her bra away to get at the wound.

"I am not sure I gave you permission." She said in a weak voice. Her eyes closed.

"Stay with me, stay, don't leave." His voice was desperate.

He realized there was the sound of something driving across the desert towards him. He knew it wasn't a border patrol vehicle.

He wanted to reach for the M16 but didn't want to let the pressure go on Maria's pumping wound.

"Don't hurt us, she's dying, help me."

He heard the vehicle door open and light footsteps come running towards him.

"Don't be afraid, we are here to help you." A strange, accented voice said from the darkness. A German shepherd ran into the light of the burning helicopter, trotted up to them and appeared to take a sentry post in front of them, ears pricked, eyes scanning the darkness beyond the helicopter. He was wearing a tactical harness.

Then a woman appeared in full combat gear, face covered, carrying a bag with a red cross on it. Strapped to her back was a strange-looking assault weapon.

"My name is Tatiana. Please hold the torch while I attend to Lt. Sánchez."

She quickly and efficiently set to work. "Are you injured, Sgt. Williams?"

His hand was shaking, he was feeling pain in his back. He heard the silent vehicle moving away. "I might be injured in my back."

A minute later, he heard a long burst of very rapid fire, the high-pitched whine of a mini gun.

"Who are you people?"

Jeeves made a noise and looked at Tatiana.

"One moment, please."

Flipping down her night googles, she swung the assault rifle off her back, took aim and squeezed the trigger. The sound the weapon made was no louder than the click of a ball-point pen.

In the distance, there was a cry in the dark and then silence.

"Good boy, Jeeves." His tail wagged and he went back to his duty.

Tatiana went back to work on Lt. Sánchez, finally giving her an injection of morphine and attaching a drip, which she handed to Sgt.

Williams to hold up.

"We don't exist, but we are here to help you. Lt. Sánchez is stabilized. She will survive," she said it in a matter-of-fact way, without emotion.

"Turn around, please let me look at your back."

He obeyed. There were several small bits of metal sticking out of the hard muscles on his back.

"You have shrapnel in your back. I am going to remove the biggest bits so we can transport you to hospital. Sergeant Williams. This will hurt." Setting to work, she added, "You are a brave man."

"He is. He saved my life." Lt. Sánchez had regained consciousness. "Who are you?"

A large, silent shape drove up close to them. It was the Unimog. Two more masked and armed people got out. They were carrying two stretchers.

"Right, I think that is the end of their drug smuggling days," one said with a British accent.

"How are the patients?"

"They will survive but we need to get them to hospital immediately."

They loaded their patients onto the stretchers and carried them to the Unimog.

Forty minutes later, bemused ER staff at the town hospital were wheeling them into the open doors as the silent Unimog drove off into the darkness.

50

Oysters and Peacocks

Alistair, Tatiana, Paloma, and Jeeves drove inside an abandoned hangar just twenty kilometers away from the Mexican border on the US side. Inside, they found three white offices the size of twenty-foot containers sitting on oversized trailers. Short, covered walkways connected each container. They went up some stairs and through a narrow door. In contrast with the austere exterior, inside looked like Kennedy space station. This was an INTERPOL temporary office. Men and women sat in rows behind screens. A digital map spanned the wall, highlighting the border between Texas and Mexico.

Misha and Stan stood up as they walked in. Dawn was just cracking over the horizon and they looked tired.

The Earl was in Europe, and he liked to keep a low profile even inside INTERPOL. Misha kept him updated.

"They will survive, but it was close. The drug dealers were tracking the helicopter and all the patrol vehicles. We heard on the police radio snipers killed two patrol men. They had a map and compass in their vehicle and they were close to the site."

"Thanks Alistair. You guys probably saved the lives of Williams and

Sánchez by good map reading and fast driving, but I doubt if we will be so lucky next time." Misha was looking at the news on a TV screen, which was showing a large truck riddled with holes. Several bodies were strewn around it.

"Nice shooting."

The banner under the images read, 'Drug Gang rivalry creates war at US border. $20 million worth of drugs are blowing in the wind.'

The image closed in on the back of the truck, which was piled high with plastic bags strapped in duct tape. The bags looked like they'd been attacked by a hundred machetes. Sunlight steamed through the thousands of holes in the truck's bodywork as the wind was swirling around, making white dust devils. Men in hazmat suits were fruitlessly attempting to shove the ragged bags into new ones, but every time they picked one up, it fell apart, causing a new avalanche.

People were lining the fence on the Mexican side, trying to breathe in the billowing dust. Gas masked Police were beating them back with truncheons.

"From our interviews with the gentlemen in Kenya, it looks like Poppy is simply renting out her system by the month. This is the third time in two weeks that the border police have reported their GPS systems going down and then their own agents being tracked. Our intel says Poppy will soon be operating in the US-Mexican border area." Misha put an image of a drone on the screen. "They also told us she is using this drone. It is a Luna X 2000, developed by the Germans. It is small, only 4-meter wingspan. It has a ceiling of 3,500 meters or 11,500ft, a range of 100 kilometers and flight time of six to eight hours. This drone costs only around $310,000." Misha moved over to the large map. There was a red dot blinking at the location where they had destroyed the truck. "Which means they must have launched it and now recovered it. GPS is now working again in the area." She clicked her mouse and a big circle appeared around the dot. "We assume that this is the center. We know from our Turkana prisoners that Poppy has built a mobile launch and recovery unit using 20ft shipping containers. The people in Turkana only knew about this one operation. The next one will be even more of a surprise. Unfortunately, that doesn't really narrow our options very much. Stan, would you like to give us an update on your anti-blocking, blocking device?"

"Yes, Misha. So, folks, we have developed a system that would not only counter the GPS blocking and tracking devices of The Mengbi Weapon, but it would also give us an exact location of the drone. Which would allow us to follow it back to the launch unit and destroy the lot—but it only works if you are 'under' the drone. That is, if you are actively being blocked by the drone. We will fit the system to the Unimog today, but unless we can find where their next operation will be and when it will be, we won't be able to do a thing. Any ideas?"

"Do we know what Dragon Poppy looks like yet... since we poached half her face off?" Paloma asked in an innocent voice.

"We don't. The prisoners in Turkana said they now only communicate with her remotely. One of the cell phones we found on them had a voice recording from her."

"Stan and I spent hours trying to come up with a location based on background noise. Sadly, there was no Big Ben chiming in the background to give us an obvious clue."

"Even if we find her, we doubt she will be with the drone launching unit. What are you thinking, Paloma?"

"I think I am right in saying if we got her phone, we could locate anyone calling her. That would give us locations, right?"

"Right, but difficult. Find Poppy, steal her phone and wait until someone calls?"

Tatiana spoke, "If we can clone her phone, that would do it."

"Agreed. So, we have two leads: Find Poppy and find the drone launching team."

All the staff were listening now.

"Right, Team A, you guys see if you can see any trucks with a twenty-foot container on the back within this area. She showed the wide circle on the map. Last time the containers were jade green with a yellow stripe but may not be now."

"Team B, let us take any communications with Poppy and try to ID a location based on sounds. Start by seeing if you can hear any birds, at least that may give us a continent."

"Tatiana, Paloma and Alistair, let's work together to install Stan's system into the Unimog."

After two hours of working on the Unimog, they were having a break, sitting down with a cup of tea.

Tatiana was explaining the Russians were great tea drinkers too, when one technician from team B came running out. She was a diligent looking girl, dressed in a tee shirt, jeans and spotless combat boots. "Sorry to interrupt your tea. We've isolated some sounds, and we have got two distinct bird calls, but they are confusing us. Please, can you come and listen? My name is Cherry."

Getting up, they trooped back into the offices and grabbed noise canceling headphones which connected to the computer the girl was working on.

Cherry pressed play and a distant, melancholy 'peep peep' made Alistair and Paloma smile. "Oystercatcher. Listen, you can also hear the sea. It's a coastal bird."

"Yeah, we used to have a joke about the oysters making a run for it and the Oystercatchers chasing after them."

Cherry played the second sound that was more like a sad, trapped cat.

"Peacock," Alistair and Paloma both said at once.

"They are on many of those in the larger, old estates in UK. They were considered an exotic thing to have strutting about your lawn."

"Yeah, we had them at home in Scotland. Alistair had me convinced for years that they had small, round, green penises."

Cherry looked confused.

"Pea-cock?" Paloma enlightened her.

Tatiana was chuckling and looking at Cherry, who was supposed to be an investigator for INTERPOL.

"Cherry, let me listen to some more sounds without the birds from the same call please." Paloma's expression had darkened.

She played the sound again after removing Poppy's voice.

"Alistair listen, tell me I am not going crazy. Listen to the sounds of the waves on the rocks. Shut your eyes." Alistair did as Paloma asked.

"It can't be Paloma. Can it?"

Misha, Tatiana, Cherry, and Stan looked bemused.

"Would you mind explaining, you are communicating without communicating and the rest of us can't understand." Tatiana was looking at the brother and sister.

"What Paloma thinks she can hear is the sound the waves are making when they hit the rocks at our family home, Wynards Estate, in Scotland. The main house is right by the sea. There is a big hole in one rock. We called it Mr. Rocking Hole because at certain tides it made a distinct sound that was a bit like our dad's music."

"Alistair, that IS Mr. Rocking Hole, and those are our peacocks and oystercatchers."

"Cherry please can you isolate that whomp, whomp sound and make it clearer?"

"Sure Alistair, just give me a minute please," she replied in a slightly dreamy voice.

Paloma winked at Alistair and nudged him—she'd seen the effect he had on girls before. He bared his teeth at Paloma.

"How and why would Poppy go to your estate in Scotland?" Misha asked.

"Don't forget, Poppy's mother was a Highland girl, so Scotland is also her home. Plus, we rent Wynards out. We didn't want to sell it, but we felt it was a waste of resources to just let it sit there empty. It is very remote with a very fast internet connection, so it is easy to disappear there..... and...." Alistair looked at Paloma.

"And maybe it's some bizarre revenge plan... I clipped off her finger and got her expelled from school and then we boiled her face off."

"Yeah, but Paloma, what could she actually do apart from blow it up?"

"Exactly. Wouldn't put that past her, would you?"

"No. Oh Bloody hell." Alistair looked mortified.

"OK Alistair, I am ready." Cherry looked at Alistair and smiled.

"Thanks."

She played the sound.

Both Alistair and Paloma pulled off their headphones.

"I can't believe it. The filthy Dragon is in our house. Let's call James and tell him to blast her face off with a shotgun."

"Paloma, calm down, you've spent all this time telling me to control my feelings about her and now you're practically foaming at the mouth. We need to clone her phone to find the next drone jamming location, and James can help us do it. "

"James is the Gillie and Estate manager." Alistair explained.

"Alistair, James is brilliant with a rifle, or a boat, but he can't tell one end of a phone from another. How about his son, young Edward?"

"Aye, you are right. Young Edward is not so young anymore, and he is a computer programmer. He still lives in the cottage with his dad, I think."

"Brilliant, let's ring him up."

"It's midnight in Scotland right now."

"That's OK, remember we used to see Young Edward going off to watch the waves almost every night, I'll bet he's still up."

51

Wildlife Photography

Paloma was right, Edward was up. It was lovely to hear his soft Scots accent. She and Alistair explained they were looking for a woman. They could describe her body (which Alistair did in more detail than Paloma said was necessary) but not her face.

Edward, who had spent most of his life taking photographs of waves, admitted that he was excited he now had something a little more interesting to photograph than seals swimming in the waves in the morning.

Years ago, they had helped Edward build a hide into the cliffs above the hidden beach of Wynards Estate. They had built it so he could reach it without disturbing the wildlife when traveling from the cottage where he and his dad lived.

Edward had used his not insubstantial income from software design to buy the best and biggest lenses for his digital camera and he often sent Alistair and Paloma beautiful photographs of the wildlife in the bay near their home.

He now sent them several pictures of Poppy swimming in the same bay. Her body was lithe and beautiful as ever, her face was now much more European, and she was blonde.

"Dragon lady has become Barbie Doll. Edward, please, can you zoom in on her right hand in that picture?"

Confused, he did as asked. The top of her middle finger was missing.

"Got you, you little vixen."

"Beg your pardon, Paloma?"

"Sorry Edward, I'll explain later."

They told him they needed to get hold of Poppy's phone to clone it.

He showed them a picture of her talking on her phone just before she went for a swim. He told them she always kept it with her towel in a waterproof bag on the beach and she always put the bag on the same rock.

"I had better show you some other pictures I took."

One zoomed back from Poppy swimming in the sea. It showed an armed guard patrolling the beach as she swam. Another showed a boat patrolling just offshore from the house. They could see men with automatic weapons in the stern.

"They banned us from the house. We can't even cut the lawn."

"Edward, you had better not take any more pictures. These people are ruthless and very dangerous. And tell your dad to steer clear. Do nothing else. We are on our way."

They said their goodbyes and cut the connection.

"So, what's the plan? Alistair gets a big horse and gallops across the beach while Poppy's swimming. Meanwhile Tatiana sneaks down while Poppy is staring at Alistair and clones the phone?"

"Thank you, Paloma. No wonder I always beat you at chess." Alistair rolled his eyes.

"Actually, the principle of Paloma's idea is good." They could hear the gears in Misha's head turning.

"But we don't need the actual horse."

Everyone was looking at Misha, waiting for the next part. She looked up and smiled.

"The Trojan Horse. Have you noticed how from the photos Poppy often goes for a walk and she collects interesting things along the beach, putting them into the bag?" Misha put up a couple of pictures of Poppy collecting.

"Next to her phone. Misha, you are brilliant." Stan was looking proudly at Misha.

"Yes, they told me that when I was a small girl."

"Sorry for us Luddites, perhaps you could explain?" Alistair was looking perplexed.

Stan obliged, "To clone a phone you just need to put the cloning device next to or very close it. Misha is proposing we make the cloning device into something she would collect on the beach."

"Then how do we retrieve the information?" Alistair asked again. They were all fascinated.

"So, we can program it to send as a burst as soon as it has downloaded all the data." Stan was looking excited. He loved projects like this.

"And then it wipes its own hard drive clean, leaving no trace of the clone. Even if she discovered the device inside, she would think it was damaged."

"Cool, thank god Edward has been having so much fun with the wildlife on the beach. Let's see what sort of things she picks up. He kindly shared 37 gigabytes of photos of her."

They quickly set to work, methodically listing every object she collected. After an hour, they had a complete list.

Tatiana put an excel sheet on the screen. Paloma toggled through the zoomed-in pictures of the things Poppy had collected. Because she was always wearing her bikini when she collected, there was often a part of her body included in the picture.

"Number one at 57% is small plastic toys."

Paloma rolled through the images, the head of a doll, a soldier, several wild animals, a unicorn, a horse, a dog, and a girl in a bikini.

"She has a very good body," Tatiana said, in a slightly admiring tone.

Alistair wasn't sure if she was referring to the doll she was she holding or Poppy. He had not forgotten Poppy's body against his skin.

"15% bits of rope."

"2% colored stones."

"Wow, no shells, she must be the only person in the world who doesn't pick up shells from the beach." Cherry was sitting next to her computer, listening.

"That is because she is actually a dragon. Dragons have no interest in shells. You can't melt shells with your breath."

Misha laughed and rubbed Paloma's back. "Let's do a horse, a model of the one they brought into Troy. She won't be able to resist. We'll leave it by the rock where she puts her bag. You can wait in Edward's hide and suck the data from there. Cherry, do you have a 3D printer?"

"Yes, Mam, we sure do."

"Great, let's get to work."

"Cherry, I need you to go to Walmart for us. You know those little rock tumbling machines, they turn rough rocks into smooth ones. We need one to age our horse, so it looks like it's been rolling around the seabed."

"No need to buy one ma'am, I have one at home, I make my own jewelry. I can show you my collection. Oh yeas, those machines are great. I love hearing the rocks rolling at night. It's so exciting when you open it up."

"That would be lovely Cherry. Just tell your boss you are on a mission."

Cherry almost knocked her chair over in excitement and rushed out the door.

By next morning, they had created a very convincing toy Trojan horse. It was light brown plastic but looked as though it had been made from lots of miniature planks of wood and had a base with holes where the wheels would have gone.

Sealed inside, Misha and Stan had built a mini phone cloning device that could be activated remotely using a UK phone sim card, which Paloma had from a spare burner phone still in its packaging.

They tested it. Cherry had bravely offered her phone to be cloned. When they got the data, she showed them her collection of photos of her two cats, Mr. Spots and Bagpuss.

"Better stop there. We don't want to use all the data downloading pictures of cats. Paloma only has fifty quid of data."

They squeezed the horse into Cherry's rock tumbler with a handful of stones and set it off.

52

The Trojan Horse

Contrary to Paloma's objections, they decided that Alistair would go to Wynards Estate on the Isle of Mull to place the Trojan horse and retrieve the data.

He would play the role of 'Jolly English Twitcher'. Twitcher being the slightly derogatory name given to earnest birdwatchers in Britain. He would wear a disguise so Poppy's men or the locals didn't recognize him.

Paloma had fun kitting him out in an anorak, tweed hat, rucksack covered in bird badges, stout boots, bushy beard, and glasses.

This had to happen fast. They were worried as they did not know where or when the next operation blocking GPS would take place. If Poppy had been paid to deploy the Mengbi Weapon to hit an airport, it would be disastrous, but they also knew all the wildlife with Askari trackers were now at risk.

Alistair got on the next plane out of Dallas that took him to Glasgow, and from there was met in an unmarked car with a silent driver sent by The Earl. They whisked him off to Oban, where he could take the ferry to Mull.

Sitting on the upper deck of the ferry, alone, apart from the wheeling gulls, he enjoyed the sea air, but he also missed his father.

His dad had taught him how to survive in the jungle, be a crack shot, and rebuild an engine, but he had never mentioned girls. He knew that when their mother died, it broke his dad's heart and something in him understood he was trying to protect Alistair by not inflicting him with advice based his own experience with girls but here he was having to face Poppy once more and it frightened the daylights out of him.

"Hey, Dad, help me out here." He shouted to the wind.

Edward was waiting at the dock in his battered Land Rover Defender. In the rear, among the bits of wool, animal feed and empty shotgun cartridges, was an old bike with a couple of loaded saddle bags.

Edward laughed at Alistair's appearance.

"You had me fooled for a wee while there Alistair, but then I saw yer walking and I said to myself, there's a soldier."

Alistair made a mental note to drag his feet and slouch.

He used the bike to ride the few miles to the estate, diligently stopping to watch the oystercatchers with his Leica binoculars whenever a car came down the narrow road. In return, the birds called their mournful cry as they skimmed the rocky shore.

The road was marked with red and white posts, a reminder of harsher winters when it disappeared under a blanket of snow.

As he cycled past his local pub, he heard the cheery sounds from inside and saw his mates' cars parked outside; he longed to duck down through the low doorway, join the fun and sit down with several pints of the local beer chased down with Tobermory malt whisky. Regretfully, he continued another two miles and then cautiously lifted his bike over a wool flagged barbed wire fence to the back of Edward and James' white stone cottage. A wisp of smoke curled up from the chimney, the comforting smell of burning wood filled the air like a soft blanket.

They welcomed him into the warm, familiar hearth of their living room. Edward spooned out a big bowl of rabbit stew, laid out three doorsteps of white crunchy bread, and poured a pint of ale. Alistair cheered up immediately. The dogs, Fergus, and Angus, settled around his ankles.

They talked of deer, sheep, otters, family, and the weather before they reached the task at hand. High tide was at midnight. As dawn struck at 4am, Alistair would place the Trojan horse next to the rock where Poppy put her bag each day, as if the tide had left her a precious gift.

He would wait in Edward's hide overlooking the beach. Edward was forbidden to join him. Alistair feared that if things went wrong and Edward or his father were in any way associated with Alistair, Poppy and her gang would not hesitate to kill both of them.

To back up the ruse, Alistair set up his tent in the walled orchard behind the cottage. After a whisky and piece of chocolate, he retired to his sleeping bag and fell asleep instantly.

At 3.45am the thinnest veil of light warmed the dark sky as Alistair unzipped the front of his tent and looked out. Warily, he pulled himself out of his warm sleeping bag and pulled on his boots. He'd dressed in dark clothes before going to sleep.

Edward had set out a flask of coffee with a shot of whisky. Warming his hands on the mug, he smiled at the thick dew that decorated the spiderwebs that crisscrossed the grass in the orchard.

Pulling on his small pack, he headed off down the well-worn path that led to Edward's hide overlooking the beach. He knew the path well and, even in the semidarkness, nimbly traversed between the tussocks of sheep cropped grass. Rabbits delicately hopped out of his way. He knew that Edward, an expert hunter of rabbits, considered these his pets and they were almost unafraid of humans.

Edward, Alistair, and Paloma had made the hide from moss-covered stones gathered from the ruined castle that had once commanded the bay. On the roof they had laid thick sod and moss, and over the years it had become part of the landscape, invisible to all but a few.

Alistair ducked under the heavy lintel, pulling aside the 'door' made of burlap, and stepped into the soft sand that they had carted up from the beach to make it quiet.

Inside smelled of damp earth, old wood, and salt air. There was a comfortable bench piled with old sacks for cushioning. There was a deep slit along one wall, deep enough so that the light never came in to flash against the mighty telephoto lenses that Edward used.

The three of them had spent many peaceful hours here as children, with Edward talking about each of the birds and animals they could watch.

Alistair knew Edward was deeply in love with Paloma, who was several years older than him. But she had always been in love with the animals they had watched together and only ever saw Edward as her brilliant wildlife guide.

The moon had long set, and the rock Alistair needed to reach was still deep in the shadow of the softly appearing dawn light. Pulling the now well-worn Trojan horse from his pack, he scanned the bay for guards. He could smell the telltale scent of cheap cigarettes and finally spotted a guard leaning nonchalantly against the walled vegetable garden five hundred meters away, the warmest place before dawn. Even the sea winds never rustle the roses there.

Backtracking along the path, he scuttled down a narrow chute that led to the beach.

The beach at the top comprised small, wet pebbles which left no footprints but crunched underfoot. Alistair timed his steps with the placid curl of the sea as it ran its rolling tube along the beach.

Reaching Poppy's 'bag rock' he rolled the little horse in a little sand and draped it in a bit of briny seaweed and then dropped it on the ground before retreating up the chute, onto the path and into the cozy hide.

He knew he had about three hours to wait before the sun warmed the bay and Poppy came for her morning swim. Lying down on the burlap, he slipped into a comfortable sleep.

53

The Pull of the Tide

Long ago Alistair's father had taught him how to set his body clock so that he could wake up without an alarm. Alistair put that skill into action.

Glorious sunshine was hitting the outer rocks in the bay. It was going to be one of those scorching summer days where sheep sought the deep shady spots, and work stopped while everyone picnicked on the beaches and rivers.

At 7.30am sharp, Poppy's confident figure appeared, heading down the path to the little bay.

Alistair tracked her with his binos. Walking ten paces behind her was a muscular man with fine features and a fit and agile stride.

As she got closer, Alistair studied her new face. The original had been the perfect blend of her highland mother and her sophisticated Asian father. Paloma was right, this was more like a cartoon Barbie doll, with overly wide eyes, lips like two inner tubes, and a nose that looked like someone had stolen it from Madame Tussauds, the wax museum. Plus, it was still blotchy from the operations.

But her body was still perfect, and Alistair could almost smell her skin.

Poppy put her bag on the rock and, almost immediately, the Trojan horse caught her attention. She squealed with delight so that even in his hide, he could hear her and felt slightly guilty for tricking her. She lifted it to the sun like it was a precious jewel.

Alistair's heart, that had healed with a thick scar from his last encounter with her, softened a fraction. Here was a woman who could buy almost anything she desired, was clearly delighted with a plastic Trojan horse she found on the beach. Alistair saw a side of her he'd never glimpsed.

Instead of putting the horse in the bag, she rinsed it off and put it on a rock by itself.

There was no way he could clone the phone. It was a good five meters from her bag.

Poppy threw off her towel and marched with a light step into the freezing water. Performing a perfect dive she powered out of the bay in a graceful crawl.

Alistair was feeling decidedly discombobulated. Poppy was having a dramatic effect on him. The last time he had seen her, she was pointing an AK 47 at him, laughing as she pulled the trigger.

After fifteen minutes, he spotted the small wake and lithe arms driving their way back to the bay. She touched the beach with her feet and walked towards her bag, water dripping off body as she went.

She called her guard over and spoke to him for a few seconds. He turned around and walked briskly away without looking back.

The beach was completely private. The only official access was through a gate which could be reached via a long, grassy path that connected to the back door of the house.

Alistair felt like he was alone with Poppy.

Watching her carefully through his Leica binoculars, he willed her to pick up the plastic horse and put in her bag. What she did was not what he expected.

Poppy laid her towel on the beach just where the sun had cast a line, and took off her bikini.

Then she did yoga.

Alistair's month went dry, his heart was racing.

The world around Poppy seemed to disappear in a vortex as he focused on her perfect body. Her skin was tight from her swim and her nipples hard from the cold water.

A noise outside the hide snapped him out of his trance and, spinning around, he stood up. His hand went to his Sgian Dubh dagger as an arm swept the sacking door aside.

The guard from the beach appeared, a look of surprise and guilt on his face.

Alistair acted on instinct, his adrenaline already on high octane. He lunged forward and drove his knife with all the force of a right jab straight at the man's neck.

The weapon sunk into flesh all the way to his hand, but the man had flinched, so the knife missed his jugular and throat. He staggered, one hand instinctively trying to stem the blood now flowing from the wound.

Alistair stepped back, balancing on his toes, looking for the next target on the man's body.

The guard moved his hand towards his back. Alistair had seen the fat Glock tucked into his belt there when he walked off the beach. Grabbing the moving hand at the wrist with his left hand, he punched the knife into the man's abdomen, again and again. Finally, the guard's legs started to go. Grabbing the sinking man's chin, Alistair drew his knife across the exposed throat, covering them both in warm blood.

The guard's eyes showed no expression as he collapsed on the sand floor, giving a final, palsy twitch before his last breath escaped.

"Bugger," Alistair said, looking at the bloody mess on the floor before glancing out to glimpse Poppy, who was facing out to sea, completing a 'downward facing dog' before finally stopping her routine and stretching.

He knew it would be minutes before they discovered the guard was missing and started looking for him. If they found the body, Poppy would probably not use her phone and it would waste the operation.

Poppy put her bikini back on. Her body was glowing. Leaning down, she picked up the Trojan horse and put it in the bag with her phone.

Hands shaking, Alistair pulled a device out of his pack and hit some buttons.

Cloning was underway.

By the time she had washed her feet in the cold water, put on her sandals and started walking back up the path to the house, he had cloned the phone. She walked close to him along the path. As she disappeared around the corner, he could smell her perfume reaching him in an invisible, exquisite cloud of femininity.

Trying to concentrate, he connected with the Ops room in Texas and uploaded all the cloned data.

They confirmed receipt with a "Well Done."

Alistair looked at the guard on the floor. He needed to move him fast, but he was too big to carry single handedly. He rifled through the man's pockets, kept the wallet he found, but smashed the phone he found in the man's belt holster between two rocks.

Running back to the cottage, he shocked James and Edward with his bloody appearance.

"You know those carts we used to move the stag carcasses from the field after we shoot them, I need one quick."

"Did you kill a stag Alistair, it's out of season, could be trouble?"

"Actually, Chinese poachers are in season at the moment, and I need to get rid of one. You chaps stay here. I can deal with it."

"No way young Alistair, Edward, you stay here."

"But Dad..." His voice trailed off; he knew the tone.

"Edward. Get the Landy ready, hitch up the trailer with the wee boat, chains, and sea fishing gear. Put the blue plastic tarp in the boat. It's a lovely day for a picnic, so don't forget pies and beer."

"Come on Alistair, the game cart is round the side of the house."

When they reached the hide, James didn't flinch at the sight of the body. Quickly grabbing the sacking from the bench, he wrapped the corpse tightly and tied it with string from his pocket. They lifted the body onto the game cart and spread sand over the blood.

"Laddie, I've been dealing with poachers long before you were even born." He said to Alistair without being asked why he was so composed.

Hurrying down the narrow path back to the cottage, they heard the familiar sound of a Land Rover backing up.

The three of them rolled the dead man in the tarp in the back of the boat, using bungy cords to secure him.

Then they hosed Alistair down.

"Ready, where shall we go 'fishing'?" James asked as he put the hose away.

"Let's go to Lochbuie, Laggan sands, there's a place to launch a boat by Moy castle."

"Great idea. We used to take you and Paloma there all the time, haven't been there for years, and it's really a deep bay."

"Good. While we drive, I'll tell you some wonderful stories about the castle."

"Aye, I can feel the pull of the tide already." James said laconically.

54

Feeding Lochbuie

Poppy made several calls as soon as she returned to the house. As the team listened in, there was a rising sense of alarm.

The first surprise was that the Askari System that had been rolled out in Kenya and was now being used to monitor elephants and rhinos across the continent was provided by a company previously owned by Henry Cheng, now by Poppy. Routed through a Panama shell company, Misha had quickly untangled the web.

This meant that governments were paying her for the Askari System, which was marketed as the ultimate answer to protecting the animals. Poppy could then use the same system to track and hunt the animals using her drones.

80% of the elephants in East and Southern Africa had already had the GPS devices installed in their horns or tusks.

"It's a simple question of supply and demand," she had said to a senior official in the Tanzanian government who was clearly on her payroll.

"I intend to reduce the supply until there is nothing left, until they are extinct, and then can you imagine how much people would pay for my stockpile of elephant and rhino tusks. And the ban on the sale will be lifted because there will be nothing left to poach. You and your people, Samuel, will become wealthy beyond your dreams."

A senior US army officer came to see Stan at the mobile Texas offices to inform him that this was now a major priority project, and the military would put their entire weight behind it. They understood the danger to National Security. Stan would stay and help the border patrol equip as many of their vehicles as they could.

While the team from the Extinct Company understood this was vital, they also knew it wouldn't trickle down to the countries in Africa until it was too late. Poppy was planning an operation now and the elephants and rhino were literally standing in the crosshairs of the poachers' guns.

They quietly packed their equipment and slipped out the back door. Only Cherry noticed them going.

Within minutes, the Grey A300 airbus taxied down the runway from where it had been parked inside a hangar and a shabby-looking Unimog truck drove out to meet it.

It was 3000 kilometers back to Panama. They needed to get back to their own Ops center.

The Unimog with Stan's system on board was strapped down by Taboga's team and within minutes, the dry desert of Texas was disappearing beneath them.

Misha had updated Alistair as he James and Edward drove the windy roads over to Lochbuie. They had decided he should stay on in Mull, but keep out of sight. They may require him to capture Poppy.

Laggan sands was as perfect as Alistair had remembered it, shaggy highland cows stood knee deep in the cool water, the battered remains of Moy castle had been renovated and a blue and white St. Andrew's flag flew proudly from one turret.

Alistair tried to imagine his ancestors meeting here, setting up the Extinct Company back in 1627.

Edward had gathered up several concrete breeze blocks and they loaded them unceremoniously on top of the tarp in the middle of the boat and then pushed it out, jumping onboard as it slipped silently into the clear water.

James pulled the toggle on the engine, and it fired immediately. As they got out of view of the shore, Alistair knelt and wrapped the chain around the ankles and neck of the guard. Then he tied it through the concrete blocks.

Five kilometers out, they cleared the headland.

"Right, let's ditch the poacher, shall we?"

James throttled back and Edward dropped the concrete blocks over side, the chains rattled after them. Finally, they rolled the body out and it disappeared into the dark water with hardly a bubble.

Alistair read out the wanted sheet from the INTERPOL database that Misha had sent him as a kind of epitaph as they headed closer to shore to do some fishing.

"Lei Keung. Born Hong Kong 1983. Arrested and sentenced to 5 years aged 16, for selling drugs and Grievous Bodily Harm. Sentenced to a further 10 years aged 18 for the murder of three prisoners and one guard. Escaped prison (aided by Cheng Gang) aged 20. Wanted for the following crimes: Illegal ivory smuggling, poaching in Kruger National Park, importing seven tons of Pangolin scales into Hong Kong. Rape and murder of eight women who he locked in an apartment, raped over several days and then set on fire. You want me to go on? It gets worse."

"No, Laddie, you and yer Sgian Dubh did the world a favor today. All those people he tortured and killed are looking down at you right now and clapping."

"Aye, and all the animals," Edward added.

Alistair pulled out his Sgian Dubh. The knife was short, the handle black. Made by a Japanese sword maker in the sixteen hundreds, it was an exquisite weapon. As a tool of The Extinct Company, it probably held the stories of the end of many a poacher. Lei Keung wouldn't be the last. He cleaned the blade with an oiled cloth.

Later that evening, when they had drunk their beer, caught their fish, and were pulling the boat up the ramp at Moy castle, Alistair swore he heard nine chairs being pushed back from a table as the occupants stood up and drank in his honor.

There was a dilemma over what to do—Poppy had already initiated what she called Askari Spear, which was to be the systematic destruction of rhinos and elephants using the very system that protected them. They knew she had assembled a team of sharpshooters to carry out the killings.

Her theory was that for every one less animal living, the price of their ivory and tusks went up. She was probably right.

They knew the first stage, Kenya and Tanzania, would start in seven days.

Arresting or killing Poppy wouldn't stop the extinction countdown.

They needed to walk the thin line of allowing her to feed them enough information for them to react to it and collapse the complete operation with no animals actually being killed.

With Poppy's naked body seared into his mind, Alistair planned an observation post over Wynards Estate. The set up reminded him of the stories he had been told of British special forces setting up OPs overlooking remote Irish farmsteads to watch for IRA operatives.

He knew that land well. He remembered games of hide and seek with Paloma and the other village children in the bracken-covered hill behind the farm. Like then, it was balmy summer weather. Unlike then—if he was caught, he'd be killed.

His camouflage was a tweed jacket, plus-two trousers and a jacket. The tweed was actually a perfect camouflage, with each island having their own pattern and colors to match the landscape. He tore some old sacks into strips and stapled them on to a rope.

Edward and James had kitted him out with plenty of food and some old army blankets to lie on. He had his satellite phone to communicate securely with the Ops center in Panama. The team would be there already. The flight from Texas to Panama would only take four hours.

He waited in the cottage's attic until darkness fell. Several times, he heard the people of the house calling Lei's name. They searched the grounds, but Edward, who had quickly installed a tiny camera, said they never located the hide.

As the last light disappeared at 10 pm. Alistair came down from the attic. James pressed a double-barreled 12 bore shotgun into his hands.

"A wee bit of insurance, Laddie."

Alistair headed up the hill. He knew where he was going. About 500 meters beyond the house there was a little copse of hawthorn trees, bent and short, in a perpetual battle against the wind coming off the sea. They had grabbed the earth with their roots and, over the centuries, created little hillocks. Under the roots, the sheep had dug their cozy nests, big enough for 3 or four sheep to snuggle in during winter storms. It was here that Alistair made his post.

The floor was flat and dry. The roots formed a simple frame over which he dropped the sacking. There was more than enough room for him to get under the bowels of the trees, even in a downpour he would be dry.

Spreading his blanket on the floor and having a last pee, he tucked in behind the sacking and got out his binoculars. All the lights in the main house were on. He could see Poppy in his father's old study. Several computers were open on the table. She was talking on the phone. He sent the images back to the Ops center.

The team knew needed to set a trap for the poachers.

It was Paloma who came up with the idea—she was desperate to get Alistair away from her nemesis. She knew Alistair could fall under Poppy's spell again and knew Poppy wouldn't hesitate to kill him.

Alistair's satellite phone vibrated once.

He picked it up. It was Paloma... speaking in a bad French accent. "Whisky, we 'ave a cunning plan, listen very carefully, I shall say zis only once."

55

Smoke and Knickers

"The ducks will fly South in winter," Paloma said in a secretive voice.

"Bloody Mary, please can you get to the plan and stop buggering about?"

"Sorry, here is the plan: we know from cloning Poppy's phone that Operation Askari Spear is going into action in seven days' time. We understand the first poaching team will go into Kenya in the Maasai Mara and the second will go into the Serengeti, Tanzania. But we need them to commit all their men and resources in the same place, at the same time. Because we only get one shot at this, we have to get as many poachers as possible and all their network in one go."

"If we miss half the poachers, they will become a problem later."

"Wait, didn't we nail everyone at The Ark?"

"That was the group based in Africa. This is basically a gang from Hong Kong. These guys have never poached animals before, but they are excellent with weapons and with the Askari System blocked and them tracking each animal, for them it will be like a video game. Their aim is to work their way across Africa. They will shoot the animals from the helicopter. They have a complete logistics network to move the ivory,"

"It looks like each team is made of about ten to twelve guys and then they have some locals to do the cutting and lifting."

"What about the local authorities?"

"They have bribed them, and we know the reaction time of Kenyan government is slow. Their aim is to cross into Tanzania quickly, where they have bribed even more people. The essence of their operation is speed. Think of it as a kind of Poaching Blitzkrieg. These guys will only take the ivory from the biggest animals. Their aim is extinction of a species."

"So, what do you want me to do?" Alistair asked.

"Poppy needs to tell both teams to go simultaneously into Kenya."

"Yeah, Paloma, you want me to walk in there and ask her?"

"Not exactly, but we need a high-quality recording of her voice so we can generate it by computer—you know, AI. Right now, we only have phone recordings and we've tried to use them but it's not working."

"So, you want me to bug the house?"

"Exactly, microphones in her knicker drawers, the full Monty."

"You know she has armed guards and one just disappeared, so she's on high alert?"

"We know, Alistair. This is risky, we've run out of ideas, but we need to catch both teams together."

"Are you sending the bugs?"

"Yup. Edward will collect them from someone on the ferry tomorrow. They are GSM bugs, so you just need to hide them and leave them. They last for 200 days. You need to record at least 30 minutes of her voice, so we get the complete range, in English and Cantonese."

"Bloody Hell fire."

"Yup."

"OK, I need to get her and the guards out of the house while I install them. I guess I need a distraction. I doubt cute seals on the beach will do it." Alistair's mind was reeling.

"For someone who murders wildlife for a living, nope."

"Drunken lads driving into the garden wall would only bring the guards out."

"True. Maybe get them to leave the house in a hurry? Remember when we set off stink bombs that Christmas, everyone ran outside?" Paloma laughed.

"Aye, now that is a good idea, a really smoky fire in the kitchen?"

"Yeah, could work, but don't burn our house down. How are you going to start it?"

"Fusebox, it's in the scullery, and the laundry chute is in there so all the smoke will go up to the next floor."

"I'm on the job. Looks like we need to get James and young Edward on the team."

"Good luck."

He put the phone away. So much a for a quiet OP. Leaving the blankets and sacking for when he returned the next night, he left his hide. As he started walking quietly away, a sheep shuffled into his nest and settled down with a contented look on her face. Perfect, now nobody would find it.

As Alistair approached the cottage, he could see through the window that Edward was still up. James woke to the sound of the back door opening. Alistair completed the story he had told them about Moy castle, explaining how he and Paloma and the team were now the Extinct Company Commandos. He told them about Poppy and what she was about to do.

Immediately they agreed to join the team.

James gave him a lesson on how to create an electrical fire using the fuse box. They needed to get lots of plastic burning in order to make toxic smoke. It would seem natural that it was the old house wiring malfunctioning.

"I need a gas mask if I'm going into a smoke-filled building."

"You forgot—I am a volunteer fireman on the island. You need a full-face mask with an oxygen tank. I've got one ready to go. I will be the one coming to rescue you."

"The smoke alarms will wake them up, plus there should be a guard on duty. Here is a key to the scullery door."

As promised, next morning a small package arrived on the ferry for Edward. He never saw who delivered it. His instructions were to leave the back door of his Landy unlocked and occupy himself elsewhere as soon as the ferry docked.

Opening the package from the Earl in the kitchen, they found seven tiny listening bugs and a jar of Gentleman's Relish from Fortnum & Mason.

Alistair made himself some toast and ate it immediately.

After that, he went on a long bike ride in his 'twitchers' outfit and actually found a pair of Golden Eagles.

Retiring to the attic, he rested, ate and communicated with the Ops center until nightfall.

When he reached his Op, he took ages to persuade the sheep to move from her comfortable spot—he had to do it without her making too much noise and alerting the guard. The lights in the house were still on. He was carrying James's face mask and a bottle of compressed air.

Finally, at midnight, the house went to sleep. A slight drizzle began and Alistair watched the guard head for the shelter of the covered bench by the walled vegetable garden. It actually had a commanding view of the house, so it was a good post. As soon as he saw that the guard was fiddling with his phone, Alistair made his way across the field to the back door.

He used the key James had given him to click open the lock and pushed inside. It was dark, and the house had the familiar smell of wood smoke. Alistair hoped he wouldn't be guilty of burning down the ancestral home, but James had insured that the local fire brigade would do some night training fairly close by. Alistair had borrowed a pair of fireman boots. James had noted that if he was going to walk from the field inside the house, he would leave footprints. Better if they were fireman boots.

The scullery, with its old hand water pump, sinks and washing machines, was just inside the back door. The electrical panel was a large grey, bauxite box, probably installed in the 1920s. The fuses were great black things, carefully labelled in purple ink from a fountain pen, his grandfather's he assumed, feeling slightly guilty: he was about to melt the lot.

He pushed a pile of plastic bags, boxes, and nylon rope on top of the box. This would be his smoke generator. They had filled some of the plastic bags with old engine oil.

He propped open the laundry chute to the upper floors.

Pulling a length of a thick cable from his pocket, he pulled on insulated gloves. He hated electrical stuff, mechanics. Plumbing was fine because you could see what was happening but electrical... The main positive and negative wires were twisted into a kind of giant screw at opposite ends of the box. He connected one end to the negative, took a deep breath, and clamped the other one with a crocodile clip to the positive. It sparked and snapped loudly as he connected it, then almost immediately the wire connections between the two went orange. The plastic around the wire caught fire and soon the flames were licking the plastic bags and, to his alarm, the wooden ceiling.

Quickly retreating out the back door, he heard the first smoke alarms make their ear-piercing chirps. The guard was already running down towards the house when Alistair reached his hidden nest. He grabbed the face mask and oxygen tank.

Even in the dark he could see thick, toxic smoke pumping out of the upper floor windows.

One, two and then three figures charged out of the front door, coughing.

"James, you'd better bring the fire brigade quick, I think I overdid it." He said into his phone, running to the house with his face mask and air bottle strapped to his back.

As he opened the back door, the flames shot out the top of the doorway. Alistair hit the floor. He was wearing damp tweeds, a good defense against fire. Crawling, he grabbed a broom and knocked the short wire he had connected. It fell to the floor, smoking like a log kicked out of the fire.

The house was full of smoke, but it helped that Alistair could walk it blindfolded, having grown up there.

He pushed into the kitchen, jumped up on the counter, and hid his first bug on top of the cabinet. He ran into the sitting room, which was full of smoke, and quickly hid another bug behind a painting of his grandfather, Major General Gordon Stuart. Alistair saluted the general and headed upstairs.

As he took two steps at a time, he heard the distant 'nee naw' of a British fire engine.

The smoke on the next floor was so thick, Alistair turned on his torch.

Poppy was using his parents' old room as hers. It had views across the bay, a big fireplace, and a generous dressing room. He shone his light along the line of drawers and realized all her clothes would smell strongly of burnt plastic. Finding the underwear drawer, he pulled it open and saw perfectly neat lines of small lacy things. Sighing, he stuck the bug under the shelf.

After hiding two more bugs he heard the fire engine crunching the gravel. He detected James's voice.

"Is there anyone left in the building?"

"Yes, Chong is still in there, he was upstairs."

At that moment, Chong appeared, wet towel over his mouth. Alistair recognized him from Hong Kong. He realized he should have dressed in a fireman's uniform, but it was too late. Chong realized Alistair was up to no good and reached for his gun. Alistair was faster, putting one hand over the man's mouth and nose, tipping him backwards to the ground at the same time he held tight to his gun hand. The weapon fell and clattered down the stairs. Chong fought hard, thrashing his arms and legs furiously, but Alistair had his knee on his chest. The smoke has already weakened Chong, so, with a wet towel covering his face, it looked like fumes had overcome him.

Alistair ran down the stairs, grabbing Chong's gun as he went. He raced to the back door until he heard the fire team burst in through the front door.

56

Time For A Wee Dram

The fire brigade had put out the blaze in the kitchen quickly. James had run to the back of the house with a chemical extinguisher and put that one down in a few minutes. The ancient wooden ceilings were charred but still solid.

"She is not a happy girl." Misha let Alistair hear Poppy from the bugs he had installed.

She was screaming at the two remaining guards for not putting out the fire faster. She said all her clothes stank of smoke and there were muddy boot prints all over the house from the firemen.

Alistair smiled at James' foresight. He would be an outstanding member of the team.

He went up to the attic to catch up with sleep.

After a few hours, Misha called in again.

"OK, Alistair, we have everything we need. We have made a very good clone of her voice. Now she needs to go offline."

He knew what this meant. Just pulling the plug on the internet wouldn't work. She had multiple communications systems, including satellite phones. He had to either arrest or eliminate both her and the guards.

"You have five hours. Alistair, can you confirm?"

"Aye, confirmed,"

He could handle the guards. It was Poppy he was terrified of dealing with. Not that he couldn't do it physically, he just wasn't sure if he could harm her if he needed to. He knew she wouldn't bat an eyelid when it came to killing him.

He went and told James and Edward. He was honest with them and told them the complete story.

"Alistair, you don't remember her, but my wife, Morag, is still in prison. She is in there for multiple murders. When I discovered what she had done, she was on the run, I knew where she had gone, she was hiding in a bothy up near Loch Spelve. We used to go there when we were courting. She had a hunting rifle, and she was an excellent shot. I knew I was the one who had to go and get her. I wasn't afraid of getting shot. I was afraid of hurting her, I was still in love with her."

"What did you do?"

"I went to see all the families of the people she killed. They hated me, blamed me. But it gave me the courage to do what I needed to do."

Alistair opened his laptop and looked at the pictures Paloma had sent of all the carcasses of elephants Poppy had ordered killed. He stored this in his head.

After half an hour, they had a plan of action.

First problem was the guard who stood outside. He had to be removed silently, but there was no way to get close to him and they had no silenced weapon.

"Longbow," James said

"You're kidding, you want me to shoot him with a longbow?"

"Alistair, you used to be the best shot in the whole of the Hebrides."

"Youth shot. I was sixteen."

"Let's go out to the back field. I think your targets are still in the barn there."

It didn't take long for Alistair to realize he was still a crack shot with a long bow.

"Aye, Alistair, yer ancestors would be proud."

The longbow was made of Yew and as tall as Alistair. The arrow tips were made to go through armor. Alistair had crafted them himself using a design from the 1600s. He wore a thick, leather arm bracer on his left arm to protect it from the bowstring as he released the arrow.

The guard was at his post by the walled vegetable garden. To hit him, Alistair had crept up to the orchard. Alistair saw he was on full alert and wearing a Kevlar vest. For a clean shot, Alistair needed the man to turn and face him.

James was standing just over the crest of the hill with Fergus, his Labrador retriever. They trained Fergus to flush out game, and he would bark madly on command.

Alistair drew the bow back, using the full strength of his shoulders with feet apart, the classic stance of an archer.

On command from James, Fergus let rip, barking furiously. The guard did exactly what they had hoped. As he stepped forward and turned. Alistair released his arrow. At less than thirty meters, his target was closer than most medieval battlefields. The arrow made a deep thud as it went straight through the Kevlar, flesh, Kevlar and finally stopped in the solid oak door to the garden, pinning the twitching body of the guard until the arrow snapped and he slid to the ground, unmoving.

Hearing Fergus's wild barks, the second guard came running out, machine pistol in hand. Alistair had the next arrow already nocked up and was drawing the bow as the guard started walking towards the barking dog.

Alistair let the arrow go just as the man took the first step down off the terrace towards the path. Instead of hitting his chest, the steel tip went straight through his eye and then reappeared out the back of his head. He instantly fell sideways into the rosebushes on the side of the terrace. There was no movement, just a sudden ending.

The sight of the arrow through the man's head was a gruesome reminder of the symbol of The Extinct Company, an Auroch with an arrow through its skull.

Sprinting for all he was worth, he reached the terrace in seconds, grabbing the guard's machine pistol and dropping his bow before he ran into the house. He called up in his most commanding voice,

"Poppy, come quietly. There is no escape. I have men outside the front and back. All your men are dead."

No answer.

Alistair began checking each room. He knew Poppy may be waiting around any corner, armed. All the downstairs rooms were empty. He ran upstairs, leaving the master bedroom for last and finally, he burst in. Posed on the bed, wearing a high collared silk Chinese dress slit up the sides to her hip, she lifted one foot and stretched, revealing her long and perfectly formed leg. Her new face was startling.

"Hello Alistair, you have been busy. Come and relax with me for a minute."

"Get up Poppy, your reign is over."

"But Alistair, I haven't even started yet."

"Get up." He lifted his weapon and pointed it at her.

"Don't be so silly, you would never shoot me."

In a nanosecond, she jumped up, pulling a sword from under the pillows. It was one of a brace of Claymore swords that was from a crossed pair on the wall.

Alistair squeezed the trigger. There was a loud click.

Poppy laughed a cruel laugh.

"They never checked their weapons. I knew those two were about to do a runner, so I spiked them!" she was advancing on him, cutting the air so he could hear it. He knew how sharp the sword was.

She sliced downwards towards his head. Sidestepping, he deflected the blade with the machine pistol and sparks flew out as metal hit metal. The blade bounced off and sliced his cheek. Blood poured out immediately.

Jumping over the bed, he grabbed the remaining Claymore on the wall. These swords were last used by the Stuarts in the fated battle of Culloden.

Poppy dashed through the door, laughing.

"Chase me Alistair, chase me."

She sprinted up the stone steps to the small tower, a relic from the house's honorable past. The steps went up in a spiral and were designed for defense.

Easily keeping Alistair back with her sword, she opened the door at the top and ran onto the flat, crenelated roof of the tower.

"Time for a duel, Alistair Gordon Stuart. Your little sister is going to miss you terribly and then I'll hunt her down."

She moved around the square roof like a boxer, staying out of Alistair's range, waiting for a moment to go in.

She was quick and light, dodging each of Alistair's thrusts with ease. She parried and moved, leaving Alistair's sword slicing into thin air.

Once he sliced across her breast, cutting through the silk of her dress and making a razor thin cut on her flesh.

"Come on Alistair, let's make it even more exciting." Stepping over the low crenelations, she advanced down the ridge of the roof like a gymnast on a beam, and then turned and faced Alistair. Staring him in the eye, she ripped off the remaining top part of her dress.

"I am all yours." A line of blood ran down her small breast. She opened her arms, sword in one hand.

As he stepped forward, distracted by the sight and barely balancing on the ridge, she switched sword hands and cut hard across left. Her sword smashed into his just as he was trying to change positions to parry her.

Alistair's Claymore fell from his hands and clattered down the roof, dropping into the rosebushes below.

His legs slipped, one on each side of the roof.

"And now YOU will become extinct." She lifted the sword above her head and, without pausing, swung it down with all her strength.

Alistair was still wearing his archer's arm bracer on his left arm, made of thick buffalo hide. He brought it up as her sword swung down at his head, deflecting the blow. The blade skidded on the bracer. As Poppy swung through with the unexpected move, the top of her body fell on to his. Alistair put his left arm around her neck and pulled her towards him, so they were in a close embrace.

"Goodbye Poppy." He drove the point of his Sgian Dubh into her naked chest. It slipped off her rib and pierced her heart.

"No," she whispered into his ear with her last breath. She shuddered, and the sword fell from her hand, clattering down the roof to join its brother below.

Warm blood from her heart soaked his shirt as he pulled his knife out.

He carried her lifeless body back across the ridge and laid her on the flat roof. He kissed her above the wound. Her skin was still warm. Standing up, he looked down at her spreadeagled on her back, bare-breasted, a moat of blood spreading around her.

Alistair made his way unsteadily down the stairs. James and Edward came running in. James took one look at Alistair and stepped over to the drinks cabinet and poured him a large malt whisky.

"You look like ye need a wee dram, Laddie."

Alistair's hands were shaking as he took the glass.

"Aye, that I do."

57

The Askari Spear

"The Dragon is slain." Paloma lifted her phone with the message from Alistair and showed it to the team.

"Good. Evil bitch."

"OK everybody, let's get cracking." Dr. KV clapped his hands together.

The team, apart from Alistair, assembled in the Ops Room at the Magic shop deep in the heart of Panama jungle.

Misha and Tatiana were imitating Poppy on the cloned phone, speaking to the Askari Spear poachers. The message was simple—converge on the Mara at once. Several objected, but Tatiana, who with her voice altered by computer, soon squashed any dissension.

The voice that came out of the computer was so remarkably like Poppy's, it was actually quite alarming.

There was an air of excitement, anticipation, and preparation.

Dr. Kitts-Vincent with a life of special forces operations and leadership behind him, was directing the show.

On one big screen was a world map. Dots representing each of the poachers tracked them, as INTERPOL shared their last known locations. Several dots had been static for months. Some were already in Kenya.

On another screen was the wall of poachers from the Hunting Guide. Photos of all the known and sometimes unknown people involved in operation Askari Spear. Each had a description.

Paloma walked over to the keyboard and put a big cross on Poppy's face and added the word EXTINCT. There was a round of applause from everyone.

There were twenty Southeast Asian men labelled 'Askari Spear Hong Kong Gang (Sharpshooters).'

Eight European and African men were listed as, 'Askari Spear Pilots' and ten Kenyan and Tanzanian men labeled 'Askari Spear Local Team Leaders.'

There were four East African politicians labelled,

'Askari Spear Politicians on Payroll.'

The last map showed the Maasai Mara and Serengeti. The map was littered with slow moving green and orange dots. These were elephant and rhino, with the Askari System trackers in their horns and trunks.

They knew as soon as Poppy's drone started flying over them, the dots would disappear to the wrong locations. The poachers would them know where each animal was and shoot them from helicopters.But once they got the Unimog with Stan's device onboard into the area, they would be able to not only track the drone but all the poachers as well.

Then they would start poaching the poachers.

The KWS Rapid Response team and their counterparts in Tanzania would make arrests whilst INTERPOL would coordinate the operation. The Unimog would be the command center and The Earl would take command.

Everyone knew that the anti-poaching units had a shoot to kill policy, so if the poachers put up any resistance, there would be no holding back.

Several of the rangers had volunteered to be 'elephants.' They would move and behave like a big, irresistible herd of elephants by carrying the trackers which would normally be inserted into the animal tusks.

They had been practicing with the Askari monitoring team in Nairobi, watching their movements. All the men and women were well versed in the behavior of the animals, so after only one day, the moving dots were indistinguishable from a herd of elephants. These volunteers were putting themselves at high risk because they knew the poachers would open fire even without actually seeing the animals. Just some movement would be tempting enough.

The Askari Spear squads were aiming to create an extinction.

Alistair flew south to the Ministry of Defense base, Boscombe Down, in England, where the rest of the team on board the Atlas A300 would fly in from Panama. From there, they would fly straight into the Maasai Mara doing a night landing at the remote airstrip.

It was cold and drizzling in England when the Atlas appeared out of the cloud. Alistair put down his mug of army tea, grabbed his bag and hurried out to the plane.

As he stepped on board, Paloma gave him a big hug and tears rolled down his cheeks as they embraced.

Many hours later, they landed in the Mara.

Driving the Unimog out of the vast aircraft, Francis Chege, the ex-army Sergeant and contractor from the Ark, along with Lt. General George Githere, met them. "Good evening, Earl, my friends, I understand you have already worked with Sergeant Chege. I asked him and his men to help us create an operations base. Follow me please, Lord Godolphin. Perhaps you would like to join me in my Land Rover?"

In the background, the Atlas was being covered in camouflage netting by Francis' men. Taboga and her team would install the mini-guns and weapons systems during the night: insurance if things went wrong.

They drove under the moon shadows of the acacia trees down a dirt road. They could smell the wood smoke, the hard dry earth, even the animal dung. It felt good to be back in Africa.

Francis Chege and his team had created a well-camouflaged camp, complete with mess tent and accommodation. Groups of the well-disciplined KWS Rapid Response Team snapped to attention and saluted as they drove past.

Parking the Unimog in the center of the encampment. Tatiana and Misha quickly set about installing Stan's device on the vehicle's roof.

As Alistair walked across to the mess tent, a red blanketed figure came grinning out to meet him. It was Leboo, Alistair's best mate from school and fellow rally driver. Alistair had hoped he would be there. The Mara was actually not under the KWS—it belonged to the Maasai and Leboo was a senior chief.

They greeted each other in Maasai and then switched to Swahili.

"You didn't expect me to miss such a hunt on our own land? These people have been destroying our heritage for too long. Our spears are sharp and our blood is up."

In the distance, Alistair could hear the rhythmic calls of the Maasai Lion Dance. They were preparing for battle.

"Leboo, these men will shoot with high-powered weapons from helicopters, they have no mercy."

"It is true, but you and I both know those helicopters will come down and the Maasai will be waiting. You and Paloma bring the birds down. We will avenge the death of our animals. We need to send a message. When the next group of poachers think about coming to kill animals here, what do you think will stop them? A picture of men handcuffed in a Land Rover or a picture of a pile of bodies with their hearts ripped out."

"Shit Leboo, you are being serious."

"It is true. You told me it is time to stop playing by the rules. It is time to poach the poachers. I don't think you meant arresting them.

Our brothers across the Mara River are waiting too."

Alistair nodded his head.

"You are right. Let me get Tatiana and Paloma."

They had finished preparing the Unimog. The system was up and running and as soon as the drone came over, they would know.

Alistair explained Leboo's idea and then asked, "Tatiana, what is the latest information we have on the attack?"

"So, from what we understand from intercepted communications, the poachers will use four helicopters. The poachers will be in the helis and they will open fire at any elephant or rhino. There will be a ground unit that will follow behind in four off-road trucks. They will cut off the biggest trunks and horns and then escape to Tanzania. We think the ivory will then be picked up to be taken to a ship waiting off Zanzibar."

"It is the men in the helicopters we want. How do General and the Earl plan to take down the helicopters?" Alistair continued.

"We know the helicopters will come in low and hover so that the snipers can shoot the elephants. When this happens, the sharpshooters and all the men in the Rapid Response team will open fire, hoping to bring them down." Tatiana replied.

"I see. How many men are in the Rapid Response Team?"

"Ten here and ten out pretending to be elephant herds."

"That's not enough. If all four helicopters hit the Mara simultaneously, there is no way that 20 men can be in four different locations at once. That's five per helicopter, chances of bringing down a helicopter with five guns is not great." Alistair looked at Paloma and Tatiana, and then added to Leboo, "So, we need your warriors."

"So, you need my warriors. I have 30 Morans, ready to fight."

"Brave as they are, how can they bring down a helicopter with spears?" Alistair had seen men trying to shoot down a helicopter with AK 47. It was hard to do.

"I have an idea."

"Go ahead Paloma, you always have good ideas." Leboo smiled at her.

"Barbed wire."

"Beg your pardon?" Alistair looked incredulous.

"And a drone."

"You're kidding."

"Actually no, the worst possible thing to do to a helicopter is to get stuff tangled in the rotors. If we hang a length of barbed wire under a drone and fly it above the helicopter, then lower it into the center of the blades, it will pull the wire, go down and make one hell of mess. Then the Maasai can nail them."

"Wow, when did you come up with that?" he looked at Paloma with respect.

"I think about things like that all the time!"

"My sweet sister."

"OK, but the only way you can do that is if we can actually see the helicopter and drone at the same time. How do we keep up with it, so we are ready when it slows?" Alistair looked at Paloma.

"*Nguruwe anayeruka*," Leboo said grinning.

"I am lost, I am sorry?" Tatiana looked frustrated. Normally, she could work things out before anyone else.

"The Flying Pig." Alistair translated.

"I am still lost, Paloma. You guys are talking about strange things. Please help me." Tatiana was holding out her hands.

"It is the name of Alistair and Leboo's rally car. They want to chase the helicopters with the rally car."

"You'll love it. I even added a special rack on the roof for my spear and shield."

"Now we are talking. How many drones have we got?" Alistair looked at Paloma.

"Four with a payload of 6kg each,"

"Wow, maybe we should add a grenade? I think we had better explain our crazy plan to the General and The Earl. Come on Leboo, it's going to be a hard sell and I need your brilliant negotiating skills." The 'boys' walked off to the Ops center doing a high five.

58

The Flying Pig and The Maasai.

"Leboo, are you sure you can wear your shuka and get your harness on?"

Leboo was struggling to clip himself into the five-point harness of the rally car's bucket seat, he was dressed in full war regalia including the traditional red shuka which the Maasai wear. Strapped to the roof of the car were his shield and spear. Strapped to the roll cage in the rear were four drones with neatly coiled, 10 meter-lengths of double barbed wire attached to each one. They had realized that the wire alone was nearly six kilograms, so grenades were out.

The Earl and General had reluctantly agreed. The 30 Maasai had each been issued with the Askari trackers that were normally installed in tusks. They decided they would make two 'herds' of elephants that were close to each other.

The Maasai took on the natural behavior of a herd of elephants with no practice at all.

Misha, who was in the Unimog command center, stuck her head around the door, "the enemy drone is airborne and jamming the GPS trackers."

Everyone held their breath to see if Stan's device worked. If it didn't, the helicopters would come with the poachers and wipe out hundreds of animals. The team would never know where they were.

After a nervous 30 seconds, Misha's hand appeared in the doorway. Her thumb was up. Everyone cheered.

Now they had to wait for the helicopters.

They dared not inform their teams by radio in case Poppy's men intercepted the message, but the Maasai had long ago developed a system that allowed them to communicate between villages across the plains. A young Moran climbed a nearby kopje and called in a high-pitched voice. After a few seconds, they could hear a distant voice responding. They would bounce this message across the Mara, reaching each team.

"Incoming." Alistair pulled on his rally helmet and looked at the iPad strapped to the dashboard. A fast-moving dot entered to the south. It was heading straight for one group of Maasai pretending to be elephants. Mingati, who had returned from Diedre's ranch in California, was in the group. Their code name was M1.

Leboo fired up the engine of the rally car. It burbled and popped, then became a roar as he increased the speed of the engine.

"They are heading towards M1. Take the Sekenani track."

The car exploded out of the camp, all four wheels spinning on the loose dirt until they found a grip. The air filled with a thick wall of dust.

The boys were enjoying themselves, despite the danger they were about to face.

"Thanks lads," Paloma shouted after them as she coughed in the dust, then added, "Good luck."

Once they hit the track, Alistair started calling out the route to Leboo, who was driving. It felt like old times, except this time, lives were at stake.

"Max. 100. Into easy right, over rocks, max. straight 300 over ruts,"

They were doing 120 kilometers per hour on very rough roads. The noise of the stones, the engine and the exhaust would have deafened them had they not had on the Pelter headphones inside their helmets.

"There, at 2 o'clock." Leboo's eyesight had been highly trained since birth. It took Alistair several seconds to see the Bell 206 helicopter flying just above tree height towards the Maasai.

They were right on its tail, exactly where they wanted to be.

The helicopter was slowing. The doors had been removed and they could see the poachers inside manning their machine guns.

They had instructed the Maasai to drop their trackers and make for cover as soon as the helicopter appeared. They hoped the poachers wouldn't notice the trackers not moving for a few seconds.

As the helicopter slowed, they heard heavy gunfire.

"M60 machine gun, I think they are trying to chase the elephants out from under the trees?"

"Or they are just warming up their barrels so they can blow the trees to pieces with that thing. Let's stop here and get the drone out."

Leboo brought the car to a fast halt, pushing them against their harnesses.

Alistair jumped out and unclipped the first drone. Leboo got the control unit out.

They laid the barbed wire in the long line on the ground.

Alistair fired up the drone and sent it skyward with its long steel tail.

The helicopter had flared back its blades and was crabbing sideways towards where the trackers were now lying. The warriors stayed hidden thirty meters from where they dropped the trackers.

The drone, slow with its heavy load, was still 300 meters from the aircraft.

Alistair was concentrating on flying the drone, which was swinging all over the place.

"Mingati!!" Leboo shouted.

Alistair glanced across to where he was looking.

One of the Maasai had broken cover and was running in a full sprint towards the helicopter. As he got closer, he lifted shield above his head and his arm pulled back with his spear ready to throw.

The helicopter rotated slightly and dropped almost to ground level. Now the gunner was facing the Maasai. He opened fire as Mingati threw his spear.

Bullets tore man and shield to pieces and slammed into the dust.

The spear clanged against the fuselage of the aircraft.

War was declared.

But the warrior had given Alistair a precious few extra seconds.

The helicopter had stopped to hover while he fired.

Now the drone was directly above the center of the whirling blades.

Instantly, fighting the downdraft, Alistair lowered the wire towards its target.

The second the steel touched the blades, it pulled down the entire length of barbed wire and drone. Alistair's screen went blank.

The aircraft immediately tipped backwards on its tail and it slammed into the earth, tail rotor madly chopping at the ground until the whole thing broke off and the main blades struck the ground, thrashing the body of the helicopter like some mad wind-up toy.

The moment it stopped moving, fourteen red figures appeared out of the underbrush and strode towards the wreckage, forming a wide circle.

They thumped their shields with their spears and stamped their feet.

Alistair looked over to catch Leboo's reaction, but he was already running towards the warriors, red shuka streaming behind him.

"Bird 1 down," Alistair said on his radio.

The deep, rhythmic noise came from the throats of the Maasai. They were going in for the kill.

The man who had been firing the door gun stumbled out of the wreckage, blood streaming down his face. He looked at the approaching

Maasai and reached for the pistol on his belt.

Pulling it out, he ran towards the wall of red warriors.

The Maasai dropped to one knee, shields in front of them, spears pointing forward with the end against the ground.

He fired wildly, screaming, eyes blinded by blood.

The red wall didn't move.

Throwing his now empty pistol at the shields, he pulled out a knife and launched himself at the wall. One Maasai stood up and drove his spear straight through the heart of the man. The spearman was Leboo.

The Maasai swarmed over the helicopter. There were no prisoners.

"Bird 2 is down."

Alistair looked at his iPad. The Rapid Response team had brought down their helicopter.

"Incoming."

Quickly, he pulled another drone out and laid the wire on the ground. He launched and let it hover, wire just clear of the earth.

Alistair heard the helicopter before he saw it.

The pilot must have spotted the smoke from the one they had downed and headed straight for it. The aircraft roared over him at tree height.

The red shukas of the Maasai and the poacher's body beside the downed aircraft told the pilot the complete story.

The incoming helicopter made a fast turn, banking sharply before coming back towards the Maasai and the stricken aircraft.

The Maasai weren't running. They had formed back into a circle and were drumming their shields with their spears.

Alistair could see the gunner in the door grinning and cocking his weapon.

He had no time to fly the drone above the helicopter.

He flew it straight under the machine then up at the pilot who was now facing him, a fraction of a second before hitting the Plexiglass, in front of the surprised man's face, Alistair sent the little quadcopter with its steel tail up through the rotors of the helicopter.

The drone slipped between the blades, but the barbed wire caught them.

The aircraft immediately and at high speed went forwards and downwards.

Crashing in a brilliant orange ball of flames 500 meters from the Maasai.

"Bird Three down," Alistair said rather shakily on his radio.

He watched as the fourth and final helicopter appear on his iPad and then almost immediately disappeared.

"Got Bird four with the Javelin." He heard Paloma's voice announce proudly.

In the distance, they heard sporadic gunfire. Over the radio they listened to the section leaders of the Rapid Response team. They were tracking the trucks. These were full of local poachers who would have cut off the tusks of the biggest animals and then disappeared across the border into Tanzania.

The Rapid Response force and Sergeant Chege's team had watched the trucks drive into the Mara and set up an ambush.

The firing finished as quickly as it had started.

"Ground units immobilized," came over the radio.

Alistair and Leboo returned to the command center.

"Hey what about the Askari Spear Drone?" Alistair asked Paloma as they appeared.

Just as he spoke, they heard the whine of the drone props heading towards the airstrip.

"Misha has control, she's bringing it in."

Alistair turned to Leboo. "I'm sorry about Mingati. He was very brave, and he gave me the extra seconds to hit the heli."

"Tonight, we will celebrate his warrior's death, we will write songs about him, he will go down in the history of our people. Long after you and I are gone, fathers will tell their children the story of Mingati, the brave warrior who attacked a helicopter gunship with his spear to save the elephants."

"The man you killed was the one firing the machine gun. You averaged his death."

"This is true, my friend. Once more the Maasai will be feared, the animals can live in peace again. Nobody will dare to come and kill them on our land."

Paloma's face peered around the door of the Ops module in the Unimog.

"Guys, come and see this video from the first drone."

Inside the cool, quiet interior, Misha and Tatiana were facing a bank of screens. When Alistair and Leboo came in, Misha hit play.

At first, they could see the side of the rally car from the camera on the drone. Alistair and Leboo running around the quadcopter setting it up. Suddenly the view whipped up into the sky, leaving the dust behind.

It flew, wobbling its way towards the distant helicopter. As it got closer, they could see a red clad figure run out from behind a tree and sprint straight towards the chopper. The drone flew directly above the aircraft just as the figure, almost directly below, stopped to draw back his arm and launched his spear. Almost simultaneously they could see the Maasai torn to pieces by heavy M60 rounds.

The last moment was as the spear hit the fuselage and the camera seemed to be sucked down into the blades of the helicopter. There was a flash of orange light and then the screen went blank.

"I think," Misha said, "that if we don't include the first part of the video, that it looks very much like that Maasai brought down a helicopter with his spear and was killed in the process."

She looked at the others to see their reaction. Everyone was smiling and nodding.

"His name was Mingati. He was a Moran, a warrior." Leboo said.

"If he had not attacked the helicopter, I would have never had time to get the drone in place, so he did bring down a helicopter with a spear in a way." Alistair added.

"I think if this video were to find its way onto YouTube there would quickly be several million viewers, all over the world, who would be so horrified that poachers from Hong Kong were coming to Kenya to kill elephants, gunning down a Maasai called Mingati who was defending those animals with a spear. I think there would be a global outrage and people would be less inclined to buy ivory."

"You are right, Misha, we can also release video of the downed helicopters and of the poachers who survived being taken away by the KWS Rapid Response force."

"Alistair, please can you get the Earl, I want to do this immediately."

59

GAS57 Pub

That night, the team and Moggy left the Maasai Mara. Their exit couldn't be described as quiet, the Atlas sounded like a storm when it took off.

They had spent a raucous evening at Leboo's Boma. The Maasai had slaughtered a cow in their honor. The Flying pig was anointed with blood and Mingati's family were given seats of honor. The Earl, General and most of his men along with Sergeant Chege had joined the celebrations.

The singing and dancing would continue until dawn.

As they climbed aboard the plane, they had brought the potent smell of wood smoke with them, it lingered in the cabin and in their clothes.

Dr. Kitts-Vincent insisted they stop for a couple of days at Saint Kitts where his family had a large and sprawling estate, dotted with colonial buildings, and blessed with several perfect white sandy beaches.

As they relaxed, swam, water-skied, and had lovely meals of fresh fish, the world reacted to the videos they had released.

By the time they had got back to Panama and were sitting under the welcome shade of the myrtle trees beside their pub GAS57, watching ships ply their way through the canal, the video of Mingati's attack against the poacher's helicopter had been viewed more than five million times and the total continued to rise.

Newspaper and TV stations fed on the information sent by Misha that gave all the facts of the poacher's hit squads coming from Hong Kong.

Global outrage of ivory hunting had manifested itself in massive marches in several capitals around the world.

China and Hong Kong were moving towards closing the loopholes in their systems that still allowed ivory buying.

Paloma stroked Jeeves' ears and took a long drink of her cold beer.

"Boy, it's amazing how much harm one nasty girl can do. Like Tatiana said, I should have finished her off in Gordonstoun. "

"Actually, despite all the battles we have had to fight on this one, I actually think we have put a long-lasting dent in the ivory poaching business. Without Poppy we probably couldn't have done it. What happened to all her money, by the way?" Alistair asked.

Misha smiled mischievously.

"General Githere received a large consignment of very useful military equipment to fight poaching in Kenya, including a Luna X 2000 drone."

"The Extinct Company now has an emergency fund to be used at our discretion."

Mingati's family will be looked after, and Leboo now has a foundation which will build and run a free school for the children of his people. It includes a small medical center.

The school will be called Mingati School. Do you know what Mingati means? 'He that runs fast'."

"Brilliant, no mention of us anywhere?"

"Not a word, we don't exist."

They lifted their beers, except Misha, who had a vodka).

"The Extinct Company. Nobis Non Est."

"One last thing. James and Edward sent us a message last night. They found fifty kilograms of high explosives in the wine cellar at Wynards. They had to get a bomb disposal unit over from the mainland to disarm it and remove it." Alistair said.

"Wow, the Dragon really was going to blow the whole place to bits."

"Yes, she really breathed fire."

THE END

About the Author

British-born author A. J. Coates has spent his life working, living and exploring Africa and Central America. His exploits have included crossing the Sahara Desert and North Africa in an old Range Rover named Fifi, entering the World Rally Championships and expeditions through the depths of the forests in Central Africa and Central America.

A. J. Coates and his wife run Cresolus, a company that specializes in creating sustainable infrastructure in National Parks around the Tropical world. Cresolus often works closely with antipoaching units. They live on the side of the Panama Canal in Gamboa with their two children.

You can connect with me on:

- https://www.theextinctcompany.com
- https://twitter.com/TheExtinctCo
- https://www.facebook.com/historicalwildlifeprotection

Also by A.J.Coates

The Extinct Company A.J.Coates
Book One in The Extinct Company Series

Alistair Gordon Stuart ex British army officer, Paloma his ace pilot sister, Tatiana KGB trained sniper and computer hacker.

They are a band of commandos that are the core team of the 1627 secret society know as The Extinct Company.

They are thrust into the murky world of organized crime, political intrigue and the illegal wildlife trade.

Some the world's most precious species are under imminent threat of extinction.

The only way they can save them is by operating outside the law, way outside.

They must become the poachers of poachers.

The Extinct Company **is a nail-biting story of courage, bravery, rebellion and battle from the new master of adventure fiction**

Murder at Stoat Barton A.J.Coates

It was supposed to be a quiet morning run along the river.

Tatiana sets off with her dog Trotsky. Enthralled by the peaceful English countryside, she is shocked when Trotsky proudly presents her with a find—a human bone.

As a sixteen-year-old Russian girl, isolated amongst once friendly neighbors and unsure who she can trust, Tatiana finds herself implicated in a murder with only her own instincts to rely on if she hopes to find the killer before they find her.

This is Tatiana who later becomes one of the core team at the Extinct Company.

Made in the USA
Middletown, DE
15 February 2023